HER CHARMING MAN

HER CHARMING MAN

GLOUCESTERSHIRE CRIME SERIES
BOOK 2

RACHEL SARGEANT

This edition produced in Great Britain in 2024

by Hobeck Books Limited, Unit 14, Sugnall Business Centre, Sugnall, Stafford, Staffordshire, ST21 6NF

www.hobeck.net

Copyright © Rachel Sargeant 2024

This book is entirely a work of fiction. The names, characters and incidents portrayed in this novel are the work of the author's imagination. Any resemblance to actual persons (living or dead), events or localities is entirely coincidental.

Rachel Sargeant has asserted her right under the Copyright, Design and Patents Act 1988 to be identified as the author of this work.

All rights reserved. No parts of this book may be used or reproduced by any means, graphic, electronic, or mechanical, including photocopying, recording, taping or by any information storage retrieval system without the written permission of the copyright holder.

A CIP catalogue for this book is available from the British Library.

ISBN 978-1-915-817-46-4 (pbk)

ISBN 978-1-915-817-45-7 (ebook)

Cover design by Jayne Mapp Design

Printed and bound in Great Britain

ARE YOU A THRILLER SEEKER?

Hobeck Books is an independent publisher of crime, thrillers and suspense fiction and we have one aim – to bring you the books you want to read.

For more details about our books, our authors and our plans, plus the chance to download free novellas, sign up for our newsletter at **www.hobeck.net**.

You can also find us on Twitter/X **@hobeckbooks** or on Facebook **www.facebook.com/hobeckbooks10**.

PRAISE FOR THE GLOUCESTERSHIRE CRIME SERIES

'All in all a good read with an interesting storyline with a clever unexpected ending.' ThrillerMan

'Always good to read an author who develops their own style of writing and I think Rachel is one of them.' Pete Fleming

'I enjoyed it immensely.' Sarah Leck

'A tantalising crime thriller.' Angela Paull

'Her Deadly Friend is a fast paced twisty read from one of my favourite authors.' JoJo's Over the Rainbow book blog

'I flew through Her Deadly Friend ... I'm looking forward to seeing where she takes this series next.' Hooked From Page One

'The writing is flawless and the plot is so twisty and original that I didn't see any of it coming.' The Book Magnet

'A good read, a shocking conclusion and I'm looking forward to book 2 in the series.' Lynda's Book Reviews

'I do love a riveting police procedural thriller! And this definitely hits the spot!' Miranda's Book Scape

'Pacy, twisty.' Janet, Two Heads Are Better than One Blog

'I hope that there will be a follow up to this novel, I enjoyed this one a lot' Steph's Book Blog

'An outstanding book.' Monika Reads

'This is another cracking read from team Hobeck who has an enviable stable of excellent authors' Lesley Wilkinson, book reviewer

'It's very twisty-turny, and full of surprises right till the end.' I Heart Books blog

'A very cleverly plotted thriller.' A Mother's Musings

'A very clever plot with plenty of twists and a fabulous conclusion.' Deb's Book Reviews

To Gloucestershire, again, for inspiring my fictional version of this wonderful county.

CHAPTER ONE

MONDAY 2ND JULY

Give her mid-morning in Costa with a large latte on the newspaper's expense account and she's calmness personified, but this is trying her patience too far. Sonia Hanson looks at her watch. She doesn't care that dawn broke almost an hour ago; she should still be comatose at five thirty in the morning.

From the bench, she surveys the cathedral forecourt. The ground is mostly tarmac, but in front of each noticeboard is a patch of manicured grass in better condition than her lounge carpet, which has been ravished by the puke and poo of three small children. If she must be kept waiting, why does it have to be here? Her recent assignment to cover the history trail's opening ceremony put her off coming again. Hours of endless speeches in the stifling heat by two National Lottery bigwigs, a TV celeb she'd never heard of and some senior clergy. Even a local councillor got on his hind legs and spouted for several minutes. Daft old goat. He rambled as much as when she interviewed him for her column last year.

Tracey Chiles slips off the lead. Hamish gives a joyous shake of his ears and prances across the cathedral green. At this time of day, he can run free and unmolested. If Tracey left it any later, she would meet the other early morning dog walkers. Hamish is still a young wee Scottie, not yet in control of his urges. Tracey shudders as her mind runs through the dangerous bitches: the overweight jogger and his basset hound; the pinstripe suit and his collie; the Barbour jacket and her whippet, and the recently bereaved elderly sisters with their one Yorkshire terrier when there used to be two. The risk of an unsuitable encounter with Hamish turns her blood cold.

The dog darts across the grass in the same general direction as Tracey, his tail almost wagging him in half. The early start is going well, despite that one moment of worry. A man standing by the lime trees, loitering. He gave her the collywobbles, the trauma of what happened in May flooding back. But she convinced herself he was just one of those lazy owners who kept well back while their dogs did their business and then went home without a proper walk. She thought she was going to have to keep Hamish on a lead after all, but the man moved towards the street. Not a dog man then – or a loiterer – just an early bird heading to the train station. She nearly called after him to say he could cut through the history trail beyond the privet hedge but decided not to. Best not to talk to strangers. What if the man turned odd?

She breathes harder as she makes her way over the cobbles towards the hedge. Hamish bounces towards her, an excitement of tongue and saliva. With a pang of guilt, she fetches a well-gnawed tennis ball out of her pocket. There are no signs to say that she can't bring dogs on the new trail, but since breaking the rules at the Georgian Gardens in May and finding a dead body, she is wary of where she walks Hamish.

The dog stands stock still, head tilted towards the ball. After a moment, he flickers one ear towards Tracey. She takes the prompt and tosses the ball onto the green. The dog bounds after it.

She's enjoying Hamish's antics when she sees a figure in the distance, coming up the street towards the green. The same man? Straw hat, pale suit, no coat. He must have taken the shortcut after all, but she loses sight of him as he reaches the trees again.

She turns back to Hamish, deciding she'll be fine to go on the history trail at this hour. It's been open a fortnight and she still hasn't read the section on Roman Gloucester. As the landlady of the nearest guesthouse, she ought to take an interest in developments at the cathedral.

But what if the man works for the Church of England? A cathedral groundsman? But he didn't look the part. No, he is a commuter, off to his office in Cheltenham. And, anyway, she'll make sure Hamish doesn't run amok in the flowerbeds or pee up the noticeboards.

"Here, son."

The dog scampers towards her with the ball in his mouth but stops when he sees the lead come out of Tracey's pocket. He drops the ball, barks and chases his tail just out of her reach.

She'll have no chance of getting him when he's in this mood and no hope of seeing the trail. Even on tiptoe, she can't see over the privet hedge that borders the display area.

Surely it wouldn't hurt to get as far as the fountain and have a closer peek? If she keeps Hamish close by, she won't need the lead.

Waving the ball in front of her, she calls, "Come on, Hamish. This way."

——————

Somewhere in the distance, a dog barks. Who in their right mind takes a bloody dog for a walk at this time? Sonia Hanson looks at her watch again. This isn't on. It wasn't her idea to have the meeting at this ungodly hour. She shouldn't have agreed, but the hack in her had taken over. Her journalist's nose has sniffed out a mint of an exclusive. As a professional reporter, she's used to putting herself out for a good story – she hasn't got this far without hard work and a hell of a lot of sacrifice. She knows not everyone shares her commitment, but she is surprised at the wait today. There is plenty at stake for her interviewee.

She yawns and takes the mirror out of her handbag. Somehow the dark circles underneath her eyes give her face more character. And the hormones left over from her last pregnancy have been good to her hair, although the curls will thin out again soon.

A caterpillar drops onto her handbag from a bush that overhangs the bench. She flicks it away with a well-aimed finger and paces to the next bench. The plaque on it proudly boasts that the Friends of Gloucester Cathedral presented it. The coldness of the seat reaches her thighs. Another ten minutes, then call it a day.

She fetches out her notebook, deciding to make use of

this wasted time. The bench is hard. Who designed these benches? Blocks of concrete overlaid with planks of wood hardly complement the modern amenity the trail is supposed to be. Sonia bets the Friends of Gloucester Cathedral never park their own backsides here.

Another yawn. God, she's tired, but not just because of this early start. She seems permanently exhausted these days. She hasn't bounced back since Tommy was born, and she's still getting that tingling sensation although she stopped breastfeeding weeks ago. Is it always like this after the third baby?

The concourse is dank and smelly, not what she expected in July. The crypt inside the cathedral would have more vibrancy. Where are the delicate fragrances of summer blooms? Instead, the air carries the tang of the old fountain beyond the archway. She draws the collar of her jacket over her face, trying to rid her nostrils of a pong like public swimming baths.

———

At the fountain, heavy disinfectant masks the faint smell of drains. Tracey supposes it's a hygiene requirement in a public space, a Euro directive no doubt. A mermaid sits atop a rock, looking even more naked than usual, as it's too early for the water flow to be turned on. Green mould threatens to infiltrate the stone robe draped over her hips. Tracey notes with some satisfaction that a piece of stone has chipped off her right nipple.

Despite the whiff and the somewhat saucy choice of fountain for a cathedral, it is a different world here. Hard to believe her guesthouse is only a stone's throw south and the railway station the same distance north. She tries again to get the lead on Hamish, but he darts to the privet hedge and barks.

She's wondering how to shut him up when he twists his head towards the archway, sniffing, body quivering.

"It's just a bird," she says. The seagull mess that has silvered the fountain and the cobbles attests to that likelihood.

Hamish loses interest and, with his snout to the ground, trots along the privet hedge. Tracey follows, then stops to admire a fuchsia bush. The buds on hers always fall off. Hamish, or dear old Victor before him, is forever bashing into them. The thought makes her check Hamish isn't causing damage now. To her dismay, he is squatting by the arch, back legs hunched forwards.

No here, wee boy, no here. But before she can distract him with a biscuit, it's too late.

———

Was this always the plan, then: get her here and keep her waiting until she gives up and goes home? Sonia folds her arms. If the interview doesn't happen, she'll run the story anyway. She isn't the one with something to lose.

Sonia tries to stamp the cold out of her feet. Who actually benefits from the new trail? Day trippers from Wales, pensioners at a loose end and drug dealers, that's who. The chill moves up her legs and takes hold of the rest of her body. Her eyes make an involuntary circuit of the noticeboards, and she reassures herself that there are no spaced-out delinquents lurking behind *Gloucester during the Reformation*.

Thankfully, Hamish's offering is hard and easy to pick up through the bread bag Tracey has with her. Deciding that Hamish has done his worst, she walks through the deep archway. When her eyes have adjusted to the reduced light in the brick tunnel, she gets a view of the first noticeboard beyond: *Our story begins on sacred ground in 679.*

Sonia cues her mini tape recorder. Still no sign of the interview getting going, but she might as well set up for it. A dog barks again, this time not so far away, making her jump. She glances across the concourse to the archway that leads through to the fountain and gets another waft of chlorine. She wrote about the cathedral grounds in her article on the history trail's opening ceremony. If she'd mentioned the fountain's unpleasant smell, they might have done something about it; such is the power of the press. She can't see through the arch, and the barking stops. Perhaps the dog isn't anywhere nearby. Sound travels further in the dead of morning.

Sick of looking at the history noticeboards, she retrieves a pen from her bag. In swift shorthand she writes the heading: *Szechwan.* Just a working title that she'll change in the final article. *Gloucester Evening News* is lucky to have her. They'll be advertising the deputy editor's post any day now. She is making sure the job has her name on it.

With a favourable wind, she'll be in post before September when Edith starts school. Alistair suggested they ask his mother to do the afternoon pickups. He would say that, wouldn't he?

No wonder they are always rowing. Alistair's mother owns a deep fat fryer, for goodness' sake. Sonia can't have Edith subjected to a daily diet of hamburgers and *Hollyoaks*. It is at times like this that she almost misses her own mother. Almost. A bedrock of stubbornness on both sides means that they haven't spoken in the years since their last argument.

Cold with bitterness, she forces thoughts of her mother from her mind. Enough now. She packs her tape recorder and gathers up her handbag. A no-show means no right of reply. She'll write the story her way. It could mean the front page. The deputy editor's job is hers.

She pulls her arms tightly across her stomach and closes her eyes. Most people would be pleased to have such a high achieving daughter. They would put her past mistakes aside. Forget them. If she could see her mother now, she'd tell her...

A warm weight on her knee interrupts her thoughts and she looks down at a black muzzle and a pair of doleful eyes.

———

Tracey hears the scream coming from somewhere beyond the arch. It dawns on her in the same second that Hamish has disappeared. Breaking into a run, she tells herself it isn't really a scream, more of an indignant 'Humph'. It sounds like a woman, so not the man she saw. Hamish wouldn't hurt anyone. Maybe cause a bit of surprise. But what if the screamer has a dog, a female dog? Hamish could be... She runs faster.

As she comes through the arch, Hamish bounds towards her. A woman stands by a concrete bench, brushing her hand vigorously over her trousers. Hamish, somehow sensing expediency, comes straight to heel. Tracey goes forward, profuse apologies at the ready.

"Keep that mongrel away from me," the woman shouts, flashing a pair of dark eyes.

Apparently detecting danger, Hamish rubs against Tracey's leg and stands meekly while she puts on the lead. It takes an age. The metal chain slips in Tracey's shaking fingers. The woman says nothing more and peers into a small mirror.

Tracey flees back through the arch, her heart hammering in her ears. Hamish trots beside her, tail drooping. It's not like Hamish to jump up. Apart from that rather unfortunate over-familiar sniff he gives sometimes, the most he ever does is offer his nose and whiskers for a pat. Her old dog, Victor, was a jumper, but not Hamish. What if the woman reports him to the cathedral? She looked so angry, face like a smacked bottom.

What is the woman doing here at this time in the morning anyway? Waiting for someone? A wave of icy outrage moves down Tracey's spine. She zips her fleece. The woman's black trouser suit looked too expensive for a lady of the night, but Tracey hasn't met many of that ilk, so she can't be sure. And at the cathedral of all places. Far worse than dogs. Head down, she hurries Hamish towards the street. They are level with the lime trees when Hamish collides with the man walking towards them.

"Sorry," Tracey yelps, one hand on her chest.

"Good morning," he says in a clipped voice and tips his trilby hat, ignoring the wet nose pressing up his leg. "What a beautiful Scottie dog." His grey moustache twitches as he bestows on Hamish a warm but tight-lipped smile. He gives him a swift pat and keeps on walking. He's gone through the archway before Tracey can think how to respond.

As she reaches the street, she thinks she hears the woman's indignant 'Humph' again. The poor man. He doesn't look like a client – far too refined. And he didn't have a dog with him. What possible exception could the woman have taken to him?

CHAPTER TWO

At eight a.m. I'm Dale Green with the Mids FM news...

Radio on, I stand in the kitchen, sipping my green tea. Although I'd rather sink a gallon of black coffee, I'm getting used to the grassy taste.

Twelve boys and their football coach, trapped in a cave in Thailand for nine days, have been found alive...

I turn up the volume, reminding myself that 'found alive' doesn't mean safe. I'd be in knots if one of those kids was Jake. The newsreader reels off stuff about divers and pipe-lines, but my attention drifts to a speck of sauce on a cupboard door. Despite cleaning every surface with Cif before I went to bed, I've missed a bit. Did Jake come down and raid the freezer for pizza? But no, the air still smells lemon fresh and my rubber gloves hang undisturbed over the gleaming mixer tap. Pink ones. Always pink now. It's been nearly two months, but I can't get finding a corpse wearing my yellow Marigolds out of my mind.

After the break-in, I gave serious thought to putting this flat on the market, but it's the only home Jake's ever known, the one my parents helped me pay for. Besides, the only actual damage was to the lounge cabinet and that was nothing a French polish couldn't fix.

The best thing to do with a violation is ignore it. I've been managing that for years.

The news soon makes way for adverts, and then the radio station returns to breakfast-time banter and bubblegum pop. Somehow I've developed a soft spot for Mids FM in recent weeks, despite one of their presenters nearly costing me my police career.

I've almost psyched myself up for a bowl of yoghurt and banana – another thing I'm trying to get used to – when Jake walks in. He's up dangerously early for college. And dangerously dressed, too, in beige chinos and a pale blue shirt.

"What time are you due in court?" I quip.

He glances down at himself. "Too much?"

"Depends what it's for. Have you got an accountancy job interview I don't know about?"

"Mum! I'm just trying to smarten up. I thought you'd be pleased."

When he folds his arms, I get a waft of aftershave and my deductive skills kick in. "You look great, love." I peer over my drink. "But why the early start?"

Pausing before answering, he looks out of the window. "I thought I'd call in on Nan and have a coffee with her first."

Gotcha! My mother runs a hairdressing salon near Jake's college. Not only does she serve the best coffee in Gloucester, she has the prettiest apprentices. The current one, Kelly, goes in for training on Mondays when the salon is closed. Jake's fancy dress must be for her benefit.

"Say Hi to Nan from me. Have a good day." Resisting the urge to tease, I reach on tiptoes to peck his cheek. He's entitled to secrets. God knows, his mother has plenty.

After he's gone, I seize the opportunity to deal with one of them. From my bedside locker I retrieve a letter, check I'm definitely phoning outside office hours and dial the number at the top.

After three rings I'm connected. *You have reached the Radiology Department at Gloucestershire Royal Hospital. Please leave a message after the tone.*

"This is Stephanie Lewis, date of birth: fourth of the ninth, seventy-four. I'm calling to cancel a scan booked for next Tuesday, the tenth. I don't need it. I'm... fine. Sorry for the inconvenience." I end the call and collapse on my bed. It's over, chapter closed. After postponing twice, the NHS must have had me down as a time waster. Now by cancelling I'm no longer their headache.

Headache. The reason for being offered a brain scan in the first place. But my migraines are getting better on their own. Elephant-strength painkillers saw me through May, and the repeat prescription I wangled out of a different doctor sorted out June. This month I'm on natural remedies. Homeopathy, essential oils, diet. Anything and everything. Something will work in the end.

The phone rings on the pillow beside me. A call back? Having got away with leaving a message, I'm out of words to deal with an actual NHS human. I turn away onto my side, but it keeps ringing. What if they don't give up? What if they call the home phone later and get Jake?

But when I sit up and grab the phone, I see the screen

flashing 'Kevin'. DCI Richards, my boss. Relieved, I accept the call, but the mobile slips from my fingers onto the bedroom floor. I scrabble after it. "Sorry, morning."

"Morning, Steph. Is there a riot your end?" Typical Kevin greeting – breezy even so soon after daybreak.

"You know me: always fighting off the bad guys." Two can tango. Then, knowing this won't be a social call, I get serious. "What's happened?"

"There's been a murder outside the cathedral, a woman. Two elderly sisters out walking their dog found her. They were pretty shaken up and rather slow in raising the alarm. Let's hope Siobhan Evans can work her magic on time of death."

He's right about needing magic. After another hot night, determining the time of death will be a work of witchcraft. And our pathologist, Siobhan, is just the woman for such sorcery.

"Be right there," I say and ring off.

CHAPTER THREE

Hands still shaking, Tracey delves into the umbrella stand on the outside porch where the door key has fallen. Her fingers find the key, but she scratches herself on the spoke of a weather-damaged umbrella. The guesthouse patrons are always leaving stuff behind. Time she got rid.

Finally, she unlocks her door. "Stay, Hamish, stay. Don't come in yet."

She hooks her heel under the doorstep, eases off one wellington boot and swaps feet to remove the other. Sucking her bleeding hand, she steps onto the tiled hall floor, but her other arm drags backwards. The dog is still on the lead.

"Sorry, son. I'm all of a dither. That nasty woman."

She bends down to release him but changes her mind. She can't leave Hamish outside on his own to dry off, not when the neighbours' bitch is on heat. The front garden is secure enough. It has to be when it's the guesthouse's only access point from the street, but even a wee dog like Hamish could scale a fence for lust, or burrow underneath.

Still leading the dog, she goes through the hall to the door marked *Private* and into her kitchen. She unclips the lead. "Stay. I need to put a towel down first."

As quick as she can, she retrieves a fraying towel from a pile on the coffee table in her parlour. When she returns to the kitchen, Hamish has settled himself in his basket under the breakfast bar.

"Oh, Hamish, not yet." She tugs on the dog's collar. Hamish lifts his eyes but nothing else, not budging. "I'll have to wipe you in there then." She kneels down, sweating. The morning is turning hot and she hasn't taken off her fleece.

"Paw!"

The dog obliges, stretching out a short front leg. Tracey works a section of towel gently over his pads and between his toes. It's harder than usual because she has to keep her other hand up to her mouth. Still bleeding.

At least the man was friendly. Quite charming. He said he liked terriers. "Other paw." The dog doesn't move. Tracey enunciates the words more clearly. She tries three times, but Hamish doesn't respond. Tracey's face is burning and a trickle of sweat touches her temple. Then she remembers and reaches up to the kitchen top for Hamish's cookie barrel. As soon as the snack hits his tongue, he offers his other front paw.

After she's repeated the titbit-induced ritual for legs three and four, something finally dawns on her that probably occurred to Hamish four paws earlier. She doesn't need to wipe him at all. She hasn't been rubbing him down after their walks for weeks, ever since the summer weather started. There isn't any wet mud left in Gloucestershire for Hamish to pick up – or requiring her to wear wellies, for that matter. The towel is still dry except for where she has trailed the edge in Hamish's water bowl. Gulping a breath and holding it, she tells herself to calm down. Forget what happened this morning. She and Hamish have endured far worse.

She drapes the towel over a kitchen chair, tosses Hamish another biscuit and peels off her fleece. Bother, blood on the sleeve, but at least it will wash. She looks down at her hands and admires the cut. They are working hands with flaking skin and dirty nails. Ideal for dog walking. She sighs. And for cleaning, cooking and hosting. She can't forget her guest-house duties.

As Hamish dozes, she switches on the radio to the reassuring voice of Dale Green. Such a nice man, she thinks, as she dabs her hand with kitchen roll. She bets he likes dogs.

———

"It stinks." Joel covers his nose with one hand and holds out the other, almost touching the smoke.

"What if it's poisonous?" Jack asks, holding a palm to his face.

"Don't be stupid," Dommo snaps, but he takes a step back with the other two.

"Is that what flesh smells like?" Joel asks, peering into the fire but not moving forward again.

"What flesh? You're pathetic. There's no flesh. I'll show you." Dommo picks up an empty vodka bottle and hurls it into the fire. All three boys jump as it shatters, throwing out shards of glass and cinders.

"What did you do that for, Dommo?" Jack asks. In fright he's grabbed hold of Joel's sleeve. Now self-conscious, he lets go.

"I was showing you there's no flesh. You can see now."

"That bottle could have exploded. Alcohol catches fire easy."

"Don't be such a girl," Dommo sneers. "Have you ever found one round here with booze left in it?"

He glances at the river. Despite it being a sticky morning, the footbridge casts a dingy shadow along the towpath. By night, it is a gathering point for Gloucester's homeless. Now, by day, people from the west side of the city are using it as a shortcut to the railway station. A stream of adults walk past, taking care to dodge the half-eaten kebab wrappings and discarded cans and bottles. Some clutch mobile phones to their ears. Others scroll screens. All seem oblivious to three twelve-year-olds in school polo shirts crouching over a smoking pile of stuff.

"Look, there's some hair," Jack squeaks, taking hold of Joel's arm again. "It's a body."

"Quiet down, Jack," Dommo commands. They've attracted the attention of a man in shiny black shoes. He slows down as he passes them but soon speeds up and returns to his phone.

"Maybe it's a dead cat," Jack whispers.

"Don't be stupid. It's a woman. There's her handbag," Joel says, shaking his arm free of Jack and pointing towards the fire.

They stare at a smoking block of black canvas and watch its plastic trim melt into the ground.

"This is awesome," Joel squeaks.

"You idiots. There's no body. It's just junk," Dommo says. Nothing so cool would happen in this dump.

He squats closer to the smoke. It's still chilly in the shade and the little bit of rising heat warms his skinny arms. The others fall silent and they watch for a while. The flames are small by bonfire standards but, given the time and place, exciting.

"Wow, did you start a fire?" a breathless voice behind them asks.

"Get lost, Alex," Dommo replies without looking round.

"I'm telling." Alex says, turning to go but not moving anywhere. He grips his school bag like a clipboard.

"We didn't start it. It was already—"

"Yes, we did." Dommo silences Joel with a punch on the elbow. "So, what you gonna do about it?" He pushes his face into Alex's.

Alex points into the smoke at a smouldering mass of black plastic. "That's one of those mini recording things. Will it still work?"

Dommo stares into the fire, annoyed that it has revealed one of its treasures to a saddo like Alex. "Why don't you pull it out and try it? I dare you," he mocks.

"I... I'll be late for school." Alex clamps his holdall to his chest.

"You've got ages yet."

Alex lifts his wrist to show the time on his watch.

"Shit," Dommo says. "Kelly will kill me." He bolts along the path away from the bridge.

The others follow, leaving the fire, past its peak, to smoulder on.

CHAPTER FOUR

INCIDENT ROOM – MONDAY 2ND
JULY, 9.30 A.M.

After battling the glare through my windscreen on the drive here, I take a moment to adjust to the gloom of the incident room. Expecting another scorcher, Kevin – or the cleaners in earlier – has opened the windows and closed the blinds. The only source of light is the projector shining a view of Gloucester Cathedral onto the whiteboard: a postcard shot of the imposing south entrance and, on the forecourt, a large area of tarmac, grass and flowering shrubs I don't remember noticing before. Likewise, the heavy memorial stones, some parallel, some at angles to each other, are oddly unfamiliar.

My colleagues are already seated and chatting among themselves. After saying my hellos, I take a chair on the back row where I hope it's not so stuffy. The headache that's threatening could still bloom despite my darkened surroundings.

I'm pretty much the last to arrive, so we don't have long before Kevin stands by the desk at the wall. In a concession to the heat, his shirt sleeves are rolled up on a fresh tan that suggests he spent Sunday out and about with Linda and the kids.

"Morning all," he starts and points at the image on the screen. "A bit of scene setting first for those who don't follow community affairs. This is the new Story of Gloucester trail, a series of benches and noticeboards about the city's history. Thanks to a National Lottery grant it has replaced the cathedral's old car park."

He gives us a moment to study the image. The coffin-sized blocks of concrete I took to be memorials must be the new benches. I can see now there are picture boards next to each one. History used to be my thing – Grade B at A level – so how could I not know about this? I really must spend more time in the city centre instead of just dashing to the bank in my non-existent lunchbreak.

Kevin continues, "The opening ceremony was less than two weeks ago and attended by the Bishop and that guy who used to present *Songs of Praise*."

"Harry Secombe?" DC Tony Smith calls out.

Kevin lets him soak up a few chuckles from the grey and balding members of the room, then he looks at DC Harriet Harris. "Do you know who he means?"

"No idea," the twenty-four-year-old replies.

"Make the jokes this century or not at all," Kevin tells Tony before getting back to his grim briefing. "A woman was found dead here at approximately six fifteen a.m. by two elderly dog walkers. Credit cards in her jacket were in the name of Mrs Sonia Hanson. Uniform went round to her home address and broke the news to her husband. Alistair Hanson has now formally identified her and provided this photo, taken at their wedding four years ago."

He projects a new image onto the screen. Even from this

distance, I can see the chic elegance of the wedding gown and the highly coiffured hair. Kevin pushes a six-by-four-inch copy into the board by the wall so that it nestles between two scenes of crime photos. On the left is a long shot of the corpse slumped on the ground by one of the concrete benches. On the right is a close-up of Sonia Hanson's lifeless face, recognisable by the same dark hair.

"Siobhan Evans has already made some initial observations."

"Blimey. She was lively with the scalpel this morning," Tony quips.

"*Initial* remarks only, not the full post mortem," Kevin explains. "Sonia Hanson was in apparent good health, and cause of death appears to be strangulation, but we need the autopsy to confirm both of these things. The date of birth her husband provided – twelfth of May, eighty-two – puts her at just turned thirty-six years old.

"He says she left the house at five. So assuming our dog walkers are accurate with the time they found the body, we can pin the murder to within an hour."

No witchcraft needed on time of death after all. That's if Alistair Hanson is telling the truth. "What do we make of the husband?" I ask.

"He says he was in the house until seven thirty when he took their children to nursery. All three were asleep until he woke them. No one can verify this. All we know for sure is he was home alone when Uniform arrived on his doorstep after eight a.m."

A cold shudder passes through me. If he's the family man he appears to be, I picture him getting back from nursery, putting the kettle on, picking up pyjamas, making beds.

Maybe getting a load of washing on before a knock at the door that will change his life forever.

But this isn't the time for sentiment, as Kevin's instructions to the detectives in the front row make clear. "Check out the family finances. Is there a nice little insurance policy on her life? He's a lawyer, works part time. See what his firm's got to say about him. Was there anything extra-marital, on either side?"

I watch my colleagues scribble notes, then I ask, "What was she doing in the city centre at five in the morning?" When Jake was little, he frequently woke me at dawn, but rather than wandering the streets of Gloucester, I'd be carrying my wide-awake toddler back to bed with me and hoping he'd go back to sleep. He hardly ever did. Payback now though. There's much delight to be had in waking a sleeping teenager.

"She told the husband she was going out early for work," Kevin explains. "When we phoned her office, her boss said she didn't start work until eight thirty, although she was a bit of a workaholic and usually in by seven thirty. That still doesn't explain the ultra-early start and why she went to the cathedral."

"Where did she work?" Tony asks, notebook resting on his crossed leg.

"She was a journalist at *Gloucester Evening News*."

Tony shakes his head. "Three kiddies and a full-time job. What a waste."

Harriet glares across the room at him. "We all know you think a woman's place is in the oven, but the rest of us have moved on."

Tony lifts his palms. "I meant what a tragic loss of a

young life. I'm as feminist as the next bloke. Do you think Nikki would be with me if I wasn't?"

I suppress a smirk. None of us are too sure how he's hung on to his current girlfriend long enough to get engaged. Maybe he just hasn't told her the good news.

"So is the husband a suspect?" Harriet asks, getting back to business.

"The feedback from Izzy and Ned is that he seemed devastated by the news," Kevin replies.

Leaning back in my chair, I feel oddly comforted. At least PCs Izzy Barton and Ned Smyth will have been gentle when they told him; they're two of our best.

"But I'd like to know what you think of Sonia's next of kin." Kevin's gaze moves across the room between Harriet and me. "Make Alistair Hanson your first port of call."

CHAPTER FIVE

Harriet sweeps up the wide, block-paved drive of the Hanson home and parks next to a blue Ford Galaxy. I let go of a deep breath. To be fair, Harriet is a good driver but I'm a lousy passenger, especially in my own car. I first let her drive it in May when my headaches were skewing my vision, and we've carried on taking it in turns ever since. I'm gradually reducing her time behind the wheel, but I have to be subtle about it. Harriet's a first-rate detective but, at twenty-four, takes it to heart if she feels undermined. Handing back the keys to my purple Golf would seem like a demotion.

The dark brick house with natural woodwork around the windows speaks of money. Hardly surprising, as this is Warwick Road in Wrenswood. Not as exclusive as some streets around here – I investigated a murder in a private swimming pool in Holly Gardens not long back – but pretty decent. Wrenswood is one of the city's wealthiest suburbs, and with this second police visit to the area in two months, maybe also one of the most tragic.

"First suspect is always the husband, isn't it?" Harriet

asks, staring through the windscreen at the front door. Two black-skinned Barbies and a white BABY born doll lie spread-eagled on the doorstep.

"Definitely a person of interest despite no obvious motive so far," I reply. During the drive here, DC Cally Lane texted me with an update. She's still checking, but hasn't found a life insurance policy on Sonia, and Alistair Hanson has no criminal record. Before we leave the car, I fill Harriet in on the details and also tell her about the phone call I took from another colleague. "Jordan says he contacted Alistair Hanson's office. According to the senior partner, Hanson is a reliable employee and there is no trouble at home as far as he knows."

Harriet frowns at me. "A lawyer gave DC Jordan Woods a straight answer?"

I laugh. "You're right. Believe nothing, suspect everything." I make a mental note not to trust Alistair Hanson, despite the multicultural toys.

Harriet steps round a child's trike to reach the door and rings the bell. I wait on the drive. Several climbing plants and hanging baskets cling to the storm porch. The lawn is neatly mown and the shrubs well pruned. Plenty of work for a freelance gardener? I can't imagine the lawyer owner getting his hands dirty.

A small woman in her mid-fifties answers the door. She's carrying a plump baby with a shock of black hair. Peeping round her legs is a toddler with the same thick hair tied in bunches.

Proffering my ID, I introduce us. "I'm Steph, a detective inspector with West Gloucestershire Police, and this is DC Harris. Is Mr Hanson at home?"

"I'm Fiona Hanson, Alistair's mother. The bairns

26

should be at nursery, but Alistair wanted them close by after... their mother..." She stops speaking and motions us in.

The entrance hall is bigger than my lounge and far more sumptuous. A mahogany staircase sweeps up the middle. A matching dado rail runs round the walls, separating two thick gold wallpapers of subtly different hues.

Fiona Hanson leads us into another room of *Homes and Gardens* proportions. Here the dado is cream and the wallpapers are shades of beige. Three white sofas look as inviting as hot bubble baths, but they are unoccupied. A man in light-blue trousers is lying on the floor with his arm around a pretty dark-haired girl. She is engrossed in a jigsaw. Despite the carpet being strewn with jigsaw pieces and Lego, I make out faded and stained patches in its weave. My guess is this young family spends a lot of time together in this room. I almost forget my preconceived notions about lawyers; there is no obvious falsehood here.

He doesn't react to our arrival, but whether he's engrossed in the puzzle or in his grief, I can't tell. For all I know neither; he could be mentally rehearsing an alibi. Wouldn't be the first dad I've interviewed who hid behind his kids.

"These people need a wee word," his mother says, enough to get his attention.

Alistair looks up and paints on a smile that does little to hide his gauntness. He kisses the girl's head and stands up. "Just do a bit on your own, Edith."

"I can't find Milo's head," the girl says. I feel my heart beat. Her mother is dead and she is perfecting a jigsaw.

"Do Doodles first," the father replies, a player in the same sad charade.

"I'll help you," Fiona Hanson says, kneeling next to the child.

"I want Daddy. Poppy will grab the pieces."

The buoyancy leaves the father's face and he seems at a loss for what to do next.

"Perhaps we could talk somewhere else?" Harriet suggests.

Alistair says nothing, but heads for the door. He's about the same height as Harriet, not tall for a man, but towering over me. Yet his shoulders sag. Perhaps grief has made him unable to fill the smart check shirt he's wearing.

We follow him into the kitchen, a vision in oak where unsightly necessities like fridge and dishwasher are hidden behind doors. Only the cooker, a dark blue furnishing with designer hood, and the Aga aren't in hiding. Without doubt, it's a room of ornamentation rather than food preparation.

"My mother's been clearing up a bit. You should have seen the state of the place before she started," Alistair says, as if reading my thoughts and contradicting them.

The three of us shuffle onto stools at the breakfast bar. "Sorry for the intrusion," Harriet says. "We just want to go over what happened this morning while it's fresh in your mind."

I wince. Whether he's innocent or guilty, some things from today will always be fresh in his mind.

"There's not much to tell. I heard Sonia get up. She'd set the alarm. The radio came on at four forty-five. *Through the night with Mids FM*. I heard her reset it for me and I dozed while she was getting ready in the bathroom. Then I heard the front door close as she went out." He pauses for breath. "I turned off the alarm to give the children a lie-in. I went back to sleep and Tommy woke me up at seven."

"No lie-in then," Harriet says kindly.

"Actually, it was. Sonia usually took them to nursery before that."

"Why was your wife going out at five a.m. this morning?"

"To be honest, I don't know. She said she had an assignment. I thought she had a long journey. It never occurred to me she was working in Gloucester."

"Did she take her car?"

Alistair shrugs. "I heard an engine, and the car is not on the drive, so I assume so. She always drives to work. Most days she'll be taking or collecting the children, too."

His answer confirms what we already know. The information came through before we left the station: Sonia's Peugeot 301 was found in Cathedral Street, not far from the murder scene. As Hanson has just said, we assume she drove it there herself, although we take nothing for granted in an investigation.

"Did Sonia take a laptop with her, or a handbag?" I ask. There was no mention of either at Kevin's briefing and her credit cards were in a jacket pocket, but most young mums carry a jumbo haul of breadsticks and wet wipes even when they're not on parent duty.

"When she was on a story, she liked to leave her laptop behind and make notes. I'll check about her bag." Alistair gets up from the stool and leaves the kitchen. We hear feet on the stairs, plus the distant sounds of a child crying. A few minutes later he's back, but stays standing. "Her black canvas handbag isn't in our bedroom or in the hall where she usually leaves it." He looks straight at me. "Is it missing? A robbery? She was mugged and killed for a bag full of nappies?"

"Just one line of enquiry. Standard, I'm afraid." I pull his vacated stool out further, encouraging him to sit. "We'll know more after the police doctor has completed her investigations." I wince again, this time at my words not Harriet's. As if avoiding *pathologist* and *post mortem* will soften the blow.

But it seems my dainty turn of phrase is worth it. He nods and sits down without further comment. I give him a moment to settle before I become a lot less dainty and ask, "Did Sonia often go out without telling you where she was going?"

A look of hurt settles in his eyes. "It wasn't like that. She didn't tell me every detail of her job just as I didn't always talk about mine."

"You are sure it was work?" Harriet asks, adding another wound.

"What else would it be?" Alistair stares at us and squeezes the edge of the breakfast bar. The word 'affair' hangs unspoken between the three of us. I sense we'll lose him if we pursue it now. I'll get Cally and Jordan to do more digging, so we can come back armed with facts, if there are any.

"What had she been working on recently?" Harriet asks, apparently sensing the same and aiming for firmer ground.

"She was the consumer affairs correspondent for *Gloucester Evening News* but she did whatever they asked her to. She was building up experience. There was a deputy editor job vacancy coming up soon." A smile reappears on his face. This one seems less forced. A man genuinely proud of his wife? Time, and more digging, will tell.

"Did she bring work home?" I know the answer will be yes. Sonia Hanson was an ambitious young woman. Ambitious women bring work home. How else would I have made inspector after my late start in the police?

"She has – had – a home study and went in there most nights after we got the children to bed."

Harriet and I exchange a glance, both sniffing potential evidence. "May we see the study?" I ask. "Is that where she kept her laptop?"

Alistair still squeezes the table edge, his neat fingernails turning pink. "But it's her work stuff in there. We have an office each; I don't go in hers." His voice trails off. Why the reluctance to let us in the study? I wonder whether he's thinking we'll discover that Sonia had secrets, or that he did.

"We'll take great care," Harriet explains, "and return everything to its proper place, but we'd like to take her laptop to our digital forensic experts."

"Nothing to worry about," I add. "Another standard line of enquiry."

"But she might have photos on there." There's a break in his voice. "Of when we got together. Of us with the kids."

"Our experts are the best," I say, and it's true – even though most of our techies still live with their parents and look like Visigoths. "In these early stages, we have to look everywhere. We want to catch who did this. We have to—"

He cuts me off. "I'm a lawyer; I know how the police operate." Although he sounds defiant, he gets up to his feet, complying with our request. "Sonia's study is this way."

He walks tall, apparently taking command of his domain. I can't decide if it's arrogance or a desperate attempt to keep control of something when everything else in his life is slipping away.

Fiona Hanson meets us in the hall, carrying the baby boy again. Although he's silent, his scarlet cheeks are stained with tears. Sounds of another child crying emanate from the lounge. "Sorry, son. They want you."

31

Alistair's shoulders sag again. His brief moment of being in charge dissolves and he looks pleadingly at me and Harriet.

"Go ahead, Mr Hanson. Perhaps your mother could show us Sonia's study," I say.

"On you go," Fiona tells Alistair. "I've put out the squash cartons and biscuits I brought with me. They might take them from you."

"Sonia gives them sugar-free..." Alistair begins, then gives up. "Biscuits will be fine. Thanks, Mum." He takes the baby into the lounge. We hear him say brightly, "Have you finished the Tweenies jigsaw yet, girls?"

To get into Sonia's study we squeeze past a baby bouncer that is hanging in the doorway. In my experience *study* means *large cupboard* but this study would make a good-sized dining room. The laptop is on a table that's pushed against the far wall. On the same table are three ring binders and a few textbooks wedged upright between wooden bookends. My first thoughts are that Fiona Hanson has been in and tidied up or Alistair has already removed incriminating material. But I dismiss the idea. From what I've so far gleaned of Sonia's personality, the desk reflects its no nonsense, organised occupant. Former occupant.

Harriet snaps on a pair of latex gloves and unfolds a bunch of evidence bags. After donning my gloves, I help her gather the files. I run my fingers along the book spines: *Whittaker's Almanac, Roget's Thesaurus, Collins English Dictionary, Brewer's Phrase and Fable*. The paraphernalia of old-school journalism. Maybe we won't find anything on the laptop if she is a hardcopy kind of woman. I pick up each title in turn, flicking through the pages and shaking them.

Nothing falls out – no secret codes, no love letters, no vital clues.

Once we've packed up the laptop and the paperwork, we turn our attention to the rest of the room. A couple of Postman Pat books lie open on the rug. A wooden train track winds its way round a leg of the desk. A plasma screen television is set into what must have once been a fireplace, with *Fun French for Five-year-olds* and *Classical Music for Babies* DVDs peeping out underneath. A sofa, draped in the same creamy yellow as the blinds, provides seating for three cuddly toys.

Fiona Hanson watches us closely, making me feel like the intruder I so obviously am.

"Your son seems to be holding up well," I say, trying to soften the atmosphere.

"He's keeping going for the wee ones but he's running on empty," she replies. "This is a big loss to him."

Interesting sentence. I wonder how consciously she has reduced the death of Sonia to the one word *this* and restricted the loss to *him* not *us*.

"How did you get on with your daughter-in-law?"

"Fine. She was my son's wife. The mother of my three grandchildren." Her reply says nothing and everything. She could just as well have stated that she wouldn't speak ill of the dead. I get the message. No love lost between the two Mrs Hansons. We need to find out why.

"It would really help our enquiries if we could build a picture of Sonia. Get to know what sort of person she was. It could help catch her killer. It won't bring her back, but it could give your son some peace of mind," Harriet says, on the same page as me.

Fiona pushes the wheelie chair under the desk. "I don't

know what to tell you. Sonia was an ambitious woman. Her career mattered more than... Her career was important to her."

"That must have put a strain on family life." I lower my voice, affecting a conspiratorial tone.

It works and Fiona confides more than I think she intended. "Alistair is a saint. Does more than his fair share of housework and plays with the children every night. He has his work, too. He's a senior lawyer."

"But they were happy..." Harriet says. She's on a fishing trip like me. I can tell by the way she keeps her eyes on the toy train while she nudges it with her foot.

"I don't know if they were. Alistair didn't say anything to me, but I could see the signs and her track record wasn't good."

Harriet and I wait, the hint of a motive in view. *Track record* usually means *extra-marital*. But what she says next isn't what we expect.

"Family didn't mean much to Sonia. She hasn't spoken to her mother for over four years. Imagine that, her own mother."

We wait again.

"Her mother is quite, well, French. Sonia's brothers run an antique place in the Quays, all vintage clothes and continental bookcases, you know the sort of thing. Sonia was due to marry the owner of the building, but Alistair came along, and Carl was history. They got married in a registry office. She wore a chic French gown but none of her family came."

"Her mother didn't like Alistair?"

"It wasn't quite that. The family had been paying Carl Bryant a token rent. When Sonia left him, he felt humiliated and put the charge up. I'm not saying Sonia should have married him, but she could have let him down gently. Instead, he had to find out she was pregnant by another man."

Although I've never met him, I know Carl Bryant is a businessman who often appears in the newspaper, handing over giant cheques to local charities. A philanthropist or just a man who likes to put on a show of his wealth? I can imagine getting dumped by Sonia not sitting well with his public image. How angry did her betrayal make him? I look at Harriet and see her already making a note of the name.

"After they declined to attend the wedding, Sonia broke off all contact with her family. If she could do that to her mother..." Fiona stops speaking, apparently leaving *what about her husband* unsaid as Alistair appears in the doorway.

"They're watching television." He moves the baby bouncer aside to enter. "Sonia wasn't keen on TV but at least it's a schools' programme."

CHAPTER SIX

After our visit to the Hansons, I discover that the stress of other people's grief can trigger migraine. I can't get Alistair Hanson's broken expression out of my throbbing head, how his mild irritation at his wife's TV rules shifted to despair that she would no longer be there to enforce them.

We pull up at the city coach park and walk down West-gate Street to the cathedral.

"Take it steady," I tell Harriet. Rushing to keep up is doing nothing for my head.

I feel her side-eye on me and can't blame her; I sound like a jobsworth. After ten years in the police force, I'm the old sweat who's seen it all before. Whether we stroll or break the four-minute mile, the victim will still be dead.

"Walking time is thinking time," I say, trying for wise and experienced while I wince with pain.

"A chance for the cogs to turn, you mean?"

"Exactly." Although the cogs in my head are grinding with rust. I feel her loll beside me, her long legs forced into a shorter stride than is comfortable.

Uniform have cordoned off Potter Street, the left turning to the cathedral. A bunch of shoppers loiter on the corner, staring down the street to the cathedral concourse with its concrete benches and picture boards of the History of Gloucester trail. In their midst stands the white tent over the location where Sonia Hanson died.

Jess Bolton, a Police Community Support Officer I met on a previous case, lifts the police-do-not-cross tape for us. Some of the nosy parkers hold up their phones. I roll my eyes at Harriet; we'll be immortalised on Facebook yet again.

"We're searching the bins, bushes and side streets for the victim's handbag," Jess explains, "and we've interviewed everyone who's wanted to pass through the cathedral concourse since seven thirty this morning. It was quite busy early on. They had to form an orderly queue. Lots of commuters cut through here from the apartments in the Quays to the railway station, as do all the shop and office workers arriving in the city by train. No one so far has recognised the photo we have of the victim. We interviewed plenty of school-run parents and people with dogs. It went a bit quiet after nine o'clock. We've spoken to a few shoppers popping into town and the mums in the playground. We could do with another trawl through there before lunch. We're expecting another rush when the college knocks off."

"Well done," I say in inspector mode and praising the efforts of my junior colleagues, even though they know they're doing a box-ticking exercise. The folk currently frequenting this area of the city won't have been here at dawn. There is an outside chance Sonia Hanson has used the cathedral as a rendezvous in the past. If we can place her here before today, we might get an ID on someone she met regularly. A long shot, but maybe.

"We'll take the playground," I say. Perhaps she used to meet a contact while she was out with her kids. I know from experience that working mums multitask. "Have you got the photo?"

Jess hands over two clipboards from the pile next to the cordon. The dark, happy eyes of Sonia Hanson shine out from the wedding photo that's clipped to both boards.

Our quickest path to the playground is round the eastern end of the cathedral. I know the route well, having often brought Jake here for a 'go on the 'ings' as he used to call it before he could pronounce the 'sw' sound. I sigh. Simpler times, when I was his world and there were no secrets between us.

We reach the path between the grey cathedral wall and the right-hand police cordon. Around the back, we go under the tape again. Ahead of us is the Guild School, all closed up as the term has already ended for private schools. Staying on the path, cathedral on our left and school on the right, we carry on to the public playground that borders the school field.

Harriet pushes open the metal kissing gate. PC Ned Smyth is already busy with his clipboard, interviewing an elderly couple who are holding onto the handlebars of a Silver Cross pram. There are only half a dozen other adults here and even fewer kids. Most toddlers must have gone home for an early lunch and an afternoon nap. A stocky man in a red football shirt pushes a boy on the baby swing. The child is too big for the seat but grips the front bar and squeals as his father pulls him backwards and lets him go with a shove.

The smile leaves the man's face when Harriet shows her ID. "He's got a cold," he says, taking hold of the seat and stopping the swing. "He'll be back at school tomorrow."

Harriet explains why we're here and shows him Sonia's photograph. He smiles and sets the boy swinging again once he realises truancy isn't the topic.

"Sorry, love, never seen her before," he says after looking at the photograph. "Is she foreign?"

"She's a local woman," Harriet says with a hint of starch in her voice, put there by the suggestion of xenophobia in his. "What time did you get here?"

"Just now, but the missus has been here a while." He points to a pregnant woman sitting on a bench. She wears a football shirt that strains even more at the seams than her husband's.

"About half an hour ago," she calls out when we turn towards her. "Why do you want to know?"

I take my clipboard over. "Have you seen this woman here?"

The woman peers at the photograph through her long fringe. The rest of her hair is crew cut short. "Today?"

"Any day." Maybe our killer is a playground regular.

"Her children are all under school age," Harriet adds as she joins us. "Perhaps they've played with your son."

"Josh is seven," she says sullenly, apparently seeing Harriet's comment as a slur on his boyhood. She looks over to where he is struggling to unwedge his behind from the swing. "Fuck's sake, Dave. Help him." She gets off the bench and moves at surprising speed. The child releases himself before she reaches him and trots off to the climbing frame.

"Nothing doing here. Let's go," I tell Harriet. Apart from the couple with Ned, there's only one woman left to question. From the back, she has a mass of grey curls and tight white trousers through which the outline of a dark thong is visible. She keeps steering her charge, a toddler in a yellow baseball cap, to the sandpit, although he's doing his darndest to escape to the slide on the far side of the playground.

When Ned turns away from the couple with the pram, the woman steps in front of him and offers herself for interview. Her big dark sunglasses make her look a bit like an owl.

"Thank you, madam," Ned says. "Just a couple of questions if you can spare a minute. I can see you've got your little lad with you."

The woman tosses back her big hair. "He's not my son; I'm his nan."

Ned does his duty and replies, "You don't look old enough to be a grandmother."

"You're too kind." She removes her sunglasses and places them on her head, hairband style. Ned puts his first question to her and we hear her predictable response. "I'm afraid I wasn't here at six a.m. At my age, I need my beauty sleep."

"Surely not," says Ned, still playing her game.

The woman lowers her voice. "Have you been doing this all morning? Don't you get a break?"

"I'll be taking my lunch soon," Ned says. Unwisely.

Moving closer, the woman says, "There's a new café in Westgate Street. Fancy a coffee?"

Ned takes a step backwards. "When I say soon, I mean I've got more interviews to do first."

"No problem. I'm dropping Charlie back to my daughter-in-law at one. I could meet you after that." Her hands find her waistband and hoist the thin trousers over her belly.

Ned is thirty-five if he's a day but quakes like a nineteen-year-old rookie facing his first drunk and disorderly. I shrug and carry on. He'll survive, but not without something I can use against him at the Christmas party. I want to walk away, but Harriet turns back to watch.

"Babe?" She drawls suddenly. "Can we have our sandwiches now?" She folds her arms and paints on a lovesick smile.

For a moment Ned looks more scared of her than the rampant granny. Then he twigs and grabs her lifeline, unconcerned with the finer details of why a police officer would be assisted by his girlfriend on a murder enquiry. "Just coming, love. I need a quick word with the lads on the concourse, then we'll meet your mum like we planned." He turns back to dismiss the woman but she has melted away, all of a sudden concerned about Charlie on the slide.

"Thanks," Ned murmurs to Harriet as we make our way round the cathedral again. "You were very convincing. I almost believed you were my partner."

"I do a bit of acting."

Acting? First I've heard of it. I glance at her but she's facing Ned.

"The uniform sets some woman off," he says. "My wife, Janet, says it's my animal magnetism. I could do without it, whatever it is."

"Acting?" I ask Harriet. "What have you been in?"

"Just am dram. The panto's coming up. I'm auditioning for..." She doesn't finish her sentence as all three of us are distracted by a man in a pink Hawaiian shirt advancing our way.

"Brace yourself," Ned whispers.

"Is this your doing?" the man says, his raspy voice swallowing his local accent.

"Good afternoon, Councillor Vale." Ned keeps an even

tone. "I'm not personally responsible for cordoning off the cathedral, but it's standard practice after an incident."

"Another flasher, is it? I said at the last council meeting we need more park patrols. It's all very well spending the money on local history, but it has to be backed up with protection." He tucks his shirt into his shorts. "How long will the concourse be closed? It's a municipal resource, you know."

"How long have you been here?" Ned asks.

The man mishears the question and answers one I assume is his favourite. "I've been on the City Council for twenty-five years. I've represented this ward, Central, for the last fifteen."

"That's magnificent public service," Ned says politely and then repeats his original question.

"Just arrived. I've been to the reference library to check the latest planning applications and I'm off home now. There are phone calls to be made. I haven't seen any undesirables about, if that's what you mean."

"So you weren't around here early this morning, say before six?"

"Good lord, constable. I know we oldies are supposed to rise with the larks, but I have my limits." He notices the photograph on Ned's clipboard. "That's the girl from the newspaper. She's a feisty one. I expect the flasher came off worse."

"You knew her?" Harriet asks.

"I make it my business to know all the city's journalists. What do you mean, *knew* her?"

As Ned explains about Sonia's murder, the little man's previously animated face pales and stills. "I don't know what to say." He points at the stained glass cathedral window. "Murdered in a place of beauty."

"How well did you know her?" I ask.

"She did a feature on me last year. A sort of 'where are they now' piece. It was well written and accurate." His face lights up, the memory of his name in print apparently restoring his energy. "I must phone David, her editor. Pay my respects. I hope you catch the monster. There's no respect for anything any more, not even human life." He makes several more utterances on the deplorable state of modern society before striding back along the path beside the cordon.

We duck under the tape and cross to where Jess Bolton is still on duty.

"Are you the front or the back?" I ask Harriet.

"What?"

"The pantomime horse."

But my joke about her acting fails to land. Her attention is on three figures in black who've emerged round the west end of the cathedral. One of them, a boy of about seventeen with black spiky hair and huge sideburns, removes two small packages from the pocket of his duffle coat. He hands one each to his companions. The girl stuffs the package up the sleeve of her voluminous velvet dress, while the other boy finds a pocket in his oversized trench coat.

"You know what they are, don't you?" Harriet whispers.

"Sixth formers?" I say.

"Drug dealers."

Ned and I exchange a glance. I know all the low-level dealers in the cathedral crowd and I expect Ned does, too. Our drugs squad keep a watchful eye, hoping for a lead to the big boys. These three kids don't figure.

"Their crime is wearing those clothes in July," I say. "Body odour is an offensive weapon."

Scowling, Harriet is about to say something when Councillor Vale appears on the other side of the cordon, having apparently dashed through the pedestrian diversion put in place by Uniform to the top of Potter Street.

"I know you're busy with this dreadful murder, but I've just remembered I really must have another word about dog-fouling. It's an epidemic," he rasps, the rushing round having taken its toll.

Ned holds up his palms as if in defence, then motions towards me. "That requires something strategic. Perhaps the inspector here could advise."

Bastard. Just because he knows I would have left him to the mercy of the amorous woman in the playground if Harriet hadn't intervened, he's passed the buck my way. I look at Harriet; perhaps she'll rescue me, too. But she drops her gaze to her feet and not before I've seen the smirk. On the opposite side of the police tape, Councillor Vale places himself in front of me. Both of us shorthouses, we're eyeball to eyeball. Over his shoulder I see Jess Bolton pointing out the detour the three teenagers need to make on their side of the cordon.

"Sorry, I can't talk now. I'm on active enquiries," I tell Vale, and to Harriet I say, "Your lead, DC Harris." I nod in the direction of the teenagers. "After you."

Because she has little guile herself, she doesn't think for a nanosecond I'm pulling her leg, and after a ninety-degree turn, she sets off like an Exocet to where the kids are disappearing from view behind the church offices. I scramble after her and clamp my arm in hers to slow her down. "Easy does it. Follow and observe."

Behind us, Ned is still protesting that dog mess requires a management response, but we're soon out of earshot as the route Jess has given the kids brings them out on Cooks Lane.

"Do you really think I'm right about this?" Harriet asks quietly.

"Having doubts?"

Harriet bites her lip but keeps looking at the group as they cross the pedestrian precinct into Quay Street. "It'll be worth questioning them. They could have been dealing at the cathedral this morning."

"Eyewitnesses, you mean?" I say, managing not to laugh. At their age they'll have been in their beds at the time of the murder. Jake rarely surfaces before eight, or later, on some mornings, making it a sprint on his bike to reach college on time.

With the multi-storey on the left, Quay Street is in shade and noticeably cooler. The trio of teens speeds up.

"What if they clock us?" Harriet asks. "When do we make the collar?"

"Not yet." The aim of my game is to put distance between us and Councillor Vale.

The teenagers turn left onto the towpath. We follow, suddenly conspicuous. We both scroll our phones, going for nonchalance. Something on the ground takes the teenagers' attention. They linger by the footbridge, where the boy with the sideburns slides the tip of his boot through the earth and kicks up a cloud of dust.

The girl loses interest in whatever they see and climbs onto the bridge. Sideburns boy follows, gets a package out of his pocket. When they turn back to the other boy, they spot us about twenty metres away on the towpath. For a moment I forget this is a yarn to wind up Harriet and I size up the 'suspects'. The boys are tall, and I can't tell whether they are skin and bone or solid muscle underneath their coats. The girl carries a fair bit of weight. The three of them could be more than a match if they resist arrest.

The second boy traces his foot through the ground where the first boy lingered, then joins them on the bridge. When they reach the middle, all three place their packages on the railings and unfold them.

Turning away, I bend almost double with the strain of not laughing. Harriet's expression remains hard, concentrating. She still hasn't twigged.

We reach the footbridge as sideburns boy drops something from his package into the river.

The girl says something. It sounds like: "We only ever get brown."

Before I can stop her, Harriet steps onto the bridge. "I am a police officer. Can I see that please?"

The girl and the sideburns boy exchange a sheepish glance. No one moves.

"Bring me your stuff," Harriet orders.

In apparent bewilderment, all three hold out their packages. Harriet peers at the heaps of breadcrumbs, realisation dawning in the flush on her cheeks. In the water below, ducks and seagulls splash and circle.

"It is wholemeal," the girl says apologetically.

Keeping my head down, I hide my grin. Then I see my feet and scowl. My black shoes are coated in a layer of silvery ash. I'm standing on the same spot that caught the kids' attention. Someone's had a fire here.

CHAPTER SEVEN

Tracey finishes watering the tiny courtyard at the back of the guesthouse. It will be touch and go whether the geraniums perk up. Bought in a fit of enthusiasm back in April, they suffer from her intermittent attention. Too much else to think about these days. And the heat keeps on. If she perspires much more, she'll desiccate. What she'll do tomorrow, she's no idea. Early morning dog walks seem out of the question, with today's trouble coming on top of the business in the Georgian Gardens in May. Hamish might have to do his business out here. She carries the plant tubs to the back wall, clearing a space for Hamish in anticipation. The effort has brought on another sweat. Time for a breather. The evening newspaper is in the kitchen.

Hamish looks up from his basket, where he's been all afternoon. Is he panting? The heat? Or the trauma after what happened this morning? Ideally, she'd sit with him on the sofa, a shared comfort for what happened, but it's too hot for that.

She gets up and runs the tap cold before changing his

water bowl. He laps messily, then settles by her chair, slobbering out more water. Tracey resolves to clean up after she's read the paper.

The table wobbles as she leans forward. She must get that broken floor tile replaced one day, but in the meantime, she might as well make some use of the sports news. She tears off the back two sheets of the newspaper, folds them three times and shoves them under the table leg. Pressing her elbows hard down, she smiles at her inventiveness. She's still got it when she wants. There was a time when she'd been handy with a screwdriver. Strong fingers. Just lately the effort of running repairs has been beyond her.

Some of the newsprint has come off in her clammy hands. The bandage she's wrapped round, over the scratch from the umbrella spoke, is grubby. She'll have another look for some plasters in a minute.

She flicks through to the TV listings on the double page in the centre. "Football again tonight. You like that, don't you, Hamish?" She taps the black muzzle. Hamish raises his brown eyes in response.

"Not much else on though." She closes the newspaper and glances at the headline: *GEN Journalist Murdered*. There is a large photograph of a dark-haired woman swathed in bridal lace. Some awful domestic, no doubt. She scans the first paragraph: *Gloucester Evening News consumer affairs correspondent Sonia Hanson was found murdered at a local beauty spot this morning.* Local? She reads the photo caption, *Sonia Hanson on her wedding day*, and studies the woman's face. Her veil obscures her hair, but her eyes stare back at Tracey, familiar and accusing.

CHAPTER EIGHT

TUESDAY 3RD JULY

The waiting room is shabbier than Anna expected. Not that she really knew what to expect, as she's never been in a police station before. Not even when her mother died suddenly years ago. Why would she?

Two banks of seats form an L-shape opposite the reception window. Yellow foam peeps out of the vinyl cushioning in places. Anna is aware of a man, unshaven, sitting in the corner where the two banks meet. She positions herself at the far end, away from him, and perches on the edge, determined not to create an unseemly noise against the vinyl.

The walls are undercoat green, pocked with Sellotape and Blu Tack. Two hardy posters are still clinging on. One is for a victims of crime helpline; the other advises Anna to lock up her bicycle. On the ceiling, a bluebottle in its death throes is making a valiant attempt to join other corpses inside the fluorescent strip light. Anna runs a finger along her seat. She finds a hole and begins to play with it but stops herself. No telling who else might have had a poke around in there.

Two young men burst through the main entrance and

slouch at the reception window until the receptionist appears.

"I forgot all about my curfew so I've come in first thing this morning," one says.

"First thing?" the receptionist says looking at her watch. "Take a seat."

Instinctively, Anna pulls her handbag towards her chest, but there is no immediate cause for concern, as the youths make no move to sit down near her. They shift their weight for a few moments and then begin pacing like caged lions. Anna notes that they are wearing baseball caps in a distinctive design favoured by that sort of person. She pictures the designer turning in his grave. There was a time when respectable ladies of a certain means wore a little of the same pattern. Anna once owned a scarf in the design but discarded it after seeing it worn as a mini skirt by a third-rate soap actress.

The thought hits Anna: there must be another waiting room for law-abiding citizens. She'll have a word with the receptionist. Discreetly of course. There is no sense in upsetting these youths. It is important not to create an atmosphere. She knows that from her work as a counsellor. First rule of counselling: defuse the situation; and the second rule: don't get involved. Misguided people don't need sympathy. She has to conserve her own energy to keep others afloat in their troubles and lead them safely to life's shore. One doesn't need to sample drowning to be a good lifeguard.

A door next to the reception opens and a young police officer enters. Smiling at Anna, she asks her to come through. When she holds the door open for her, the gesture goes some way to stifling the disappointment Anna feels on seeing the lack of stripes on the uniform. She expected a more senior officer, but at least the girl has manners.

At the end of a dull corridor, the police officer leads her to an interview room and motions her to a chair at a bare table.

"I'm PC Izzy Barton. How can I help you, Mrs Gittens?"

"Gold. I'm Anna Gittens-Gold." Anna folds her arms. The lack of attention to detail doesn't bode well. Names clearly aren't the girl's thing. Izzy must be short for Isabel, but why call herself that? It rhymes with dizzy, only a step away from ditzy.

"My apologies," Izzy Barton says, not sounding the least bit contrite. "I gather this is about your husband."

Well, at least she's got that right. "I'm sure there's some perfectly logical explanation," Anna says, "but he has disappeared."

Izzy Barton seems to choose her facial expression carefully, a patronising mix of concern and sympathy that she must have practised on other women making such a report. The girl hasn't yet realised Anna isn't like those other woman – not alarmist, or distraught, just sensible.

"When did you last see him?" the police officer asks.

"When he left for work yesterday morning."

"And you've not heard from him since. No phone calls or texts?"

Anna shakes her head neatly.

"Have you tried ringing round friends and family?"

Anna presumes the girl is going through the motions, asking the right questions, listening to the answers, no doubt planning on telling her – gently – to come back in a couple of days if he still hasn't turned up. Anna lowers her eyes a fraction. "We are a very close couple, constable; our outside interests are naturally limited. I phoned the Centre. They say he arrived at work as normal and left at around four, but he didn't come home."

"The Centre?"

"The Cross Care Centre. Gerald's a counsellor. We both are. I phoned again this morning but he hasn't gone into work today."

The girl frowns. "You are both counsellors? So weren't you at work yourself yesterday?"

"Gerald and I are job share partners. He works on Mondays and Tuesdays. I do Wednesdays and Thursdays." She slows her words; she and Gerald have explained this so many times over the years she's in danger of sounding robotic.

PC Izzy Barton pauses and composes her features. Anna can tell she's building up to something. "Forgive me for asking, but has he ever disappeared before? I mean, gone away without telling you where he was going?"

Anna sits up straight and speaks carefully. "The nature of my husband's work has frequently taken him away. He has often been unable to tell me where he was going, but he always kisses me goodbye before he leaves."

"I didn't realise that counsellors went into the field as it were," the police officer replies, biting her lip.

"In his other job. His main career. The counselling is more of a hobby really, although it is a vocation, too. It is for both of us. Good counsellors are born and not made," Anna says with not a little pride.

"His main career?"

"He worked for his government, a military photographer."

"*His* government?"

"He's Australian. He retired five years ago, but still gets called upon to advise now and again. He flies out to war zones to give briefings in theatre."

"Have you checked with his, er, government that he's not on a mission?"

Anna narrows her eyes. Is that a smirk the girl is hiding? She's not the first to be sceptical, but surely police officers should keep an open mind. "Gerald has to keep that part of his life secret. But he'd have told me if he was flying off somewhere. As far as I know he's still in Gloucester and something has happened to him."

The young officer straightens her expression and hesitates, as if deciding how seriously to take this. Anna waits, aware that she is scowling.

Finally, the girl commits. "Can you give me a description of Gerald and explain more about his army career?"

Anna reaches for her handbag. "I've brought in a photograph of him. It's from the Cross Care Centre brochure. As you'll see, he's smart, distinguished. Grey hair and moustache, very neat. Five feet ten. When he left for work yesterday, he was wearing a light suit and a straw trilby hat."

CHAPTER NINE

Our enquiries reveal that Fiona Hanson's information about her late daughter-in-law's family is out of date. After Sonia jilted Carl Bryant and he put up the rent on her brothers' antique shop, they struggled on for a couple of years, but in 2016 they quit the city centre for Hucton.

While Harriet runs background checks on Bryant, DC Tony Smith and I are making a call on his former tenants in their newish suburban location. Tony closes his driver's window as we join a queue of traffic under the railway bridge, a traffic fumes catch point. I sit in the semi-darkness, silently willing the lights to change before Tony – already warned by DCI Richards for his Miami Vice tendencies – sticks the blue light on the roof. He's leaning forward, sunglasses pushed up on his head – only a rolled sleeve away from the full Don Johnson. His hands are clenched, apart from his forefinger, which drums on the steering wheel. Instead of the police light, he settles for his car's music system, which he turns up.

I turn away and close my eyes, trying to block out the

bass thud that's duetting with my migraine. Pretty sure he's cranked up the volume to test me out. Everyone knows about my bout of headaches a few weeks back. Not everyone believes me when I say they've cleared up. Thanks to Foreigner at full belt, my head's throbbing again. They might be 'Cold As Ice' but I'm sweating like a hog, pain so intense I might puke.

But his upholstery is saved a green tea and yoghurt makeover when the traffic light changes and he kills the music. We emerge in Warren Hill. Although no longer in the shade of the railway bridge, the sun has lost its radiance here. The concrete frontages of the Royal Mail sorting depot and the kebab house emit gloom. We drive on past stone-clad terraces and a huge building of metal and tinted glass. A gymnasium, an incongruous invitation to health and fitness.

Traffic is still heavy, but Tony weaves onto and around the ice-cream factory roundabout and takes the exit onto Ermine Street, the old Roman road and straight two-mile run out to Hucton. When we get there, Tony punches the address we have for Sonia Hanson's family business into the sat nav and we leave the prosperous main drag. After a series of right and left turns, we arrive at Hucton Parade, a row of shops on a newish estate of town houses and flats.

"How the mighty have fallen," Tony mutters, as he reverses into a loading bay in front of Clarke's Furniture Emporium and Minimart.

The brothers' business stands between a fish and chip shop and a vape shop, beyond which are two boarded up units. Certainly not the flashy shop front of their previous premises in the Quays. On the opposite side of the road is an area of scrub grass where a group of young people sprawl in the sun. Two lads wave lager cans; the girls huddle over a litre of Lambrini.

"It's not even eleven o'clock," Tony says. "Oh to be young." He picks up the phone. "DC Smith to Control. Send a patrol to Hucton Parade. Some kids breaking the alcohol ban. They look too dozy to give any trouble, but you never know." He replaces the handset and peers up at the shop front. "Looks like Sonia's brothers have gone down the convenience store route. What's the betting they live over the shop?" Then he puts his seat back, stretches his legs and gets comfy with his hands behind his head.

"What are you doing?" I ask.

"I'll wait here to give Uniform a hand. You're all right to interview on your own, aren't you, boss?" He looks me in the eye and raises his eyebrows.

Another test. Tony is one of the least observant detectives in the West Gloucestershire force, but he's read my headache right. Ignoring the pain, I open my door ready to get out. But when Tony cranks up the music again, my pain turns to anger. "I'll go solo, but it could be embarrassing for you."

Tony turns my way. "Embarrassing?"

I keep gazing through the windscreen, pleased to watch the morning drinkers dump their cans and bottles in the bin and form an orderly queue at a bus stop. Tony can't even get them for dropping litter. "With your appraisal coming up."

Tony sits up. "That's not for ages."

"We inspectors have long memories."

Scowling, Tony gets out and slams the door. As we approach the Clarkes' shop, the fury bounces off him in waves. I'm not one to pull rank. Promotion is nine parts hard work to that vital one part right-time-right-place luck, but

Tony's been asking for it since my headaches became known round the station. All of a sudden, the kidder is too good at spotting another kidder.

He's also right about the shop being more convenience store than antiques. Inside it is cramped with high shelves of groceries and narrow aisles. The place smells of Weetabix and washing powder. Not a whiff of the French-polished furniture I was expecting from an antiques emporium.

There's a queue of customers at the checkout, where a young assistant in a faded orange apron is packing a trolley bag for a pensioner. Ever subtle, Tony steps in front of the next customer, another elderly lady with a basket of cat food, and waves his ID card.

"Police. Where's the boss, love?"

"Stockroom," the assistant says mildly, as if policemen ask her that every day. Without looking our way, she lifts the cat lady's basket on to the counter.

The room at the back is where the furniture is stored. And it really is a case of storage rather than display. Tables upended on other tables, stacks of non-matching chairs, a plastic tub of elderly silk scarves, a tray of costume jewellery, a tailor's dummy balanced on a wicker cabinet. On the far wall are boxes labelled Tewkesbury Mustard and precarious towers of loo rolls. I try not to breathe too loudly in case I start a cascade.

"All right?" A man appears around a dark-wood wardrobe, carrying a cardboard box.

"Mr Clarke?" Tony asks.

"Who wants to know?"

"We're the police. We need to speak to the family of Sonia Hanson."

The man looks late thirties, forty at a push, but the

expression that comes over his face makes him old and ugly. "That person has no family here."

"Are you her brother?" I ask.

"I'm working."

"Perhaps we could speak to your mother if she's here."

"My mother has no daughter." He drops the cardboard box with a thud. When he sets about opening it with a key from his pocket, it's clear he isn't planning to resume the conversation.

Tony has had enough, and the rage that's been simmering since I ticked him off bursts out at the man. "You're right there, mate, seeing as Sonia was murdered yesterday."

My headache runs hot and cold. What if Uniform haven't told him yet? There are procedures for informing next of kin. We can't always stop the media getting ahead of us, but there's no excuse for our own cockups.

But the man carries on dealing with the box. "Two policewomen visited us yesterday evening. We already have that information."

I sigh, relieved and also shocked. Never before have I heard a relative describe the news of a bereavement as 'that information'. This guy clearly didn't like his sister, but is dislike enough to kill?

"Jerome?" Another man enters from the back of the stockroom.

"They want to see Maman," the first man replies and then speaks in French. It's been a while since my GCSE but I get the gist. Younger brother, Jerome, is asking the newcomer to decide whether to accommodate our request.

"I'm Olivier Clarke. Come this way," the second man says. He is short and stocky. Below his t-shirt sleeves, his arms are an odd mix of muscle and flab, the result, perhaps, of years of collecting antique furniture and more recently lugging boxes of Doritos and eating their contents. He leads us through a door at the back of the stockroom and up a bare staircase.

We step into a well-furnished lounge. The pieces are lightwood and modern but too big for the space, no doubt more evidence of the family's move to humbler accommodation since the fallout with Carl Bryant. Without another word, Olivier sits on the sofa next to an elderly woman who is dozing. She wears a pink dressing gown with thick black socks and no shoes. The coffee table next to her is a shrine to old age: a glass of orange squash, various medicine bottles, spectacles and a copy of *Paris Match*.

"Mrs Clarke?" I ask, puzzled. This woman looks well into her eighties.

Another woman comes into the room. "I'm Monique Clarke."

I look straight into a pair of dark eyes. It's like facing an older version of the photograph on the CID office wall. The mother is chic, well-preserved mid-sixties, although the dark circles below those dark eyes suggest crying or a lack of sleep, or both.

"You are here about Sonia," she says, speaking with a precision that her sons' local accents have lost. "I can tell you nothing."

"I'm sorry for your loss and for troubling you at this difficult time. But anything you can tell us about your daughter could help our enquiries," I explain.

Olivier Clarke grunts something. Tony gives him a challenging glare. He glares back but says nothing more.

"I know little of her life," Monique says.

59

"Don't you care?" Tony blurts, that anger I stoked still not under control.

Monique looks him in the eye. "My daughter died for me four years ago."

"Sonia dishonoured this family," Olivier chips in.

"It might help if you explained what happened," I suggest. Surely marrying Alistair Hanson wasn't a point of no return? He might not have been a millionaire like Bryant, but many mothers would be happy to welcome a lawyer as son-in-law. Frankly, given my great age, my dad would marry me off to an estate agent if one showed interest.

Monique speaks again. "You think I should have been happy she made a love marriage. No doubt we would have accepted it in time, but there are ways of doing things, of picking the right moment. She gave no thought to anyone but herself." Her arms hug her body. "My husband had not long passed away and money was already tight. It was Sonia who left us. She wanted it all: marriage, children, a career. Ambition ran like a poison through her veins. She became a cobra, striking out at everyone. The first person she bit was herself."

I'm at a loss for how to respond, unable to see Sonia's decision to marry for love as anything other than completely normal.

"Is this Sonia's grandmother?" Tony asks, moving towards the old woman, who is still dozing on the sofa. "What did she think of Sonia?"

Monique sits down beside the woman. With Olivier on her other flank, the elderly lady has two bodyguards. "My mother is having a nap, and she doesn't speak English," Monique says quickly, but the woman is awake now and has understood the word 'Sonia'. She purses her wrinkled lips and makes a low, sucking sound, saliva brewing. She projects the spittle onto the coffee table and babbles. As the babble becomes a wail, the animation of her limbs increases. Olivier catches the glass of squash as the sleeve of her dressing gown knocks against it. He takes hold of her arms and draws her towards him. She lets herself be held and her wailings turn to sobs.

Throughout the outburst, Tony has been running his fingers through his hair. Now everyone looks to him for the next question. But he has no plans to ask more. "Right you are," he says. "We'll be in touch." He hastens to the door of the flat.

I thank them for their time and follow him out. There's a story here, but these people are too raw, too bitter to reveal it today. I'll return with a decent colleague for the interview and after a hefty dose of paracetamol for my head.

CHAPTER TEN

INCIDENT ROOM – TUESDAY 3RD JULY,
2.30 P.M.

The windows are still open, but the incident room has reached gas mark four and the sweat on my scalp feels like it's sizzling. There is no projector show to illustrate this briefing, but such is the intensity of the sun through the closed blinds, we are in daylight. On the board, more notes and photographs have appeared beside the images of our victim. Among them is a beaming Carl Bryant handing over one of his bountiful donations to a couple in evening dress.

Kevin points at him. "What have we found out about Jilted John?"

Tony chuckles. "Sir, you said to keep the jokes this century."

"You sound like a Gordon," Kevin fires back.

Those old enough to remember the seventies' one hit wonder give a round of applause. Even Tony claps, admitting defeat.

"Anyone got anything?" Kevin returns to his question.

Harriet checks her notebook. "Carl Bryant is a big noise in Gloucester. A portfolio of retail properties and a major shareholder in the rugby club. His P.A. has fitted me into his diary for an interview tomorrow afternoon."

"Nice of him to find the time," Kevin says. "It's only a murder enquiry after all. Steph, go with Harriet. We don't want him playing the big 'I am'. As the victim's ex, he is a person of significant interest."

"Right-oh, boss," I say and notice Harriet bite her lip, apparently crestfallen at not being trusted to go it alone.

"Can I just get something straight?" Tony says, tapping his fingers with his pen. "The victim was born Sonia Clarke, and her married name is Hanson."

"Correct, Tony," I say, breaking into a smile. "I'd say her husband is of Scottish extraction."

"So where does the French stuff come in?"

I outline what should have been clear from our visit if he'd been paying attention. "Sonia's late father was an Englishman, John Clarke. His wife, Sonia's mother, is Monique, a French woman. All three children – Olivier, Jerome and Sonia – were born here but brought up bilingual. Sonia's grandmother is the elderly lady we met, Marie Fournier."

"Could it be a random racist attack?" Tony asks. "I mean, we hate the French now, don't we?"

I wait a beat for the punchline, and when it doesn't come, I ask if he's serious.

"We've voted leave, right? This could be a savage expression of what someone thinks of our nearest neighbours."

I rub my head in my hands. It's bad enough hearing nothing but Brexit on the news without Tony bringing it to work. "Not even extremists have resorted to pitch forks and flaming torches at Dover."

"What about keeping it in the family, then?" Tony says,

flying a different kite. "A revenge killing. Those brothers detested Sonia for marrying Hanson."

"What, four years and three kids later? Isn't that a delayed reaction?" I ask. Why bother to kill their sister now when Carl Bryant, the ex-fiancé, has long since cast them adrift in Hucton?

"You've seen enough families in this business, Steph. Simmering cauldrons that can catch fire at any time."

I nod. He's got a point. There's certainly something going on in the Hanson/Clarke family.

Kevin moves on. "We've had no luck so far with the interviews at the cathedral. Plenty of folk pass through – dog walkers, commuters, shoppers. But no one admits to being up bright and early enough to see the victim. Uniform are still searching for the victim's handbag. She had credit cards in her jacket but no cash or keys. There's a handbag somewhere. Until we find it, we can't rule out a simple robbery as the motive.

"Siobhan Evans has completed the post mortem. Sonia Hanson was in good health, about twelve weeks pregnant and strangled. It was an expert manual strangulation. Whoever did it knew what they were doing."

"Man or woman?" I ask. Monique's fingers were dainty and manicured, but her sons had fists like burnt hams.

"It was our old faithful: medium-sized hands. Siobhan has confirmed that the victim died between four and six yesterday morning. So accepting for the moment the husband's version of events that she left home at five, we have a narrow window of sixty minutes. I'm still hoping Uniform will turn up a witness. Someone must have seen something. This time of the year it's light at that time."

There's a knock at the door. All the detectives jump. No one ever knocks, just barges in or stays away in droves.

"Sorry to interrupt, boss." It is PC Izzy Hutton. "I've got a missing person. A bit of a funny one."

"Funny?" Kevin cracks a smile. "Not sure this is the best occasion, but we could do with a laugh. What have you got?"

"Wife says husband didn't come home from work last night."

Kevin folds his arms. "Like what you did there. This is where I say, 'You must be joking, constable.'"

Izzy nods as if she was expecting the brush-off but carries on. "The funny bit is that he used to work undercover for the Australian government. The wife says he's had private jets from Brize Norton. I thought it might be political. Here are the details." She hands over a sheet of paper and a photograph.

"Political." Kevin rolls the word around in the same way he pronounces "Budget Cuts". It seems to leave a nasty taste in his mouth. "Okay, leave it with me. I'll see what I can do."

Defying the heat, Izzy all but sprints out of the room, no doubt making her getaway before Kev drop kicks the misper back to her.

"I wonder if Alistair Hanson knew his wife was pregnant. He didn't mention it," Harriet says, getting back to business.

Kevin drops the photo and Izzy's paper on his desk and turns to Harriet. "Good question, and one you can put to him when you and Steph interview him again."

Harriet scribbles in her notebook, then looks at me. Her solemn face says we get all the good jobs.

CHAPTER ELEVEN

WEDNESDAY 4TH JULY

It's seven thirty and, with the news headlines on Mids FM, I'm Dale Green. An estimated twenty-three million watched England's footballers' win over Colombia to reach the quarter finals of the World Cup. Police in Salisbury say a man and a woman are critically ill in hospital after exposure to the nerve agent Novichok, some four months after Russian defector Sergei Skripal, his daughter and a police officer were similarly poisoned.

I sip my green tea, pondering the ramifications of both news stories. Will there be new operating practices for all police forces under the threat of chemical attack? And why wasn't Jake, who watched the match at his mate Bradley's, more effusive about the result? Instead, when he got in last night, he apologised for being late due to the penalty shootout, poured himself an avalanche of Coco Pops in the kitchen and took the bowl to bed without once looking me in the eye. He hadn't backed Colombia, had he? An illegal bet with his friends. There was no blurry-eyed sign of drugs, no smoke-stink on his clothes and no tinny alcohol breath. What else could it be?

I listen as the radio plays interviews with jubilant fans and overexcited commentators bent on reliving every kick of the match. I can well believe twenty-three million watched. When I popped out to the corner shop last night, the streets were as quiet as a zombie apocalypse; every household seemed to be indoors watching.

Carrying his empty cereal bowl from last night, Jake comes in. "Morning, Mum."

Now I'm proper worried. Since when did he retrieve dirty bowls from his room without two days of my nagging? "How was the match?" I ask.

"Yeah. Great. Four-three on penalties. Really great."

That's all he said last night. I decide to probe; not for nothing am I a detective inspector. "Who was your man of the match?"

Facing the sink, he runs the tap on his bowl. "Jordan Pickford made a brilliant penalty save from Carlos Bacca."

Isn't that verbatim the news report I just heard? Some-thing that people like me, who didn't watch, might repeat. I clear my throat. "Jake, can you come and sit down a minute?"

"Let me just..."

"Leave the washing up."

Slowly he shakes excess water off and puts the pot on the draining board. He pulls out the chair opposite me and sits well back from the table.

"I don't bite," I say, motioning him forward.

Finally, he looks at me, but there's no smiley response to my joke, only alarm in his eyes. At that moment my mobile pings on the table and Kevin's name flashes on the screen.

"Better read that, Mum. Could be important." He stands up. "See you tonight."

"Wait. What about breakfast?"

He taps his belly. "Still full. See you." And with that, he's gone.

———

Harriet and I approach Longton. Kevin's text was new orders. Word from on high – overriding his decision to concentrate exclusively on the Sonia Hanson murder – to give attention to the 'political' missing person case. The wife, Anna Gittens-Gold, has given her address as St Levens, as do most residents of the old part of Longton, keen to distance themselves from the 1990s housing sprawl that has attached itself to the suburb.

"What do we know about the missing man?" I ask Harriet, as I haven't made much effort with background reading, concentrating instead on the statements on the Hanson murder.

"He works part-time as a counsellor at the Cross Care Centre in town. He's ex-Australian armed forces."

After the story about Novichok on the morning news, my mind goes to terrorist revenge or a spy who knew too much. "Description?"

"Five ten, medium build. Grey hair and moustache. Fifty-six years old."

"Fifty-six?" Not old by any means, but it must be a while since he was on active service. "How old's the wife?"

"I've got her date of birth here," Harriet says, looking in her notebook. "That would make her fifty-one."

I ease off the accelerator, turn into Maple Gardens, a quiet side road dotted with parked cars, and squeeze between two in a manoeuvre that I would not have attempted yesterday with my headache. So far this morning, I'm migraine free despite my concerns about Jake. I switch off the engine and look up at the bungalow. "Doesn't the Ozzie army pay well then?"

"What do you mean?"

"It's quite compact, not exactly Wrenswood."

"Pensioners downsize, though," Harriet says matter-of-factly.

A cough sticks in my throat. The way twenty-somethings see the world never ceases to terrify me. Even my parents, a decade older than the Gittens-Golds, are not out to pasture and still occupy a four-bedroomed home.

We walk up to the bungalow, and I hear Westminster Chimes resonating through the hall as Harriet presses the bell. No reply. Encouraging. If no one's home, we can get back to the Hanson case. Gerald Gittens-Gold has been gone all of five minutes. Meanwhile Sonia Hanson is on ice in the mortuary, mourned by half her family and loathed by the other half.

But the door opens on Harriet's second ring. A woman towers over me. Silent. Imperious. When I present my ID, I feel like an eight-year-old showing my spellings to teacher. When she motions us onto the doorstep, she's still tall; even Harriet doesn't reach her eye level. Well preserved is the description that comes to mind. With taut skin pulled over a large nose and mouth, she is striking in a mannish kind of way. She is slim, wearing a white linen jacket and navy slacks.

"Come through to the lounge." When she smiles, her mouth displays an expensive array of bridgework. Gold by name and nature. Her high heels clack on the wooden floor.

The lounge is neatly ordered but with an unmistakeable aroma of stale cigarettes. Harriet and I take seats on a dark green leather sofa. Mrs Gittens-Gold assumes position on a matching armchair. Four arty sunset photographs and a black-and-white wedding picture occupy the wall behind her. Seeing Anna beaming out in her white dress and veil is another reminder of Sonia Hanson. Harriet should be out showing the dead woman's photo to possible witnesses.

Anna fixes her gaze on me. "What news do you have?" I'm no longer thinking teacher, more headmistress.

"Nothing so far. I'm afraid I'm here to ask you questions."

"Don't be afraid, inspector. I'm an experienced counsellor. I'm not going to be fazed by a few questions. I deal with far worse on a daily basis." She tilts her head to one side, now reminding me of a psychiatrist in a TV drama.

"Thank you, Mrs Gittens-Gold."

"Do call me Anna," she says, still playing therapist.

"Anna, I understand your husband helps out as a counsellor, too."

"We're not volunteers, if that's what you're thinking. We are *professional* counsellors." She enunciates the words slowly, dipping her head. "The Cross Care Centre is an independently run service. We provide bespoke counselling for the problems of today." She seems to be addressing the room.

Harriet must be thinking the same; she turns to see if anyone has come in behind us.

"What kind of problems?" I ask.

"Our work is confidential," Anna says simply.

Put in my place, I lose the thread of my questioning, but after a pause, Anna fills the gap.

"Marital difficulties, including sexual deviance, sexual abuse, drug and alcohol abuse, self-esteem issues, depression. Gerald and I specialise in marriage guidance. We are able to put the experience of our own successful relationship to good use for others." She nods again. This time it seems to be in anticipation of something. I sense she's waiting for our acknowledgement of her skillset or her long marriage.

I don't oblige. "Have you always been a counsellor?"

"I suppose I have in a way. People have often been drawn to me. Even at school, the other girls found me good at problem solving. When they got in a fix – boyfriend trouble mostly – I soon put them straight. I got a first class honours degree and was head-hunted into the business world, but I moved into professional counselling after I married."

"What did you read?" Harriet asks.

"Read?"

"At university."

"Electronic communications. I worked in the industry for a while, then found my calling in advisory work."

Harriet and I exchange a glance. I think we're both finding it hard to cast this woman in the role of listening ear. "Do you like counselling?" I ask.

"The rewards are unimaginable. But it would be better if people didn't wait until they were in crisis. If they came to me before that, I could show them how to understand themselves better."

I study the unflinching contours of her face and can't imagine her clients doing anything other than obeying her every word. Maybe she should have been the army commando in the marriage. "Tell me about your husband's previous job," I ask.

"I'm afraid I can disclose even less about that. It was all very hush hush. He advised some of his country's most senior military figures."

"What kind of advice?"

"He never discussed his work with me." Her tight pale curls quiver. It's hard to tell if they're natural or out of a bottle; probably out of a bottle at her age. My mum would know. I wait and she duly plugs the pause again. "Reconnaissance, intelligence, photography. He was an expert photographer."

"Did he take those?" Harriet points at the prints on the wall.

"A little hobby of his. As you can see for yourself, he was the best in his field."

I'm no expert but they seem pretty good. He must have used a special filter to get the perfect muted colours.

"And you last saw him when he set off for the Cross Care Centre on Monday morning. Have you checked whether any of his clothes are missing? His uniform perhaps?"

"You don't wear uniform when you're undercover. Besides, he retired some years ago. He worked latterly as a civilian advisor to the army. He was a colonel before that." She tugs her sleeve with pride.

"Would you mind if I had a look at his belongings? Sometimes a fresh pair of eyes can see something unusual." We've got nothing useful so far, but maybe a nosy through the missing man's personal space will inspire.

"Be my guest. Search the whole house. Nothing is missing. You think he's gone off, don't you? Well, I can assure you he doesn't have another woman and you won't find him

72

hiding in the broom cupboard. When are you police going to widen your search? He could be lying in a ditch somewhere or have lost his memory. People do, you know." She sniffs and stands up.

"Of course," I say, even though I'm not one to buy memory loss as an explanation. I've not come across one genuine case among countless suspects who've claimed amnesia.

"Look wherever you like," Anna says. "The bedroom's across the hall. I'll make some tea. Or would you prefer coffee? I can't stand the stuff myself but Gerald drinks it by the gallon."

I decline both but Harriet says tea would be fine. Anna leaves us in the hall and goes to what must be the kitchen. It is a long hallway with a high ceiling that gives the bungalow a regal air. Rugs covered the parquet in the lounge, but the hall floor is bare and badly pitted as if under constant attack by stiletto heels. Along one wall are several framed certificates. One announces that Anna Gittens-Gold has successfully completed level three self-defence at the Gloucester Adult Education Institute. Hanging on another wall are three fading black-and-white photographs of young women in various theatrical costumes. One photograph under the caption 'More St Maur's, 1983' depicts a chorus line of girls dressed in long silk shorts. Another – 'Wild About Harry, 1984' – shows a line of half a dozen dancing girls in bobbed wigs and twenties dresses. The third is of a tall girl in a long dress, the train of which is held by four other girls – 'Snow White, 1985'.

The bedroom, carpeted in the same honey colour as the walls, smells like the lounge. Maybe the walls were white at one time before tobacco invaded the pigment. The tang catches my throat and I cough. Like every reformed smoker, I'm an evangelist who can't bear even a whiff these days.

A double bed takes up most of the length of the bedroom. To the left are a pine wardrobe and two chests of drawers. Either side of the bed are identical cabinets, and another wardrobe is squeezed between one of the cabinets and the window.

Harriet opens a chest of drawers. The bottom drawer is full of ladies' pyjamas. Drawer two holds t-shirts, and the top drawer contains neat piles of silk pants with rolled up lacy bras tucked in front. Everything is neat and expensive, quite unlike the riot of colour and cheap cotton that inhabits my cupboards. In the pine wardrobe we find a regimented line of women's clothing: linen and tweed skirts, trousers, blouses, jackets and two coats, a Jaeger label on one. The base of the wardrobe is stacked with shoeboxes with Italian-sounding names.

In the other cabinet, I'm not surprised to find three neatly filled drawers of men's clothes: underpants with an electric razor tucked down the side, polo-neck jumpers and pyjamas. The husband is as neat as the wife, except he has shopped for comfort not trend, 'St. Michael' appearing on most of his labels.

The clothes in the other wardrobe are similarly immaculate in their storage: cotton shirts in white and pastel shades, several grey trousers and jackets, one full-length coat. The shoeboxes are all Clarks – size seven, quite small for a man but way bigger than my size fours. On the inside of the wardrobe doors are rails crammed with cravats – lime green paisley pattern, red polka dot, lilac silk.

The bedside lockers in the Gittens-Gold residence reveal nothing of interest. Men's handkerchiefs and a two-week-old

Sunday Telegraph in one, women's handkerchiefs and a counselling journal in the other. An emptied ashtray on top of the left-hand one and make-up tubes on the right break the symmetry.

"Look at this, Steph," Harriet calls out, and I follow her voice to the bathroom.

There's a plywood shelf over the bathtub, hinged at one end so it can lift like a flap whenever the Gittens-Golds require a bath. Harriet opens a built-in cabinet, revealing what looks like the contents of a well-stocked chemistry lab with numerous small bottles variously labelled as B/W developer, stop bath, fixer and wetting agent. Behind the shower curtain we find a large plastic tank as well as several shallow trays and an odd-looking piece of equipment like an overhead projector. The rest of the bathroom meets the same orderly standard as the bedroom: two toothbrushes, two flannels and two towels. In place of blinds are heavy black drapes.

Back along the hall, we head into what appears to be a study. There's a computer, a telephone and a bookcase containing a few books on counselling and a couple on military history, but it is mostly decked out with trophies and tankards. I make out that a couple are self-defence prizes. Others are awards for photography. One engraving reads: 'Photographer of the Year 1984'. Another is for 'Subiaco Town Snapper 1981'.

In the kitchen, Anna has made the tea.

"You must find it a bit of a nuisance when your husband uses the bathroom as a darkroom," I say.

"Not really. He only does his own developing in winter."

"Why's that?" Harriet asks.

The older woman's head tips to its usual condescending

angle. "It has to be dark, of course. He's put up black-out curtains but it's only good enough at night."

"Doesn't that rather limit his military work if he can't process film in the summer?"

Anna peers down her nose. "My dear constable, he doesn't use our bathroom to develop high-level reconnaissance photographs for the Australian army. There are facilities in theatre. Besides, it's all digital these days. Gerald uses wet film for fun." She pauses, perhaps long enough to check that Harriet's cheeks are glowing with the level of humiliation she intended, and then drops the subject. "I hope you find him soon," she says, opening the fridge door and fetching out a plate of raw meat. "I bought him this steak. I'll have to throw it out soon. I don't eat flesh. I suppose I could offer it to someone at work."

"Are you going to work? What if your husband comes back here?" I ask.

"Not after two days. Something has happened. I'm certain he can't come back until he's found."

"Could he be staying with friends or family?"

"We are both orphans. We only have each other."

I watch the broad, middle-aged hand transfer a tea bag from one china cup to another. Little Orphan Annie – seriously?

"How long have you been married?"

Anna clears her throat and sips her hot tea. "Twenty-five years. That's why we are able to devote ourselves to counselling. We have so much experience to offer. I'm fortunate to have achieved in widely different disciplines. Gerald's the same. You must have seen our magnificent trophy collection."

"Where did you meet?" I'm struggling to like this

woman. Maybe if I can flesh out her background, some sympathy for her predicament will return.

"Australia. I was at university there. We fell in love. We tried to fight it, of course. Long-distance love and all that. But we couldn't stop our feelings and we married within a year."

"Whereabouts in Australia did you live?" Harriet asks.

Anna fixes her with another steely stare. "Do you know Australia well?"

"Not at all. I just wondered," she replies, cheeks flushing again.

Anna sets her cup on the kitchen top. "I studied near Brisbane at a private university with an excellent reputation. I finished my degree and we came here. Because of the unique nature of Gerald's work, he was able to move to Britain and still continue. There was an international agreement with the Ministry of Defence to fly him out of RAF bases at Brize Norton and Lyneham."

As she speaks, I again feel that Harriet and I are being addressed as members of a larger audience.

CHAPTER TWELVE

"What did you make of the grieving widow?" I ask Harriet when we return to the car.

"How do you know she's a widow? It's less than forty eight hours since Gerald was seen at work."

"He's either dead or with his mistress – in which case he'll be dead when the wife catches up with him."

For once Harriet laughs at a joke. "I know what you mean. She reminded me of a Victorian school ma'am. I thought she was going to give me detention."

"Maybe that's the answer. Case solved. She's detained her husband in the basement. Permanently."

We both laugh now, but as I accelerate to forty on the northern by-pass, I mentally review the layout of Anna's bungalow for evidence of a cellar. A daft idea, but stranger things have happened.

"Perhaps he's skipped the country," Harriet suggests. "I didn't find his passport, did you?"

I shake my head. "Not under his own name, he hasn't.

Kevin got Tony Smith to run a ports and airports check. No one named Gittens-Gold has passed through."

We travel in silence as I take a right at the A40 roundabout onto Causeway. The road runs above the oldest part of the city. Merrywell is a community imbued with a hearty dose of Dunkirk spirit, thanks to its perilous location next to the floodplain. People look out for each other here. When the river burst its banks on 13th February, beleaguered gym and office workers abandoned their own flooded premises to bail out the waterlogged Merry Well Restaurant so that the owner could reopen the next day for a fully booked Valentine's evening. When our kids were little, smiling council workers in waders would carry Jake and Bradley in their pushchairs through the flooded streets while Terri and I stepped across hastily erected duckboards. We 'endured' this for three years in a row. Even though we both lived in Tufton with flood-free access to the city centre, we came up to Merrywell. As single mums, the help from the council workers was the nearest we got to chivalry. Every girl wants to be a damsel in distress now and again.

Harriet yanks her mobile phone out of her pocket as it rings. "Yes, boss. We've just interviewed the wife of the misper. Nothing much to go on so far." She runs her fingers through her tidy blonde hair. "Do you want us to start follow up interviews at his place of work?"

My grip on the steering wheel tightens. Why did she put that idea in Kevin's head? It shouldn't be our priority. But judging by what she replies next, it sounds like I don't need to worry.

"Sonia Hanson's workmates?" she says into the phone. "We're on our way to see her ex-fiancé now." Above the hum of the engine, I hear the murmur of Kevin's voice. He has a lot to say. "So you want us to go straight to the newspaper office after we've interviewed Bryant? Will do, boss."

Smiling, she puts the phone away. "We're back on the Hanson murder full time. Kevin wants statements from all of Sonia's journalist colleagues by close of play today."

CHAPTER THIRTEEN

The place looks like a spaceship: strips of pink lights, silver walls and matching seats, black floor. A glass counter displays ice cream in colours so luminous I suspect manufacture in Chernobyl. Techno music drills out of the speakers – not loud enough to trigger a migraine but enough to piss me off.

"Why here?" I ask Harriet.

"This is where his P.A. set up the meeting."

"Carl Bryant is a background witness in the murder of his ex. His office would have been better. Or have you got designs on a knickerbocker glory?"

Harriet looks down but not before I see the eye roll.

A man in a red-and-white striped apron and a straw boater is wiping down the far end of the counter. He looks up. "Take a seat, officers. I'll let Mr Bryant know you're here."

Harriet and I exchange a glance – are we that conspicuous as coppers? But when I look at the empty tables, the lack of other customers makes his deduction reasonable, except in one small detail. Why does the ice-cream seller know Bryant's business?

"Is Carl your boss?" I ask.

"I'm the owner." He sighs. "But I'm also the tenant. He owns the building."

"Got you," I say and wonder what rent he pays for this off-city-centre site. Being so far from the main gate streets doesn't seem good for business. Maybe it picks up when the schools kick out at three p.m.

We take a booth under a pink spotlight that makes Harriet's sensible, blonde haircut look edgy. There's a laminated menu card on the table with images of sundaes and waffles even more garish than the stuff at the counter.

The man brings over a tray and sets down two cappuccinos and two glass bowls glistening with scoops of vanilla ice cream and dripping chocolate sauce. "Mr Bryant's treat while you're waiting."

I fancy a coffee and might have reached for it, if it wasn't for the threat of headache. But there's no way we're playing this game. Keeping us waiting and trying to sweeten us up has bumped him along to suspect in my eyes. "No thanks," I say simply. "Can you ask him to come out now?"

"He's not here," the man explains. "But I've texted his secretary to say you've arrived." He heads back to his counter.

"Can you take these away, please?" I call out.

When he reloads the tray, he nods with a hint of a smile in his eyes. I'm sensing he approves of our refusal to indulge. Not as much of a lackey to the landlord as he first appeared.

Bryant keeps us waiting fifteen minutes. He arrives in a crisp, short-sleeved shirt, but when he gets inside the air-conditioned parlour, he puts on the jacket that is draped over his arm. Linen, navy, expensive. He holds out his hand to me. "You must be Inspector Lewis. And may I say more attractive than your TV namesake."

I shake his hand, ignoring the variation on the joke I've heard a thousand times. "This is DC Harris."

Harriet waves in greeting, then returns her hand to her notebook, dodging the handshake.

Although not a heavy man, Bryant manages to take up the whole length of the bench opposite. He also leans over most of the table top, his forearm perilously close to a blob of chocolate that dribbled from the ice-cream bowl. I will his fancy sleeve towards it, but at the last moment he puts his arm up to summon the other man. "Gio, can I get an iced coffee? What else would you like, ladies?"

"Nothing for us," I say, not bothering with a thank you.

Putting his hands behind his head, he sits back. "How can I help?"

"Sonia Hanson."

For a second the flashy confidence leaves his face. "I knew her as Sonia Clarke, but when I heard it on the news, I recognised the name. We were close once."

"How did your relationship end?" Harriet asks, pen poised.

"Badly." He blows out the word in a sigh. "She was the love of my life, but I read her wrong. She wasn't the girl I thought she was." He smooths each sleeve, but they wrinkle again as his hands go back behind his head. "I ended it as soon as I found out she was seeing Hanson behind my back. You can't blame me. What could be worse for a man than an unfaithful partner?"

A dead one, I say silently. This same love triangle has turned worse for Alistair Hanson, the widowed father of three. As Harriet asks Bryant more about his breakup, I study him. Neat dark beard, good haircut. Early forties. Not unattractive. Those twinkly green eyes must have closed many a business deal and charmed a good few women into his bed.

I interrupt Harriet. "Have you found love again?"

He breaks off his reply to answer me. "Love is hard to find, don't you think?" The eyes stop their twinkle to glance at my bare ring finger. Despite the air con, heat sweeps through me. It feels like I'm the one being interrogated.

Harriet helps me out with a change of subject. "How did you get on with Sonia's family?"

"Madame Clarke was never mother-in-law material. I've sometimes wondered what Hanson makes of her. Maybe it's the French way. She would be aloof whenever I met her but insisted on planning every detail of our wedding, even though I was paying. I heard Chère Maman broke contact with Sonia after we split up, which I could never understand, because she barely spoke to me when Sonia and I were together. One confusing croissant for sure."

"What about Sonia's brothers?" Harriet asks.

"Olivier and Jerome were fine until the split, but they cut up rough when I increased their rent. Said it was extortionate and refused to pay. They've got some temper on them."

"Temper?" I ask, although I can hardly blame the Clarke brothers for getting stroppy with a landlord who lobbed a stupid-fold rent increase at them out of spite.

"As soon as my relationship with their sister ended, I withdrew from any personal involvement with our business dealings. But Jerome threatened one of my property managers with an étagère when he went to collect unpaid rent at their shop."

Harriet notes down *étagère*. No doubt she'll google it and let me know.

"How did the brothers get on with Sonia?" I ask.

"They were never close. She used to say they resented her not joining the family antiques business, even though it was down to her relationship with me that they got a prime retail unit. They never acknowledged the support she gave them in that respect."

"You said they reacted physically, brandishing a..." I pause.

"An ornamental shelf unit," Harriet says, looking up from her phone. I silently thank the police gods for giving me a DC with speedy thumbs.

"Did Olivier and Jerome ever get physical with Sonia?"

"Not that I saw," he says. "As I understand it, they've been giving her the silent treatment for the last four years."

"Is that what you've been doing, too?" I ask. "Or have you seen Sonia since your break up?"

He smooths the sleeves again. Waste of time. Even top-rate linen crinkles, apparently. "I do my bit for local charities and they sometimes like me as the front man for photo opportunities: guest of honour; after-dinner speaker; master of ceremonies. Occasionally she was there in the press pack but we didn't speak."

"Did she ever give you a bad write-up?" Our next interview is with Sonia's editor at the *Gloucester Evening News*. Is this all about the power of a journalist to skewer a reputation? I make a mental note to find out what Sonia had to say in print about her ex.

"Nothing doing there, inspector," he says, reading me again. "My P.A. scans the local newspaper on my behalf and tells me of any negative publicity. She hasn't shown me any of Sonia's work." He leans forward, still missing the chocolate globule. "I understand you have to explore all avenues, but my connection to Sonia Clarke ended the day she told me she was pregnant with another man's child. It was easy to sever all contact. I can't abide cheats." The left sleeve gets a push to reveal his smart watch and remind us he's a busy man.

"What about—" Harriet begins.

"Just one more question," I say over her. "Where were you on Monday morning between five and seven?"

"I wondered when you were going to get round to that," he says. "I spent Sunday night with a friend, left at seven thirty and went straight to the office. I'd rather not give a name. She's married."

I fold my lips shut between my teeth. What was that about cheats? Pot and kettle.

"I'm not proud of it," he says, as if reading me again. "But when you've had your heart broken once, it's easier to choose options that you know aren't going anywhere." And he gives me another stare that looks right through me.

I stand up. "We'll be off now, but you'd better warn your friend we might well be back for her name."

As I lead Harriet away, I hear him summon the other man again. "Cancel the coffee, thanks, Gio. And you might want to wipe away these chocolate stains before the afternoon rush."

CHAPTER FOURTEEN

"It's called a Whot-not in English, in case you're interested," Harriet says as we reach the car. It's the first time she's spoken since we left the ice-cream parlour.

"What?"

"Whot-not," she deadpans. I grin but she keeps her features straight. "The piece of furniture Jerome Clarke threatened Bryant's letting manager with. According to an antiques website, it's a light shelving unit for displaying ornaments. Hardly a lethal weapon, but evidence of a tendency to violence. Shall I go to Hucton and give the Clarke family another shake?"

"Not now. We're interviewing Sonia's colleagues at the newspaper next."

"But you don't need me there, do you?" She's hovering away from the passenger door as if reluctant to get in. "If we split up, we can cover more ground."

I open my driver's door, but she doesn't move nearer. Why has she picked now to go lone warrior? "We need more background before we tackle the Clarkes again. If you try them now, you'll get nothing more than Tony and I got yesterday."

Nodding as if my ruling comes as no surprise, she goes straight for an alternative. "Let me go back on the misper then. We hardly scratched the surface of Gerald Gittens-Gold. I can get more from his wife."

"We don't know we've got a case there yet, whereas time's ticking on Sonia Hanson's murder."

Harriet folds her arms. "You'll get more out of her colleagues without me."

I shut my door again without getting in. "What is this about?"

"Nothing." She colours. "We can achieve more separately, that's all."

I check my watch. Truth be told I could get through the *Gloucester Evening News* interviews quicker without an enthusiastic golden retriever at my heels. "We'll meet back at the station afterwards for a debrief."

"Of course, thanks." I'd expect more excitement in her voice at the prospect of flying solo, but she sounds relieved. She sets off out of the car park.

"Wait. Don't you want a lift?"

"No need," she says and speeds up without turning round.

———

'Glouc ter Evening New' reads the chipped grey lettering that clings to the shabby brick façade of the newspaper office. The receptionist is friendly enough – small and middle-aged and better preserved than the building in which she works. She's unfazed by the sight of my warrant card. If anything, she seems excited. The whiff of a news story must rub off on all the newspaper staff, not just the hacks. She summons the editor, David Oakley.

Appearing almost immediately, he comes into the reception with an outstretched hand and a solid smile. A pleasant looking man, medium build. If I saw him in the street, his casual trousers and round-necked t-shirt would suggest to me council worker or teacher rather than journalist.

Even in his working environment, Oakley maintains the demeanour of a civil servant. He leads me to the newsroom, chatting all the way about the hot weather and the England match. The untidy desks and miles of computer cable put me back in the CID office. There's even the same ragged assortment of personnel: a man with grey hair pecks at a keyboard; a younger man leans back on his chair and gazes out of the window; a thick-set man gnaws on an untidy sandwich, and a girl on the telephone twists strands of blonde hair with a manicured finger.

"Have a seat," Oakley says, pushes a swivel chair towards me and perches on the side of a paper-strewn desk. "I'm camping in here until my office has been redecorated. We're doing the place up ready for the new deputy editor. Roger's leaving at the end of the month." He points at the grey-haired keyboard pecker. "We'll get the advert out soon."

"Was Sonia Hanson in the running for the vacancy?" I ask, launching into the interview. Always the best way; it avoids giving the suspect time to read me. And Oakley might be a suspect. A few well-placed questions should give me a better idea.

"Poor Sonia. I phoned her husband. Nice guy. What can you say to him? We're a newspaper. We deal in the tragedy business every day, but this one's close to home. Everyone's in shock. It's the story no-one wants to write."

"Indeed." I wait a beat and then prompt. "The vacancy?"

"I'm sure she would have applied for the deputy's job. She was ambitious."

Sensing Oakley has answered two questions in one, I make a mental note: yes, she would have applied, but no, this editor would not have made her his deputy. "What was she like to work with?"

"Sonia was..." Oakley speaks slowly, picking his words, "tenacious. She worked hard for her stories. She was our consumer affairs correspondent. This basically meant writing the weekly consumer file column. Members of the public would phone in with their horror stories – cancelled holiday flights, badly fitting double-glazing, lost postal items, the usual stuff. Sonia would investigate. She'd phone up the companies and get their side of the story. She often managed to get compensation out of them when they'd previously been uncooperative. Such is the power of the press."

I'd rather know more about how she got on with her colleagues, but see another line of enquiry. "So she wouldn't have been popular with these companies. Had she had any particular run-ins recently?"

"She did her investigations over the phone and rarely had to visit premises. Many weren't local anyway. She might have kept notes on computer. You lot took hers away yesterday. I doubt her arguments were any more heated with companies than they were with anyone else."

"So she did have arguments?"

Oakley sits further back on his desk, dislodging a pile of paper and taking a moment to restack it before answering.

"She was tenacious. A hound after a hare as far as her work was concerned."

Tenacious – that word again. "Did she work on anything else?"

"Our theatre reviews. She went to see something at the King's Theatre about once every three or four weeks."

My mate Terri entered her Year 10 drama group in a schools competition at the King's Theatre a couple of years ago. I remember how she raged against the faceless *Gloucester Evening News* critic. "Where does he get off?" she said. "They're school kids." Neither of us knew the stinging review of *The wannabe Ibsen that failed even to resemble The Inbetweeners* was written by a woman. Somehow that makes it worse. I feel a guilty twinge of relief on Terri's behalf that Sonia won't be writing any more.

"Sonia wrote what she thought," Oakley is saying. "I can get you copies of all of them as well as her Gloucester Reunited features. They've been running for about six months."

I mishear. "United? She covered the football?"

"Reuniting local people with their school friends. She got them to meet up with their old mates and interviewed them about how they'd changed or stayed the same. A 'Where are they now?' thing. She featured ordinary people like her hairdresser, a girl from the health food shop, and the manager of her children's nursery. The articles are... they were very popular. She's... she was always on the lookout for new people to feature. She also did local celebrities like the town crier, the mayor and a couple of councillors."

I wince, recalling our encounter with Councillor Vale by the cathedral on Monday. "Was Sonia kind to her subjects?"

I ask. Vale had sounded tickled pink with what she'd written about him.

"Actually, she was. They were very light-hearted pieces. Despite her..." Oakley faltered.

"Tenacity," I suggest.

"Yes, quite. She could write with surprising warmth and humour."

"Yet she wasn't in line for the deputy editor job, was she?" Ambitious, tenacious, hardworking, but sadly deluded if she'd been expecting a promotion.

"I anticipate several internal candidates, and it will be advertised externally, too." As I thought, the answer is no.

"Who are the other candidates?" I ask.

"I'm guessing Gerry will apply." He looks at the man who is staring out of the window. DC Tony Smith to a tee. "And I think Lauren's going to have a go." The blonde is still working her finger through her hair. Despite this interference her locks remain straight and shiny.

I request copies of all of Sonia's work from the last two years. I'm the details girl. Something to read at home while Jake watches football.

"Happy to help. Sonia was one of our own. We'll do anything to get the bastard." He pauses. When he restarts, a slippery smile replaces his earnest expression. "Now, inspector, what have you got for me? Have you found any leading suspects? What's the motive?" The civil servant sheds his skin and reveals his journalistic innards.

"Our investigation is ongoing," I reply.

"Don't give me that several-lines-of-enquiry waffle," Oakley says. "We're entitled to an exclusive on this one. It's what Sonia would have wanted." He speaks without a hint of irony.

When I don't reply, Oakley tries a different tack. "Obviously, I'll be keeping a close personal eye on this one and writing up everything I know. This interview included."

Normally the threat of making me look an idiot in print would be water off a rubber duck, but it's not long since a radio presenter accused me of murder, so that duck isn't quite floating again. A diversionary tactic pops into my head. "We've got another case. A missing person's enquiry."

Oakley eyes me suspiciously, smelling the distraction. "Give me some details. It should just make tonight's late edition."

"It will have to be tomorrow. I'll get the press office to email you a photo. It could be big." I don't for a minute think Gittens-Gold doing a runner will amount to anything, but I'd love to be a fly on the wall when his missus Anna goes all-out frantic wife on Oakley if he tries to interview her.

Oakley suggests I speak to the other journalists now, no doubt hoping one of his newshounds will tease from me the lowdown on the Sonia Hanson case. He asks which colleague I want to talk to first. Still rattled by Oakley's threat to feature me in the paper, I opt for keyboard-pecking Roger Smithson, the retiring deputy editor. He looks the most harmless. I'll work up to Gerry and Lauren later, when my nerves are back in check.

"Poor lass," Smithson says, rubbing a knotty finger around his eye socket. "She'd got three little kiddies at home. Did you know that?" He looks at me. "Of course, you know that. You detectives are in the questions game, same as we are."

"Was she good at her job?"

"She did very well, more than competent I'd say. She was always on the look-out for leads and would put herself out to chase up a good story. She did a lot of chasing, did Sonia, if you know what I mean."

Is he implying she chased romantic partners? My gut feeling is that sex was the last thing on the mind of this busy working mum. I think of the reference book in her study. "Do you mean she was a good, old-fashioned newshound, tracking leads?"

"There was nothing old-fashioned about Sonia. She was a good writer in today's style, up on all the latest trends. Left some of us standing, did Sonia. She was a proper modern lady reporter." Smithson sighs out the expression and rubs his eye again. At a rough guess, I reckon 'lady reporter' translates as 'bitch of a journalist' and figure it's worth confirming with a direct question.

"How did you get on with her?"

I don't get a direct answer but it's enough to confirm Smithson's feelings. "She had her ways, I have mine. Different generations have different approaches. I'm sorry I can't be more help. If you don't mind, I'm up against a deadline." He spreads his gnarled hands in the direction of his desk. "We're in the grips of the summer show season. It was Upton last weekend. I judged the children's poetry competition," he says proudly. "Baz might be able to tell you more about Sonia. He's more her generation."

The last few crumbs of Barry 'Baz' Reid's sandwich stick to the front of his shirt. He's opened a bottle of Lucozade Sport. Suspecting it's the nearest he gets to physical exercise, I do my best to quell a wry smile when Baz introduces himself as the newspaper's sports reporter.

"It's going to be a good season for City. I've just filed the story about the new coach. You can read about him in tonight's edition. He's a Cheltenham lad. I always said they should go for a local, or fairly local anyway. The last one was from Basingstoke. Not a hope. I can get you tickets for tomorrow's pre-season friendly if you like."

The second offer of the day that's easy to refuse. Just as Bryant's coffee and ice cream would have been likely to trigger a migraine, so would standing on the terraces in thirty-degree heat. I explain I have a murder to solve before I can watch any sport.

"You're not into footie, then? We've got a couple of girls coming up from the juniors. One of them's a pretty decent keeper, too."

"What can you tell me about Sonia Hanson?" I say, getting back to business.

Baz takes a swig from his drink and does nothing to stifle the belch which follows. "From what I could see, she got on with her job. Always had her head down. She never said two words to me. Didn't like football either. Or rugby. You'd think she would, being French. They're starting a women's team round here. What do you think of that, eh?"

"I haven't really been following." I'm not about to go there with Barry Reid. He might be playing the brain-dead armchair sports fan, but he is still a journalist. It would take only one unguarded comment to find myself quoted on sexism in sport. I close the interview and move on to interview Gerry Donnelly, whom I pigeon-holed, quite correctly it turns out, as DC Tony Smith's understudy. I ask him how well he knew Sonia.

"Not *that* well, if you know what I mean."

I ignore the innuendo. "What did you think of her?"

"I didn't think of her." Donnelly's eyes make an involuntary glance across the office to the luscious Lauren, and I've a shrewd idea how his mind is working.

"Sonia was a good-looking woman, too," I say. "Weren't you in the least bit interested?"

"Sure, at first. Put a pint of beer in front of a bloke and he's going to try and sup it, so I had a sniff but there was nothing doing. I don't do ball-breakers."

"And that's what Sonia was?"

"Tough as old bollocks. She could tear the arse out of..." He pauses, apparently remembering the woman is dead. "But she was a sound journalist."

His gaze strays out of the office window towards two Chinese girls who are attempting to park their Ford Ka in the car park. Until Tony Smith met his fiancée, Nikki, he'd had the same wandering eye. He was the scourge of the CID office for a while, but it was all talk. Irritating but not dangerous. Similarly, I sense, Gerry Donnelly would chance his libido with everything in a pair of heels, but if one right-thinking female – like Sonia – gave him the brush-off, he'd just stroll along to the next one. Sonia wasn't a big deal to him. I have no further questions. Donnelly will live another night to cruise the wine bars.

I keep the last interview brief, too. Lauren Chambers tries playing coy, pulling her long fringe forward and peering through it. But fooling no one; there isn't a coy hair on her shampoo-advert head. At least she has the guts to admit that she and Sonia weren't friends. It is the funny thing about murder victims I've found over the years. They instantly became model employees and salt-of-the-earth workmates. Death confers virtues lacking in life. Lauren, to her credit, goes as far as admitting they didn't 'get each other' because Sonia had 'tension issues'. Tucking hair behind her ear, she tells me, "I said she needed to chill out more, but she never did. I guess that's just the way she was wired." I can only imagine how the hardworking mother of three would have taken that piece of advice from Little Miss Blonde In A Bottle.

I pity Sonia working her skin off for a gutless editor. How could Oakley possibly consider Lipstick Lauren for deputy editor? She doesn't look any older than Harriet Harris. If this near-teenager had got the job while Sonia was still alive, Sonia would have been the one justifiably contemplating murder.

I'm back in the foyer, signing out with the receptionist, when Oakley finds me. "Before you go, can you just give me anything? Off the record."

"You'll know as soon as we have something," I say and walk to the door.

"I'm not asking as a journalist, but as Sonia's boss. Her friend."

"Thank you for your time, Mr Oakley," I say flatly.

He follows me outside, around the building to the car park, lobbing out questions. "What's you main line of enquiry? Is it to do with her work here? Can you confirm you have a suspect in mind?"

I stop sharply and he skids to a halt, almost banging into me. "Goodbye for now, Mr Oakley," I say. "No doubt we'll be in touch."

Somehow he takes this as the threat I intended and he goes back inside. It's not until I've driven off and parked two streets away that I think about his behaviour. I've attended a fair share of press conferences and endured the usual badgering, but Oakley is in a different league. He practically chased me like a paparazzi doorstepping a celeb. Why? Does he have a vested interest in knowing how the investigation is going? Is there a reason to stay one step ahead? I pick up the radio set.

"Contol, this is Steph. Can you run PNC checks on a bunch of suspects?" I spell out the names of the newspaper editor and his staff. That might shake things up. There's nothing like a bit of 'previous' to loosen the tongue.

I put the car in reverse, planning to avoid the city centre. Oakley and co. are probably as pure as the paper they write on. Perhaps Oakley's keen interest is merely concern to get justice for one of his own. But I can't see him going that extra mile for Sonia Hanson. Maybe he would for lazy Gerry or blonde Lauren, but he's made it pretty clear he had no time for Sonia when she was alive. There'll be a tasteful period of mourning before he breathes a sigh of relief at her passing and puts her out of his mind for good.

Before I've forced a U-turn into traffic, my phone goes. Kevin. I park again and answer.

"Can I have a progress report?"

"I've talked to Sonia's colleagues at the newspaper. Something's off with the editor. Could be something, could be nothing, but—"

He cuts me off. "What about the misper?"

"Gittens-Gold? What about him? Harriet's getting chapter and verse from his wife right now. She'll deserve a commendation for that one."

I laugh but he doesn't laugh back. "Can you catch up with Harriet? The super wants a senior officer to be seen to be working on it."

I'm about to ask why, then I remember the Australian military connection. Superintendent Thomas must be getting nervous. Personally I think the wife is over-egging her husband's role in covert ops, and I suspect Kevin thinks the same, but we're neither of us paid to see the politics. Or cover the West Gloucestershire Police Force's rather large back-side. I'm happy to let Thomas pull rank.

"On my way, Kev." I abandon the U-turn and head north through town to St Levens to join Harriet's interview with Anna Gittens-Gold.

CHAPTER FIFTEEN

I draw up outside the Gittens-Gold bungalow as Harriet is leaving the front garden. The sight of my purple Golf makes her speed up towards her car. For a moment I think she's going to drive off, but she thinks better of it and comes along the pavement towards me.

But there's no friendly greeting when I get out. "I thought you weren't interested in this one," she says, accusation evident in her folded arms. "I said I was happy to handle it."

"Boss's orders. The big boss." And daft though the case seems, I'm starting to wonder if Naomi Thomas has a point. On the way here, I checked in with the station. Gerald Gittens-Gold hasn't used his credit card or a cash-point machine since Sunday and his passport hasn't popped up at any major port or airport. The man has disappeared into thin air.

"If Superintendent Thomas is worried about our public image, won't it look like right hand left hand if you to go back in there and ask Gerald's wife the exact same questions I've just asked?" Harriet says.

"Fair point." And Anna Gittens-Gold strikes me as the kind of woman to tell the world what she thinks of the police handling of her husband's disappearance. I might not have given David Oakley his exclusive for the *Gloucester Evening News* on the Sonia Hanson case, but he could run this misper story with a police incompetence angle. "What did you get out of her?"

"More of the same. She talked me through his recent movements up to when he left for work on Monday; who she contacted when he didn't come home; the limited knowledge she has of his undercover work; and what a complete gentleman he is. Admired and respected by everyone who knows him."

I take a minute to think. Chances are Anna has put on the same show as last time. I don't trust the woman, but whether she's outright lying or just carried away with her self-importance, I can't tell without another crack at her myself. Yet, as Harriet says, going back in right now would look bad. The wife is best left to simmer for a while. But I have another idea. "Have you spoken to the neighbours?"

"Not yet."

"Come on then." I lead Harriet past the bungalow to the pair of semis next door. "Let's find out how charming it is to live over the fence from him."

Harriet rings the bell. After a pause, an elderly couple open the door together. The man is small, dressed in a shirt and sleeveless pullover despite the heat. The woman, also small, hovers close behind. She wears a Beefeater gin apron over a cotton dress. They keep the door half-closed as if to shut it in our faces if they don't like what we're selling.

Holding out my ID, I make our introductions. The door doesn't move until I mention Gerald and they fling it wide open.

"Come in, ladies," the man says, hobbling along a narrow hallway.

The wife moves ahead into another room and reappears with a kettle. "Tea or coffee?"

"That would be lovely," Harriet replies.

But I cut her off. "We've just had one, thanks." Despite this case possibly having legs after all, the limbs on the Hanson case are longer and in need of more urgent surgery. We're more than forty-eight hours into a murder investigation with nothing to show. Sipping tea on what might still turn out to be a wild goose chase is not a good use of time.

I notice the woman's swollen skin pressing against the top of her slippers. "But we can sit for a moment if that's easier."

"We spend all day sitting," the woman says. "Let me just..." She puts the kettle back in the kitchen and returns without it.

It seems we'll be doing the interview in the hallway and I wonder if I should have agreed to refreshments, so we could be shown into the lounge. Harriet clearly thinks I should have; her expression is granite.

"What can you tell us about your neighbours?" I ask.

"Has something happened?" the man says, and I wonder how useful this is going to be. If Anna hasn't even mentioned to these people that her husband is missing, I'm not picturing close neighbourliness.

"Mr Gittens-Gold hasn't been home for a couple of days. We're just checking it's nothing untoward."

"I wouldn't worry. The colonel is tough," he replies. "A

character of true courage. You'd never know to look at him what he has to endure."

"Very brave," his wife adds. "We once invited him – and Anna, but she couldn't come – to supper. I've never seen a man tuck into a meal with such relish. He'd just got back from an assignment. He said he was delighted to be eating proper food again after weeks of surviving on army ration packs." She grips her arms across her apron. "All those hours he has to spend sleeping in a tent, half-awake, wondering if enemy soldiers are creeping through the darkness, ready to run a knife across his throat."

"Easy, Chrissie. Don't upset yourself." The man squeezes his wife's shoulder. "I couldn't do his job. All those parachute jumps. Not until I've had my knees done anyway." He grins and attempts to stand up straighter.

"He's a nice chap," Chrissie says. "He pops round for a cuppa and chat, even when he's only in the country for a few hours. The tales he has to tell. They make my blood run cold."

"Is he still going on assignments?" Harriet asks. "His wife told us he had retired."

The woman's face clouds and she stares down at her hands, then glances at her husband. His downturned eyes don't make contact. Eventually he looks at Harriet. "I'm afraid we don't always remember. Our memories... We lose things... Get the time wrong. Old age, I suppose."

"I'm sorry," Harriet mumbles. "That must be—"

"Not to worry. You've been very helpful," I say brightly. There's no point in asking them whether they saw Gerald leave the house on Monday. Days of the week have probably fallen victim to the early stages of dementia. I blink away a tear, remembering my nan in the later stages. I hope the disease is kinder to this couple. "We'll leave you in peace. Do you see much of Anna?"

The husband chuckles. "We nod over the recycling bins."

"She's pleasant enough," Chrissie says. "But I'm sure she thinks we're a bit beneath her. When we invited them round, she said she had a prior engagement, but I've often wondered if it was just an excuse. If you cut her in half, there'd be the word *snob* running through."

"Maybe he's done a runner," her husband chips in.

"Jonnie, you can't say that to the police."

"Why not? If anyone was going to pull a vanishing act, a special forces commando would know how."

We leave the couple speculating on whether Gerald's skillset fits his current absence. Similar thoughts run through my mind, although I also wonder why they think an Australian army photographer is another Rambo. Is their thinking muddled or is Gerald as much of a fantasist as his pompous wife? His neighbours offered him good grub while he doled out helpings of cock and bull?

There's no reply from the adjoining semi, so we head to the neighbour on the other side of the Gittens-Golds. We meet a young woman backing out of her porch with a pushchair. When she explains she's running late to pick up her son from nursery, we conduct a brief interview as we walk with her.

"My Tom loves listening to Gerald's stories," she explains. "The things he had to do. And in such terrible conditions. We saw him once with a streaming nose and red eyes. I thought he had a cold but he'd been doing a military exercise in the Australian desert. Caught in a sandstorm. He's an all-action hero to Tom. I better get a move on now. The children will be out any minute."

When she speeds up, we let her go. No point in racing in this heat to end up with a thumping migraine and more tall army tales.

Back at the cars, Harriet makes to get in hers without saying goodbye. I beckon her into mine and we sit with the engine and air con on while we debrief. Or at least while I try to. Harriet's in a mood.

"I'll write up my interview with Anna and you can read it later," she says. "What the neighbours said about Gerald tallies with her description of him."

"But what's your gut telling you?" I ask. "Anything churning in there?" Something's nagging me. This whole case smacks of 'vasectomy syndrome'. It's a pet theory I'm forming that I'll explain to Harriet sometime when her face has stopped looking like stewed lampreys. "What's up with you?"

"You want me to speak now?" She stares through the windscreen. "Is that so you can shut me off again?"

"I stepped in back there because Alzheimer's is a mine-field. People don't always want sympathy." My nan spent five years in denial and two in oblivion.

"I don't only mean just now. You've been like it all week. On Monday, I rescued Ned from that cougar woman in the park, but straight away you laughed at me for following the teenagers."

"They were feeding the ducks."

"We know that now, but you should have let me speak to them. What if they'd been by the cathedral early on and seen Sonia's killer?"

"How old do you think they were?"

"Seventeen, maybe."

"I have a son of that age and I can assure you his sleeping

carcass never sees a dawn. Cast your mind back a few short years. Weren't you the same at that age?"

She looks out of her passenger window, turning her back to me. "I didn't sleep much as a teenager."

Crap. How could I have forgotten? Her father, an off-duty policeman, was murdered when she was sixteen. Before I can think how to apologise, Harriet saves me with another rant.

"Even the DCI belittles me. I set up that interview with Sonia's ex-fiancé, but Kevin said you had to come. And you spent the whole time interrupting me."

I think back to Carl Bryant at the ice-cream parlour. Kevin had made a good call sending me, too. No way could Harriet have managed Bryant alone. "I am the senior officer."

"What happened to 'Don't call me Inspector Lewis, just Steph will do?' Aren't we a team?"

"Of course," I say. Maybe I should have let her drive off and calm down before having this conversation. "I value your judgement. Absolutely."

She looks at me. "So if I make a suggestion, you'll let me follow it through?"

"Such as?"

"Anna Gittens-Gold talked about their jobs as counsellors. What if Gerald's disappearance is about that rather than his army past?"

"Go on." At last a line of enquiry that doesn't sound barmy. According to Anna, the army career is five years in the past. Harriet is right to concentrate on Gerald's current work colleagues.

"I'd like to go to the Cross Care Centre to interview them," she explains.

The digital clock on the dashboard catches my eye. Time

is still ticking away on Sonia Hanson. "We're back on the murder case for the rest of today, but we could go tomorrow."

Harriet's sigh and eye roll say it all. Am I really that domineering?

"But you can lead the interviews," I concede.

Without thanking me, she opens her door. "I'll see you back at the station then."

As I watch her drive away, I resolve to give her wriggle room tomorrow. Maybe Gerald's colleagues can shed light on aspects of the missing man's life that are unknown to his wife. But as the couple work in the same place, I have doubts.

CHAPTER SIXTEEN

Sally Parker chops courgettes and tosses them into the pan with the onions. She turns down the heat under the rice and takes another swig of her wine. Why not? Everyone should have a bottle of chilled Chardonnay on a Wednesday night, and a decent meal. She prides herself on never having resorted to a takeout. She couldn't even if she wanted to. There isn't as much as a fish and chip shop in the village, and the Indian restaurants in Gloucester don't deliver as far out as Klox. The only times she's dined on monosodium glutamate have been round at Tim's. The nearest he's got to preparing a gourmet meal for her is ordering a Chinese from an app and dealing with the ring pull on a can of Fosters.

The cat starts mewing outside, unable to get through the cat flap she's forgotten to unbolt. When she opens the back door, he slinks past her into the kitchen, leaving a freshly slain mouse on the doorstep.

"Oh, Fool, darling, another gift. You shouldn't have," Sally says.

Out of a cupboard, she fetches a tin of chicken and

scoops it onto a plate on the floor. The cat crouches on his haunches and devours it. By the time Sally has sieved her rice and mixed in the stir-fried vegetables, the cat has licked up every morsel of his food and is drinking from his water bowl. Sally carries her meal and her wine glass through to the lounge. She brushes aside the remote control and sits on the sofa. The cottage might be too small to have a dining room but she doesn't do TV dinners. Even though she lives and works here alone, it is a self-imposed standard she insists on. Sitting through onscreen football with Tim is her one exception and probably not any more. Time to call it quits with him.

It seems to be the end with Gerald, too, the cheese to Tim's chalk. Not really her type, but she'll miss his thrilling conversation over chaste suppers together. It is his age, she supposes. The generation that eats with the television off, sips expensive red wine and doesn't expect sex for dessert. Not that she knows anything about Gerald's habits away from her. She's never been invited to his and has never asked to visit, assuming that's wife and children territory. And after the shock of bumping into him at that counselling place this week, her suspicion about his home life has grown. Not red flags exactly, more like dishcloths on a washing line. Such a letdown. The evenings they met were a riot, alive with hot possibilities, including making Tim jealous enough to suggest getting engaged, but seeing Gerald in his daytime setting was an ice-cold wake-up.

The cat has followed her into the lounge. He brushes against her legs and then explores the room, rubbing his nose against the stalk of the standard lamp and the bookcase, laying his scent. She takes her meal back to the kitchen to add salt and fetches the rest of the Chardonnay. When she comes back, he's taken up residence on the sofa where she's been sitting, and she has to shoo him off. He glares at her for a moment, but soon begins a fastidious primping routine that takes in every inch of his thick, grey fur.

Thirsty on the hot evening, she refills her glass and watches. These days he has a coat worth grooming. It was a matted clump of dirt slung over a bag of bones when he came to her. He appeared on her doorstep on April the First, hence the name.

Fool completes his ablutions and trots back into the kitchen. Sally goes after him and opens the back door. He lingers by the honeysuckle, nosing between the petals before stalking away into the night. *Typical man – gets what he wants then goes.* Fool – it isn't the cat that deserves that name.

Tim has already been and gone today. She still has to make the bed again before she can sleep in it. He came over mid-afternoon on his way back from a job in Whitminster. He couldn't stay long, had to get to the builders' merchants before it closed. No time for a coffee or a cosy chat – a courtship. She shouldn't have let him in. She was still upset about what happened on Monday. It doesn't matter that his not turning up at their appointment probably saved her some explaining; the fact is he put work first, above their relationship. "Sorry I didn't make it, but I had a tricky customer. When she wanted an extra coat of gloss on all the skirting boards, the meeting went clean out of my head," he protested when she broached it again today while they were getting dressed. "It's a new business. I have to be flexible. There'll be time for us soon, I promise." But all homeowners are tricky, aren't they? Tim never had any intention of making their meeting. The decorating job was a convenient excuse. But

Sally has simmered down since Monday and barely reacted to his well-worn defence today, limiting her fury to no goodbye kiss and the door slammed behind him. Despite her fear of losing a man she thought was The One, the need for flaming rows and make-up sex is palling.

But things with Gerald have come to a sudden stop, too. He left abruptly after dinner last week. Something she said, she thinks, although she can't for the life of her think what. It's not as if she does much talking in his company, happy instead to hear about his army career. In a rare gap in the conversation she offered a few anecdotes about her work as a translator, her cottage, her school days. At some point she noticed his expression had locked. Pupils wide, mouth gaping beneath the thick moustache. Soon afterwards he feigned an important text and left. Tears of shame hit the sink of water as she washed up their supper pots. Although she'd been stood up a few times, she'd never had a guy run out during a date before.

It's stupid when she thinks about it now. Ironic, even. When she bumped into Gerald at his workplace a few days later, she was the one who bolted. She goes back to her meal and drains her glass. Neither man is right for her. Tim only wants sex, and she's still no idea what Gerald wants. Not her – that's clear now. As she pours the rest of the wine, she picks up her meal. Time for lots of quiet nights in. No racking her brains for something intelligent to say to Gerald; no keeping her legs shaved for Tim. Freedom to relax in her own company.

Across the room, the light is flashing on her answerphone.

Tim!

It has to be. He wants to try harder. He'll suggest coming

over on Saturday. With the heatwave forecast to continue, they'll have a walk in the village and out to open fields, take a picnic.

Or Gerald wanting to bring over another bottle of his expensive red wine to rekindle their friendship, maybe take it further. She'd rather it be Tim, but mustn't cut her options. Heart fluttering, she presses the play button.

It's a message from her publisher asking her to bring forward a deadline on an anthology translation and make significant changes. It will mean another week cocooned at home, all devices turned off, no time for play. New humiliation pricks her eyes; she's no one to play with anyway. She storms into the kitchen, scrapes her stir-fry into the bin and fetches another bottle of white from the wine rack. Too bad it isn't chilled.

CHAPTER SEVENTEEN

THURSDAY 5TH JULY

We leave the car in the theatre car park in Wellington Street and Harriet leads the way on foot to the Cross Care Counselling Centre. Her mobile phone provides directions, even though we both know it's in Eastgate Street, one of the four main thoroughfares in Gloucester city centre. But she's twenty-four and her generation don't blow their noses without sat nav telling them where their hanky is.

It turns out to be in a courtyard beyond the Access medical surgery where I sought help for migraines a couple of months back. Feeling suddenly guilty for having cancelled my scan appointment, I put my head down and speed across the square.

Automatic doors at the counselling centre swish open on a foyer that looks like my bank. As well as the same high ceiling and grey carpet tiles, it's got two long queues of people. The bank to a tee. Their strategy is to keep customers waiting until they give up and do their business online. Turkeys voting for Christmas come to mind. I don't suppose it's the same story here. I'm surprised to see so many people in need of counselling and prepared to present themselves in public. I never would. Not now, not ever, and not eighteen years ago. Counselling tells secrets. A cold shadow creeps along my spine.

A woman comes out of a side door and opens another desk with a 'General Enquiries' sign. We reach her before the other queues have time to react. Not for nothing do coppers take an annual fitness test. She is a forty-something woman with mid-brown hair and party make-up. Her smile remains friendly when Harriet shows her ID.

"I'll let Rosemary know you're here," she says and clacks her acrylic nails over a keyboard. "Please have a seat."

We move to a couple of utilitarian sofas. Soon after we sit down, another woman pushes open a glass door and calls us through.

With more grey carpet and three more sofas, the room beyond feels like another foyer, but smaller. The woman introduces herself as Rosemary Davies, Head of Centre, and motions us to take a sofa each. She slides neatly onto the third sofa. There's no desk so I'm guessing her office proper is through the door behind her. We must be in the area where she sees clients. The glass door separating here from the main foyer doesn't seem very private, but perhaps it's designed with the security of the therapist in mind. As a police officer, I know what it's like to be in a confined space with a member of the public who's asked for help but turns unexpectedly nasty.

Rosemary Davies crosses her legs, cups a hand over her knee and leans towards me. "What would you like to know, inspector?"

"My colleague has some questions," I say and nod at Harriet. I've promised her this rodeo.

Her notebook already on her lap, Harriet makes a start. "I'm enquiring about one of your counsellors who hasn't been seen recently."

"This is about Gerald, isn't it? He still hasn't turned up. Poor Anna." Rosemary looks at me again while she's speaking, but I make a point of turning towards Harriet, letting her keep the lead.

"When did you last see him?" she asks.

"It would have been Monday."

"How did he seem?"

"Absolutely fine, but I didn't see much of him, as we both had clients all day." She smiles at me again, a woman used to dealing with the person in charge. She oozes authority, and I don't kid myself she thinks I'm on her level. If I was here with the DCI, she'd be giving him the eye and ignoring me.

Harriet presses on. "Did anything unusual happen during his shift?"

Rosemary smooths a crease in her linen dress. "Not as far as I know. He worked as normal until four p.m. on Monday but didn't arrive for work on Tuesday. Anna, his wife, phoned me shortly after nine enquiring after his where-abouts. She said he hadn't come home on Monday night. I advised her to ring you." Another smile my way.

"And Anna works here, too. Is that right?" Harriet asks.

"They share a post, specialising in relationship guidance."

"And how does that work? A married couple working together? Any tensions?" I ask and score a daggered look from Harriet for interrupting, but I want more than the surface stuff Harriet is getting. Do Mr and Mrs G-G clash over therapy plans or is their front so united they gang up on colleagues?

"They are extremely professional," Rosemary replies. "They tend to allocate clients separately but always brief each other. Second opinions are so helpful for counsellors."

"Besides this week, have either had any absences recently?" I'm thinking undeclared health problems or pulling sickies for away days with a lover. Work might be going well, but what's happening in the margins?

"Obviously I can't go into staff personnel files, but I'm not giving away any confidences if I confirm that, until this week, Gerald's attendance record is excellent, as is Anna's. She even returned to work this morning despite worries about Gerald. She is currently upstairs with a couple in the Relationship Suite."

Harriet looks up from her notes, clearly as surprised as I am that Anna is here. Wouldn't the errant Gerald be more likely to reappear at home? Why isn't she pacing the photo-lined hall of her bungalow?

"If you have questions for her, she'll be free in about forty minutes," Rosemary says as if reading our thoughts. Maybe that's what counsellors do: know what's going on in clients' heads and draw it out.

Calculating what time we can see Anna, Harriet checks her watch, but I don't want to waste the whole day on this dubious misper when the trail on Sonia Hanson's killer grows colder by the hour.

"That won't be necessary today," I say.

Harriet frowns but carries on. "Getting back to Gerald, you say he had clients all day on Monday."

"That's correct." This time the woman turns her smile on Harriet. "But I'm afraid I cannot tell you their details," she says, from warm to officious in a single sentence. "It's confidential."

116

In spite of herself, Harriet looks at me, wanting help. For the devilment I don't respond. I've ways and means of getting sensitive information out of tinpot bosses but not today. The quicker Harriet's questioning stalls, the sooner we get back to Sonia Hanson.

Although Harriet has reddened, she finds a second wind. "If Gerald works here on Monday and Tuesday, what does he do for the rest of the week?"

"I can't tell you that either. You'll have to ask Anna. Anything I know about Gerald, I know because I'm his manager. I cannot disclose information about my staff."

"Anna told us he used to work for the Australian government," Harriet ventures.

"Then you already have that information," Rosemary replies. "I can't say more than his wife has apparently already told you."

Harriet sighs. "And I don't suppose you'd tell us if he had any disagreements with colleagues or clients?"

"My staff get along famously. As for relations with clients, they are trained to recognise problems at an early stage. Signs of transference crop up now and again. Sometimes the client transfers feelings he or she has for a parent or partner onto the counsellor. Gerald has never reported anything of that kind, although I wouldn't be able to give you details even if he had. It would be..."

"Confidential," Harriet fills in. "So no chance of a list of his clients for the last month or so? To eliminate them from our enquiries."

"Naturally not."

Harriet is clutching and I itch to take over.

Despite the odds, Harriet perseveres. "Can you at least give me an idea of the type of client?"

"Type? Our clients come from all walks of life. At least one in ten people suffers from depression or stress at some point in their lives. We would never categorise them by type."

I'm about to break my promise and take charge when my phone vibrates in my pocket. I use the distraction to avoid hearing Rosemary Davies parry Harriet's next futile question. It is a missed call with a follow-up text. My fingers jitter as I scroll; I've been waiting days for this ring back.

"I've got to take this." Pressing redial, I bolt to the foyer.

"Tewkesbury Kinesiology," says a bright male voice when my call is answered.

"Can I speak to the...... kinesiologist?" I say. Is that what they're even called?

"That's me, Gregory Peters. How can I help?"

Answering his own phone? Is that a sign of an amateur set up? Does it matter? I've been down the traditional route and got nowhere. "You just tried to phone. I'm hoping to get a consultation, well a chat, I'm not sure..."

"Are you Steph?"

"How did you know?"

"The last number I dialled. I'm glad you got through. I'm ringing prospective clients all day. Bit of a backlog. What do you need to know?"

I look around the Cross Care foyer. There are still queues and noise. No one can hear me but I still lower my voice. "I get headaches. Migraines, I think. Not all the time, but..."

"What treatment have you had so far?"

"Pretty much everything." *Except the brain scan.* "I went to a homeopath but she said I'd have to come off my painkillers. I have a busy job and couldn't take the risk. And

I've made dietary changes but I'm not sure if they're working."

"They can take time. I might be able to suggest more. Through kinesiology the body communicates its physical, nutritional or emotional needs. Practitioners like me test muscles at energy points on the body to identify the root causes of health issues."

I've never heard the like, but after months of on-off and mostly on pain, I'd let Harry Potter have a go. "When can you fit me in?"

"I've nothing until September, I'm afraid. It's the back-log. But after an initial consultation, you'll be in the system and will probably only need a couple more sessions."

I make the booking and end the call, disappointed at the delay but unsurprised. I'm at the point beyond expecting anything to work. *Except a brain scan.*

Through the glass door, I see Rosemary Davies stand up and hold out her hand. An expert terminating the inter-view. She must have years of practice at dismissing clients when their forty-five minutes are up. But Harriet stays seated. I silently urge her on, though I sense she's no match.

The receptionist at the enquiries desk has dealt with her queue. She smiles and calls out, "I hope you find him."

Walking towards her, I wonder if she'll answer a few questions or put down the same confidentiality barrier as her boss. "Do you know Gerald?"

"He's a lovely bloke. Down to earth." She lowers her voice and points at the ceiling. "Not like *her*."

According to Rosemary, Anna Gittens-Gold is upstairs in a consultation. I check that's who the receptionist means.

"Yeah, that's her. Puts on airs and graces. A vegan for

119

goodness' sake, and teetotal. What does that tell you? She's no business being a counsellor."

Before I can work out how an abstemious lifestyle rules out that particular career option, the receptionist explains. "Counsellors need to have lived. How else can they empathise? Anna wouldn't throw a rope to a drowning man. She reckons she's a technology expert, right, but when I was new and didn't know how to work the computer, she told me to use the manual. And she's a gossip. Always talking about the clients. Not like Titfer. He's discreet. Don't get me wrong, he talks about himself a lot but keeps his mouth shut about the clients. I don't know what he sees in her."

"Titfer?"

She gives an embarrassed laugh. "That's what we call Gerald behind his back. Titfer Tat – rhyming slang for hat. He always wears a straw boater. His clothes can be a bit fancy, too, sometimes – cravats and stuff."

"Does he wear a hat all the time? Even with clients?" It could be worth mentioning headgear in a public appeal if it comes to that.

She nods. "Mostly. I expect he's going bald. Bound to be at his age. I suppose he wore a military cap on his missions."

Through the glass door, Harriet is staying seated but Rosemary is still on her feet. Harriet's tactic looks unlikely to prolong the interview. If anyone's going to find out anything here, it's me with this receptionist. "Could I take your name?"

"Julia Paget."

"Thanks, Julia. And you know he went on military assignments?"

"Everyone knows. He worked for the Ozzie army." So much for Rosemary Davies's confidentiality pledge. "He's lived here for years but still has a bit of an Australian accent – although I've never heard him say 'G'day'. I don't suppose she'd let him." Her eyes roll to the ceiling again.

"Has anyone other than clients ever popped in to see him, a friend maybe?" And I'm thinking a lover.

She shakes her head. "Even when he goes clubbing, he's on his own mostly."

I blink. I would swear the lipsticked mouth said clubbing. "What does Gerald do in his free time?"

"He's got his photography, of course. That's part of his army work. And he set up a portrait studio here to do our photos for the office brochure last year. Apart from that, there's just the clubbing as far as I know. It started out as a joke. After I split from my boyfriend, I asked Titfer to come to Taboo to help me drown my sorrows. I didn't think he'd come but he did. Got really into the dancing. Not a bad mover for an old bloke, for any bloke really. I've seen him there a few times since, laughing with the girls."

I've already warmed to this chatty woman but I like her even more now. She's about my age and still at the boyfriend stage. Not a husband or wife or even a partner. We share the sadness. No, the freedom.

"Does Anna go clubbing with him?"

"Nah, but I bet she knows about it. They're definitely close. Tell each other everything. He's no blabbermouth but he does tell *her* all sorts. When I told him my boyfriend had chucked me, she knew all the details the next day. I reckon him going clubbing is a bit of a giggle to them both."

"When he's at the clubs, are there particular other clubbers he likes to spend time with?"

"It's not like that. Titfer is a gentleman. He's loyal to her, though I can't think why." The finger goes upwards again.

Through the glass, I see Harriet concede defeat and shake Rosemary's hand. When she comes out, I thank Julia for her help and we leave.

"Any joy?" I ask when we get to the car.

Harriet shakes her head. "Should we request a warrant to search their files?"

"What do you think?"

"There are no grounds, are there? This place is a dead end."

"Not entirely," I say, thinking of my conversation with Julia, as I fasten my seatbelt.

CHAPTER EIGHTEEN

Dommo closes his bedroom door and drops his school bag on the bed. Jutting out his lower lip, he blows his face and feels the warm air through his damp fringe. His scalp has been sweaty all day and his underarms stink. A fleeting worry about his sweatshirt crosses his mind. This heat means he's taken it off somewhere. At school? *Shit.* When did he last have it? What if he dropped it on the towpath on Monday? Kelly will kill him. She paid for it out of her wages. Then he remembers he didn't have it with him; the fire warmed his bare arms. But it's not on his bedroom chair. So where?

He finds it hanging in the wardrobe. Kelly must have done a tidy up before she went to work. *Double shit.* Did she look under his bed? Heart thumping, he hits the floor, lifts the bedspread and stretches his arm as far as it will go. His fingers touch the strap and he relaxes. Her tidying hasn't extended this far, but it's a reminder that he needs to find a better hiding place. Reaching further, he teases the handbag towards him.

When he caresses his cache on his lap, the burnt material stains his polo shirt and trousers. Can he get the clothes into the laundry basket for Kelly to wash without her noticing? Mentally he rehearses a plausible explanation. Joel and Jack were mucking about by the school bins where someone had left a pile of ash. They rubbed it on Dommo for a laugh. Yeah, that would do, although he isn't keen on mentioning ash. Too close to the truth.

Upending his school bag, he finds a pen and prods the burnt bundle with it, like he's seen TV detectives do at crime scenes. Claiming a dentist's appointment, he raced away from Joel when the end-of-school bell rang on Monday and went back to the towpath to gather the remnants of the fire.

He lifts the handbag flap, plunges a hand inside and pulls out the treasures one by one. The recorder thing first, a misshapen block of plastic with three metal buttons on a melted frame. Dommo moves on as it's obvious it won't work, and the fact that stupid Alex saw it first tarnishes its worth.

The hairy-furry stuff creeps him out and he lets go of it sharpish. Likewise the straw-coloured crescent, the rest of which the fire has eaten away. Tears prick his eyes. It reminds him of the hat his grandad used to wear. He probably still does, but Dommo hasn't seen him since the row he and Mum had on Dommo's eighth birthday. Mum said it was just one drink to celebrate, but Grandad said she'd had her last chance.

The final prize, a notebook, is more intact. The metal spiral at the top is bent and several pages are scorched but readable. As he leafs through, he realises he's holding his breath. He exhales, trying not to make a sound even though it doesn't matter. Kelly is still at the salon and Mum's in front of the telly, dead to the world, with a tennis match blaring.

Too bad the words in the notebook are in code, but he's got IT tomorrow. When Mrs Barrow isn't looking, he could go on the internet and find a way to decipher it. Just as long as she doesn't pair him with Alex. No way is that saddo sharing in this.

CHAPTER NINETEEN

The afternoon in the CID office is hot, airless and dodo-dead. We're all at our desks, following up enquiries and collating evidence, but any progress on the Hanson case seems extinct. Almost everyone who knew Sonia had a reason to dislike her, but there's no concrete evidence and no witnesses, apart from the usual cranks who come out of the woodwork for every major crime from the Great Train Robbery to Shergar's disappearance. DC Tony Smith is convinced the motive is a family rift and he's scouring their social media posts for proof of nefarious intent. According to him, the Clarkes are honour-killing material, whereas I thought they were just sad when we interviewed them on Tuesday. The French grand-mother's outburst encapsulated what they were all feeling: an agonising grief, clouded by bitterness and hurt.

My inclination is towards Carl Bryant, Sonia's dumped fiancé. He doesn't strike me as someone who takes humilia-tion well, but he also strikes me as a man of decision, a hard-nosed businessman who gets things done. If he wanted to exact revenge on Sonia, would he wait four years? There's something we're missing. My gut says not all key witnesses have been found, and with each passing day, they have more opportunity to blend into the Gloucester landscape.

Harriet sits opposite, prodding her keyboard. She keeps stopping to adjust her monitor. The thing has stood stock still for weeks, but now it requires her constant fiddling. Hunching over my notes so I can't see her fidgeting, I start to type a summary of the Hanson case. But when my fingers transfer the details to screen, *Gittens-Gold* stares back at me in 12pt Times New Roman. I stab the delete button and type the correct name, but... Where is Gerald? My mind isn't so much wandering as making a route march to the wrong case.

Admitting defeat, I push away on my chair and rub my eyes. My energies should be on the three tiny Hanson children who've just lost their mother, not on a man who divides his time between parachuting behind enemy lines and chatting up girls in clubs. Not much difference between the two activities, perhaps. Both require a heck of a nerve and a touch of disguise – camouflage paint for one and a daft hat for the other.

What's the wife's game, returning to work? Anna Gittens-Gold should be out of her mind with worry about her husband, but I can't get beyond the performance she gave us in her pristine house. The study was lined with photography trophies but there were no ornaments, no souvenirs of Gerald's overseas trips. When my mate Terri and I were kids, we sometimes went to her aunt and uncle's house. They collected mementoes from everywhere that the uncle ever toured with the army: Bavarian barometers, Polish pottery, brass donkeys from Gibraltar. I'd assumed that all military families were the same. Did Anna make Gerald chuck his out, or were neither of them interested in trinkets?

I send Terri a text, thinking she'll see it after she's finished teaching, but she replies immediately.

Marking YR10 monologues. Please interrupt.
I reply: *Haha. To grade or not to grade... Did you ever meet your Uncle Phil's army pals?*
She fires back straight away: *One or two I think. Am I helping with police enqs again?*
I confirm this: *You're never off the suspect list. Drinks tomorrow? I'll explain.*

We've been going to the King's Head on a Friday night while it's light enough to walk the mile there and back in daylight. There's no reply. She must have got busy with her marking. Then I see she's typing.

Not this week. Sorry.

I look at my screen, surprised by the knockback. She's typing again.

But we're still on for Sun lunch right?

My parents have invited Terri and Brad as well as Jake and me to a roast. But her text is a puzzle. Normally she'd be more expansive about her plans. Instead she's deflected to Sunday. What's the secret? Must be a date. I text back.

Looking forward to it.

Sunday lunch will be a chance to put my interview skills to use on my day off, me thinks, and find out what she's up to.

After the text exchange, I try to work but still find Harriet distracting. She pulls her keyboard forward, pushes it back, nudges it sideways. When she sees me looking, she snatches her hands off the desk and chews her pen for a while. Then she leans over her workstation, clicks a few buttons and picks up the phone.

"Good afternoon. I'm Detective Constable Harriet Harris. I'd like to speak to the tutor who runs your self-defence courses."

I look up, puzzled. Our police training is better than any adult education course. If she wants a refresher, she only has to ask. But as I hear more, it becomes obvious her call is related to our misper case.

"The level?" Harriet flicks through her note book. "I believe the student in question did level three... Yes, if you could..." She turns more pages as she waits on the line. "With Jiu Jitsu, really? If you could ask the tutor to give me a call back, that would be great. I'll give you my direct number."

She returns to her keyboard and we carry on working, both of us silent against the low noise of our colleagues. But it's not long before she's reading her notebook again, scrabbling through the pages. After a few minutes, she makes another phone call. Even from here, I can hear the cut-glass tone of the woman who answers.

"Good afternoon, Mrs Gittens-Gold, this is DC Harris..."

The voice on the line reaches a higher pitch.

"You haven't heard from your husband ... I see ... You would have notified us immediately ... I understand." Harriet's neck has reddened. "I've another reason for the call. Do you know which clients he was scheduled to see on Monday?"

Good thinking, Detective Constable. More than one way to skin Rosemary Davies's tight-lipped cat, but I can hear Anna's sing-sing protests down the line.

"If you could have a think whether he said anything ... Confidential ... I see." Harriet looks at me and rolls her eyes. "Thank you. I'll keep you informed."

She rings off and fills me in, although I've got the gist. Just like her boss, Anna can't break confidentiality rules, but she'll try to remember any general comments Gerald made.

We work again, but every time Harriet is poised to recommence typing, she moves the keyboard. The damn thing is going to end up on the floor at this rate. I come out of my document and find the number for the Cross Care Centre. I might have let Harriet run the rodeo there this morning, but it is time for me to break in the horse.

A receptionist, not Julia, answers, and puts me straight through to Rosemary Davies. "Good to hear from you," she says. "I've got five minutes before my next client."

"Excellent," I reply, refusing to be irked by her attempt to set the timeframe. "This won't take long. I need the names of the clients Gerald saw on Monday."

"As I explained, not two hours ago..."

"Indeed. You were most helpful." My jaw tightens. I hate bullshitting but it has its uses. "What I'm going to tell you now is confidential." I hear the in-breath. I've piqued her interest by speaking her language. "There is a possibility that Gerald Gittens-Gold has been murdered." I feel several pairs of eyes swivel my way. I'm suddenly the CID office floorshow.

"Surely not," Rosemary gasps down the phone line.

"We have to consider whether one of his clients is involved."

"But... we know where they live. They wouldn't..."

"I'm sure you do what you can to vet them, but we don't know the motive for Gerald's disappearance. It could be a vendetta against the Cross Care Centre itself." Now I sense the mouths of my audience fall open. Tony Smith has folded his arms. God, I'm good.

"But if you don't know the motive, you can't assume it's a client. I can't just divulge private information." The words are decisive but I sense her wavering. Time to close out with flattery, and a sting.

"Of course. I have no doubt that, as an experienced manager and counsellor, you can vouch for the integrity of everyone who comes through your doors. I admire your professionalism, even knowing culpability could rest with you if your team is endangered."

Another intake of breath makes her cough.

I lower my voice. "You have my word we would approach the clients with the utmost discretion."

Silence. Down the line, I hear the tapping of computer keys. "Do you have a pen?" she says eventually. She reads out the names and addresses. I note them down and thank her.

After acknowledging a ripple of applause from my colleagues and a wolf whistle from Tony, I pass the note to Harriet. "Arrange the interviews with that lot. I'll come along." I stand up, fancying a walkabout. Time to visit the police press office to discuss releasing Gerald's details to the media. If Harriet is so hung up on this misper, she can wade through all the responses a public appeal today would get.

Harriet smooths out the address list and gives me a look I can only describe as pissed-off gratitude. I let it pass. Whatever rank we are, the ones above us are both irritating and necessary. There are times I can't get info without Kevin going into battle for me, but I still resent him for it.

But I can't resist lobbing another superiority bomb over my shoulder as I leave. "I may have another job for you. Tomorrow night. I'll let you know."

CHAPTER TWENTY

When the letterbox rattles, Hamish scuttles to the porch, skidding on the tiled floor. He retrieves the rolled-up newspaper, hurtles along the hall to the open kitchen door and relinquishes the prize at Tracey's feet.

She bends to tickle his silky throat and watches joy spread through the dog's body. He shakes his hips from side to side, wagging his tail against her legs. Tracey sits at the kitchen table, tears off the back page and folds it under a table leg. Perhaps sensing a new ritual forming, Hamish takes her actions as a cue to settle in his basket.

"Clever wee boy," Tracey says. He's worked out she won't move for a long time. No chance of anything to eat or a friendly pat. It's been the same every evening this week. Tracey tells herself she's putting him first by delaying the evening walk until the heat has gone out of the day. Yet this new urge to scour the news isn't about killing time until they venture out. It's another kind of killing she has in mind.

The newspaper is damp where Hamish's slavering jaws

have made contact but it's still readable. The headline is about cuts to bus routes, but Councillor George Vale – folded-arm stance and a frown into the camera – is vowing to overturn the decision. Tracey wonders how serious the plans are and whether Vale, Gloucester's greatest self-publicist, has planted the story himself. Not bothering to read the detail, she glances down the page.

"Well, the nasty lady's murder is still on the front, but only just," she tells Hamish. The dog doesn't react. To her human eyes, he looks uncomfortable with his paws sticking over the side of the dog bed and his head resting on the higher edge, but his eyes close for a doze.

Tracey reads the article. There's nothing new. Police are pursuing several lines of enquiry. She exhales deeply. Maybe the woman outside the cathedral wasn't as nasty as she seemed. Just not used to dogs. Perhaps Tracey was too harsh in her description. Not that the police were interested. The officer who took her call treated her like a dotty dame.

Yesterday, coverage about the dead woman extended to pages two and three. Life and times stuff in the absence of anything concrete on the murder hunt. Easy for the newspaper to print as she was one of their own reporters, apparently. But today, when Tracey flicks through as far as the TV listings, there's nothing more.

When she turns back to page two, she gasps and Hamish gives a start.

Local man missing. The photograph is shockingly familiar. He's even wearing the same straw hat. "It can't be."

Hamish lifts his head, excitement surging from nose to tail. He sits up, and Tracey realises she's used her eager, time-for-a-walk voice.

"I'll have to phone the police again first. They'll think I'm a crank. Do you think Mummy's a crank, Hamish? If you do, stop wagging your tail."

CHAPTER TWENTY-ONE

INCIDENT ROOM – FRIDAY 6TH JULY, 10.00 A.M.

If Death wore sunglasses, I'd be her doppelganger. No sleep last night; no life left in my bones this morning. Even my headache is tired. Instead of throbbing, it leans heavily against the inside of my skull. Hence I'm keeping my shades on as I quit Kevin's office and go to the incident room. He suspected nothing when I offered to take this morning's briefing on his behalf. It was easy to keep my expression neutral when the top half of my face was doing a Jackie Onassis impression.

It wasn't just heat that kept me awake. Jake arrived home after eleven p.m., pleading another homework session at Brad's, even though there's precious little to study this late in the summer term. It's a shame I'm not meeting Terri tonight, as it could be a chance to swap notes and check whether the boys are playing one mum off against the other. But Terri seems to have got a better offer. Maybe she was on a date last night, too, and hasn't a clue where Brad and Jake were.

At the incident room door, I take a breath and prepare to deal with the third reason for my insomnia: a phone call I took in the office just as I was leaving last night was someone from my recent past I hoped never to hear from again.

Inside the room, the blinds are down, the lights are on and it's party time. The desk by the overhead projector displays a large cake that Tony Smith is cutting with a fancy knife. A few detectives line up for a slice. Others, who've already been served, chomp away, with paper serviettes close to their chins to catch crumbs. All are laughing and chatting.

"Want a bit, Steph?" Tony calls. "Nikki made it."

"It's Tony's birthday. He's forty-four," Harriet explains. Unnecessarily. Even with a migraine, I've sufficient detective skills to deduce that Tony's fiancée has been baking for good reason. And given Tony has been two months older than me the whole time we've served together, I know his age.

When a piece is passed to me, I wrap it in its serviette and put it in my bag. "I'll have it later, thank you." I'm off chocolate for the duration, and I can hardly scoff Tony's cake when I'm about to use him as a scapegoat.

Pointedly, I stand close to the desk to address the room. "I won't keep you long."

Tony speeds up serving the cake and everyone takes a seat.

"Where's the DCI?" Harriet asks.

"He's in with the Super and has asked me to lead." I say, putting my spin on how I was in his office first thing, telling Kevin about last night's phone call and persuading him that he, or the Super, or another grown-up, might want to announce the latest development to the press before it leaked. That was only part of the reason for my urgency; I needed to orchestrate who did the follow-up enquiry, and the easiest way was to make sure I ran the morning briefing.

"There's been a breakthrough thanks to a diligent

member of the public, who phoned here late last night. It's good to know someone's on the ball." My implied criticism gets their full attention and they stop chewing. "Does the name Tracey Chiles mean anything to any of you?"

Harriet swallows her cake. "It rings a bell. What's the context?"

Shit. I forgot Harriet was with me when we visited Tracey's guesthouse two months ago. I move on quickly. "She is the vigilant citizen who saw both Sonia Hanson and..." I pause for effect. "...Gerald Gittens-Gold outside the cathedral at twenty to six on Monday morning."

The hardened coppers gasp like excited children. Here's a surprise lead. They like surprises, especially with party food.

"Tracey Chiles first phoned us on Monday evening, less than twenty-four hours after Sonia's murder, to say she'd seen the victim that morning. For some reason we didn't do anything about it."

There's a shifting of weight in seats. They must be wondering if this is a breakthrough or a bollocking, but I have to keep up the 'rottweiler with a sore arse' act, so they don't challenge me. I don't want any of them remembering Tracey Chiles's involvement in our previous investigation.

"She tells me that when she phoned on Monday she spoke to a detective constable." I shoot a look around my colleagues. "She says he was cocky."

As I hoped, every pair of eyes swivels to the birthday boy. He wipes his mouth, leaving butter icing on his chin. "You know how it is," he says. "There have been dozens of calls. Even now that one doesn't stand out as a priority. I could hardly hear her for the dog in the background."

"She might be a crank, Steph. Have you checked her

out?" says Jordan Woods, on the other side of a sugar rush and suddenly Tony's best mate. But I don't mind the show of solidarity because it leads to where I want the interview allocation to go.

"You might be right," I say, "but my nose tells me that she's genuine. I'm going to see her straight after this. Thank God she rang back when she saw Gerald's photo in last night's paper. We might never have made the connection otherwise. Superintendent Thomas is making another press appeal later today. Let's see who else can place a man answering Gittens-Gold's description near the scene of Sonia Hanson's murder."

"What have we got on Gittens-Gold?" Tony asks.

Harriet looks preoccupied and I worry the cogs are still turning on how she knows Tracey Chiles. Needing to distract her, I ask her to brief us on what we've found out about the missing Gerald.

She's on it with confidence. "His wife says he left for work on Monday morning and she hasn't seen him since. She phoned his office on Tuesday morning to be told that he'd worked Monday but hadn't turned up on Tuesday. That's when she came to the station and spoke to Izzy Barton."

"There you go, then," Tony announces. "If the wife saw him at home on Monday morning, he wasn't at the cathedral. Tracey Chiles got her sighting wrong."

"Anna isn't sure what time he left because she was asleep," Harriet explains. "But he normally left around eight thirty. He works at the Cross Care Centre as a marriage guidance counsellor two days a week, but he has a military background. He's an Australian national and apparently used to do undercover work for their government. There was a reciprocal agreement with our MOD to fly him out of RAF bases to East Timor and the like. His wife hinted that he still does jobs for them now and again, but she's adamant that he hasn't gone off on one now."

The East Timor bit is news to me. Harriet has done more digging than I realised, but I still don't buy it. "There's something not right about this army stuff," I say. "We've talked to the neighbours. They all know too much."

Tony swallows a mouthful of cake. "Meaning?"

"How much do you tell your neighbours about your business? These days, most folk in the same street hardly pass the time of day, but Gerald gives his neighbours chapter and verse on his derring-do." I ask Harriet whether she's checked out his military record.

"I've got nowhere yet," she says. "Australia House referred me to the Department of Defence in Canberra. I was passed from extension to extension until I got a retired colonel in personnel who told me they needed the application in writing. He faxed me the form and I've faxed it back. God knows when I'll get a reply."

"Keep on it," I say. *Keep on it all while I deal with Tracey Chiles.* "Anything else?"

Harriet faces her colleagues. "I didn't get much out of Rosemary Davies, the manager of the Cross Care Centre where he worked, but with Steph's help..." Her neck takes on a pinker tinge. "Davies gave out the names of the three sets of clients Gerald saw on Monday, the last day he went into work. I haven't got hold of one couple yet, but I've fixed to interview the others at home tomorrow morning."

"I'll come with you," I say, kissing goodbye – again – to a Saturday lie-in. "I spoke to the receptionist at the Cross Care Centre. She confirmed that he had some kind of army career and that he is an expert photographer, even doing the

Centre's annual brochure. She also reckons he likes going to nightclubs."

"Clubbing?" Tony says the word as if actually battering someone with a blunt instrument. "How old is he?"

Harriet points to the birthday cake. "Asks the man halfway through his fifth decade."

"Gerald Gittens-Gold is fifty-six. We'll all be that old one day if we're lucky," I say. "A regular on the club scene, apparently. Likes dancing and flirting with the young 'uns. The Cross Care Centre receptionist says it's all harmless, just a bit of fun."

"Harmless, my arse," Tony says. "The dirty sod is holed up in some hotel with a girl half his age. Maybe he attacked the journalist because she found out and was going to tell the wife."

"That's a bit far-fetched, isn't it?" Harriet says.

"Did Sonia Hanson go clubbing?" Jordan asks.

"I doubt she'd have had the time. She was a workaholic and she had her family," Harriet replies.

"Maybe it's just coincidence Gittens-Gold was near the cathedral. He could have fancied an early stroll to work. It was a warm morning," Jordan says. "Unless there's another connection? Journalism? What was Mrs Hanson working on?"

I fill them in on Sonia's writing responsibilities as explained to me by her boss, David Oakley.

The theories come in thick and fast. "Maybe someone wrote to her consumer affairs column to complain about the dodgy marriage advice Gittens-Gold had given," DC Cally Lane suggests.

"What about this?" Jordan says. "He was in a play and

she ripped his performance to bits in a review. He attacked her out of humiliation. Did he act?"

"His wife, Anna, did a bit at school. There are pictures on the wall in their house. Maybe she still does, although she didn't mention it," Harriet says.

"Maybe Sonia featured Gerald in her Gloucester Reunited column but no-one had anything nice to say about him," Jordan says. "He got angry, went to confront her and killed her."

"What is there on her laptop or her work computer?" Harriet asks. "Wouldn't a connection show up in her files?"

"As soon as Forensics get round to it, we'll be the first to know," I say.

"When will that be?" Jordan asks.

"It's Forensics we're talking about," I reply.

Jordan rolls his eyes. "No holding our breath then."

"How likely is Gittens-Gold to be the killer?" DC Darren Ayres asks. "Only one witness has placed both him and Sonia in the general vicinity of the cathedral at roughly the same time."

"Sonia's autopsy showed an expert strangulation," Cally chips in. "Someone in the Australian SAS would know how to do that."

"Australian reconnaissance," Harriet clarifies. "He was never a Ninja."

"We've got to establish or rule out a connection between Sonia and Gerald." I nod at Darren, Jordan and Cally in the front row. "The DCI and I want you to follow up all the stories Sonia worked on in the last year: consumer affairs, Gloucester Reunited and the theatre reviews. Take a column each. I'll forward the links." Oakley finally arranged for Sonia's articles to come my way late last night, when my head was throbbing too much to make a start on them.

"There might not be a connection, not in life anyway," Harriet says. She peers at me through her fringe.

"Go on," I say.

"Maybe he isn't the murderer but another victim. What if he saw who attacked Sonia and had to be silenced?" Sitting up straight, she warms to her theme. "Or maybe he was the intended victim and Sonia saw what happened to him. Maybe it's the motive for his murder we should be looking for."

Even though I'm impressed by her lateral thinking, I crush the theory. "Several witnesses, including his boss, say he went to work as normal that day. He was seen alive and well at the Cross Care Centre several hours after Sonia died."

"Exactly. There's no crime scene to investigate," Tony pipes up. "The guy did a runner between work and home. As far as the Hanson murder goes, my money's on a family feud. There are all the hallmarks."

"What hallmarks are those – that Sonia's family is half-French? Five minutes ago you said Gittens-Gold did it to cover up an affair."

"To be fair, Harriet, it's a viable line of enquiry," Tony argues. "The Clarke brothers hadn't spoken to their sister for years."

"And it could just be a robbery gone wrong," I remind everyone. "Uniform haven't turned up her handbag. Open minds, folks."

I break up the party with a final allocation of duties and ask Cally and Harriet to wait behind.

"Close the door," I tell them.

"If we are going to get anywhere with this, we need to know more about Gerald Gittens-Gold as well as Sonia Hanson. We have to delve into their private lives, meet their friends, go to the places they went, do the things they did. How would you feel about some undercover work tonight?"

The two young detectives grin at each other, eyes glittering.

CHAPTER TWENTY-TWO

The smell of dog hits me as Tracey Chiles opens the door.

"Come in," she says without asking for ID. I guess that's what comes of running a guesthouse: strangers welcome. But she might want to work on first impressions. I remember from last time that her skin was weather-beaten, but today it's heart-attack red and her hair probably hasn't seen a comb since she got up. The checker-patterned hallway floor, which was immaculate on my previous visit, has a dusting of dog hairs, partly concealed on the black tiles but unsightly on the white.

Suddenly a yapping black fuzz of legs shoots out from somewhere. Jumping up, its muzzle finds me and it isn't shy with it.

"Stop it, Hamish." Tracey pushes the dog's nose away. "He hasn't been out today because next door's bitch is in season." She grabs the dog by the collar and places her other, bandaged, hand on its rapidly moving rear end. She barricades the dog behind a door marked 'Breakfast Room' and the yapping changes to a whine.

"We'll go into my parlour but I don't want to leave him for long."

The parlour could best be described as work in progress. A pile of ragged towels on the coffee table and a clothes horse of woollen socks by an unlit electric fire. The windowsill resembles uncharted jungle. I identify a cheese plant and a couple of African violets. The rest is tangled rainforest, coated in a layer of Gloucester dust.

"Sit where you like." Tracey sighs, as if having a visitor is all too much.

I step over a couple of rubber dog toys and nudge aside a chewed blanket to reach the ancient sofa. A large patch of its base has changed from dusky pink to black, presumably where it has endured assault by wagging tail. As I sat down, my shoulders feel hot. Slants of sunlight stream through two large rips in the net curtains. I have probably picked Hamish's favourite spot on the sofa and parked my one decent pair of linen trousers on the hair-covered cushion.

Tracey folds into a winged armchair that's too worn and large for the rest of the room. I recall there's a stag's head on the stairs. Perhaps the chair would look better up there.

The dog's frustrated yelps reach us.

"He wants to play in the front garden," Tracey explains, "but I can't let him out on his own. Dogs try quite hard to get at bitches on heat."

"I know blokes like that," I say.

Tracey squints at me. "You came here before."

So she's recognised my humour but not my face. My gob has got me into trouble again.

"Do you think I'm jinxed?" she says.

I think she's being flippant back, knocking me a sideways insult about being the detective who turns up on her twice.

But she looks out of the window and her eyes water as she keeps talking. "For forty-eight years, everything was normal. There have been ups and downs – a divorce, a few bereavements, but this year... You read about these things but you never expect them to happen to..." She tails off and looks at me.

It's my turn to glance at the window. Coppers think a lot about the effects on their mental health of being around murder, but when have I given a thought to members of the public on the periphery of a case? In May, during the reign of a serial killer, this woman found the body of one victim at a local beauty spot and provided another with bed and breakfast prior to his demise. Two months later, she's caught up in another murder. Is that why the guesthouse looks a mess and the front garden is overgrown, bushes overhanging the pavement? Did things start to slide after her first encounter with serious crime?

"How's business?" I ask. "Are you fully booked for the school holidays?"

"A couple of my regulars will be here in August, but I haven't advertised this year." She kneads the fingers of her injured hand against her other palm. "I didn't get round to it somehow."

"What happened there?" I ask.

"It's nothing," she says, sitting on her hand in its grubby bandage. "Just a scratch. I couldn't find any plasters."

The dressing resembles shredded cabbage. More evidence of how she's struggling? My presence can't be helping. I get to the point. "I just need to go through what you saw on Monday morning."

"So you think it was him? The man I saw." She wraps her arms across herself. "I only saw him for a few seconds, but he was quite pleasant, even when Hamish started sniffing him. It's an embarrassing habit a lot of dogs have. Hamish usually only does it to women. Like just now. Sorry about that."

"No problem," I say, recalling how the same dog climbed up my leg when I first saw Tracey in the Georgian Gardens in May, after she found a body.

I show her the copy of Gerald's photograph, which our press office distributed to the media.

"That's definitely him. I remember his smile, tight lipped. I thought he was going to be angry like the woman 'til he spoke."

"Sonia Hanson was angry?" This was news. So much for Tony Smith's defence at this morning's briefing that Tracey's phone call hadn't stood out as a priority. Where's due diligence when it's needed? "Perhaps you can go through it from the beginning."

"I wanted to walk through the Story of Gloucester outdoor exhibition. I thought with it being by the cathedral it would be safe... I always pick up after Hamish and there's a poop-a-scoop bin by the main entrance. I take plenty of plastic bags with me, empty bread bags mostly. But I won't go there again. Frankly, I don't know where I'll go. Poor Hamish. He's such a good dog. He's..."

"And you spoke to Sonia Hanson?" I move her back on track, wanting to get this done before the quiver in her voice cracks wide open.

"I was coming through the arch from the green to the history trail when I heard her shout. Hamish had run off somewhere, so I followed the noise. A woman was standing by a concrete bench, dusting down her clothes. Hamish must have jumped up at her and she was furious. Called wee Hamish a mongrel. Imagine that? I put him on the lead and left. The woman didn't say any more. I thought she was... waiting for a client. Well, those women are always angry, aren't they? I didn't know she was a journalist. And a mum."

"And the man?"

"On the way out of the concourse we sort of bumped into him. He said 'Good Morning', patted Hamish and called him a beautiful dog. Even doffed his hat, a straw trilby. You don't get manners like that often. His voice was cultured, a bit colonial-sounding. He seemed such a refined man."

Now I know for sure she's not the crank Tony suspected her of being. This description matches, and even suggests an Australian accent, a fact not revealed to the media. She really did see Gerald.

"And that's the last you saw or heard of either of them?"

"Apart from the second shout. That came afterwards. Hamish and I were on the path by then. I thought she was annoyed with him like she had been with Hamish. It never occurred to me she was in danger. If I'd gone back... Hamish is no guard dog – that wouldn't work in a guesthouse; you can't have a dog that bites visitors – but it might have scared him off. She didn't like dogs, but even so, she didn't deserve... I can never understand people who don't like animals. They're much nicer than people. When was the last time a dog murdered another dog?"

I find myself nodding. In my line of work we see attacks of all kinds. Whenever dogs are involved, it's usually the human owner's fault. I can't think what to say and am grateful to Hamish when his desperate whining gets the better of Tracey and she says she must go to him.

Standing up, I hand her my card and tell her I might need to get in touch again.

At the front door she says, "By the way, did you get that stuff to his next of kin?"

My hot skin chills, knowing immediately what she means. Harriet and I called here during the May investigation to collect the belongings left behind by the deceased guest.

"We forwarded everything to his family in Liverpool," I assure her. Off our patch and out of my life. No one but me – and my super-bloody-sleuth boss, DCI Kevin Richards -- has so far found out that the murdered man was my son's father. And by taking charge of this interview with his former landlady I'm making sure it stays that way.

CHAPTER TWENTY-THREE

After I leave the Loch Lomond Guesthouse, I go back to the station to collect Harriet.

"Any progress?" I ask as I retrace part of my route through town. It will be easier to concentrate on what she says and still drive safely by avoiding the bypass – or the Nürburgring as it's known to Gloucestershire's white van men.

"Still nothing back from Canberra. It's the middle of the night there now, so I sent another email and left an answerphone message." She looks at me. "Only a short one."

"Fine with me," I say. I don't pay the police phone bill.

"I also tried the Australian High Commission in London again, on the off chance I'd get through to someone different, but they still couldn't, or wouldn't, tell me anything about Australian undercover manoeuvres even if their operatives set out from British soil as Gerald is supposed to have done."

"Keep trying. We've only the wife's word for his military past. I'd like it confirmed officially. Anything else?"

"I'm checking Carl Bryant's alibi."

"Brave," I say, recalling Bryant's reluctance to name the married woman he'd been with at the time of his ex-fiancée Sonia's murder.

"It wasn't as hard as I expected. I phoned his P.A. on a hunch that proved right. It's her job to organise flower deliveries for Bryant's girlfriends. With a little 'this is a murder enquiry' coaxing, she gave me the name and address."

"And does it check out?"

"I've arranged to meet the girlfriend face to face. Bryant has probably already briefed her on what to say, but I'll see if I can read her."

"Okay, but don't spend too long. My gut tells me she won't want to risk her marriage on a lie for a lover. She'll either confirm or deny as truth dictates and want to get the hell out of it."

"Right," Harriet says tightly and looks out of her passenger window.

"It's the priorities game," I tell her. "You know that." I admire her initiative in contacting Bryant's secretary though. I'm about to compliment her when an oncoming car strays across the white line. I swerve left and hoot. The driver corrects his path with a one-handed grip on the steering wheel, his other hand giving me a two-fingered salute.

"All set for tonight?" I ask instead, seeing an opportunity to thank her in advance for the interviewing at the city's nightclubs she and Cally Lane are going to undertake. We need to get an angle on Gerald Gittens-Gold. His apparent love of clubbing will be a good place to start.

Harriet clears her throat. "About that. Cally can't make it."

"What does that mean? Sometimes dates have to be

cancelled. She knows that, right?" It takes young detectives a while to twig that work will get in the way of a social life.

"It's her parents' silver wedding. She wanted to tell her mum she had a last-minute shift change, but chickened out. Family party. Relatives coming from abroad."

"Fairs," I say, recalling my parents' ruby anniversary a few years ago. Slap-up dinner at Bondend Hall; seventies disco; second cousins I hadn't seen before or since. "Cover as much ground as you can. I appreciate you might not get to all the clubbers who knew Gerald on your own."

"On my own?" Her voice ups its pitch. "Can't you allocate another colleague or let Cally and me do it tomorrow night?"

"We can't always be there to hold each other's hands, and time is against us. With Gittens-Gold tentatively linked to Sonia's murder, we either make it stick or move on. Quick as you like."

"Right," she says again.

That is the end of our conversation. We travel along the section of riverside that's yet to be developed – no cafés or boat trips or quayside promenade, just dilapidated warehouses with brickwork blackened by schoolboy arsonists. But a family of swans doesn't seem to mind. Two white parents and five grey teenagers make the most of this deeper section of river that is unaffected by the drought.

When we loop east, away from the waterfront, the city casts off its urban drudgery and we soon reach Wrenswood, Gloucester's land of milk and property. Bougainvillea flourishes on high brick walls that obscure views of large detached houses. I turn into Warwick Road and park on the Hansons' drive. I step out of the car and brush dog hairs off my backside for the third time since the visit to Tracey Chiles.

The toy trike and Barbie dolls are still where they were when we visited on Monday. Despite the glorious summer weather, none of the Hanson children seems to have ventured outside.

Alistair Hanson answers the door. His shoulders still sag and he's aged five years in as many days.

"The children have gone to nursery for a few hours. I'm trying to keep things normal." The word 'normal' sounds like a swear word. "My mother has gone to Tesco. I can make us some tea."

He leads us into the kitchen. If anything, it's even cleaner than before. Perhaps evidence of how his mother is channelling her energies at this terrible time.

"Have you brought back Sonia's laptop?" he asks, eyeing Harriet's bag.

"Our experts are still working on it," I say. *Some hope.* Our Forensics department goes at one speed, and it ain't fast.

After he's flicked on the kettle, Harriet shows him the photograph of Gerald Gittens-Gold. For a moment I think I see a flicker of recognition on his expressionless face, but then it's gone and he stares at the image impassively.

"Did he kill Sonia?" he asks.

"A witness saw him near the cathedral early that morning. That's all we know. Please think hard whether you've seen him before."

"I don't think so," he says, not taking his eyes off the photo.

"He has a slight Australian accent," Harriet explains. "He's five feet ten. We believe he often wears that hat. He works in town at the Cross Care Centre. He's a counsellor."

"Counsellor," Alistair echoes. He seems to be about to

say something else but he hands the photograph back to Harriet. "I don't think he has any connection to Sonia."

Harriet makes the tea while Alistair and I go into the lounge and I give an update on the case. I feel like a second-rate Superintendent Thomas, putting on a front of progress where there is none. Alistair listens, not once interrupting or querying. Grief seems to have overwhelmed his faculties as a lawyer. I fleetingly wonder if the same would have happened if he had been murdered and Sonia had been the surviving spouse. Would the journalist in her have become derailed by bereavement? I lose my thread as I catch sight of the Hansons' joyously stained carpet. How will the children's faculties be affected? When will they feel joy again?

After Harriet brings in the drinks, she occupies the stalling silence with questions about Sonia's background. Nothing new emerges, but she raises a smile from Alistair when she asks about their wedding.

We hear the front door open and Alistair's levity vanishes. "That will be my mother." He blinks off a tear, no doubt remembering that the sound of a key in the door will never again be his wife. "I'd better help her unpack the car." He stands up.

I say we'll be off. "There is just one more thing I have to ask you." I take a breath and pause until he has sat down again. "Did you know Sonia was pregnant?"

At that moment, Fiona, weighed down by two carrier bags, pushes open the lounge door. "Oh, son. I'm sorry," she says.

Alistair Hanson's face does a tour of pride, excitement and despair. "I knew it," he whispers. "She'd been feeling run down. I thought it might be that but she didn't say. I'm not sure she even realised herself." His voice crumbles and he begins to sob.

When I was a kid I used to fantasise about the moment I'd tell my husband we were expecting a baby. He'd whisk me into his arms, lay me on the sofa and shower me in kisses. In reality it never happened. When I realised I was pregnant, there was no husband to tell. But, even though it was my first, I felt the symptoms early on. Surely an experienced mother like Sonia would have seen the signs of a fourth pregnancy? Was there a reason she hadn't shared the news with her husband?

"I'm really sorry, but I have to ask," I say as gently as I can. "Would the baby definitely have been yours?"

Fiona drops her shopping and locks arms with Alistair as he weeps. She glares at me. "I questioned my daughter-in-law's loyalty to her family, but I never doubted it to my son. Not once."

"Thank you," I say. "We'll see ourselves out." I swallow but can't get the nasty taste out of my mouth. I hurry ahead of Harriet, not bearing to have her look me in the face. Soulless bitch that I am, my eyes are glistening. It's not just the shame of upsetting the husband; it's my envy of the departed wife. Sonia Hanson had her cake and ate it. Career, children and a loving husband to mourn her.

CHAPTER TWENTY-FOUR

If we found the interview with Alistair Hanson difficult, it was a picnic compared with our visit to the Clarkes. At the minimart in Hucton, the same cashier in the same tired orange tunic directs us to Jerome Clarke in the stockroom. Not only do the furniture pieces and bric-a-brac still reside, unsold, in the same cramped spaces, the same boxes of groceries are stacked on the back wall. Jerome Clarke even sports the same scowl when he sees us. Bereaved families I've dealt with often talk of their lives going into limbo following the death of their loved one, but I sense this suspended animation predates Sonia's murder. It's not her death that's had a profound effect but her marriage. Her split with Carl Bryant to wed Alistair Hanson and the family's forced move from their antique shop in the Quays have cost them dearly.

"Most of our orders are online," Jerome says as he sees me glancing around. Even the customers are staying away in droves.

I explain why we are here and Harriet shows him the photo of Gerald Gittens-Gold.

"Never seen him. He looks like a clown," Jerome sneers. "Is that the best you can come up with?"

He doesn't accompany us when we request to go upstairs to the flat, and we find ourselves alone up there with Marie Fournier.

As I came with Tony last time, Harriet has no knowledge of the old woman's spitting hostility towards her granddaughter. Smiling gently, she shows her police ID. "Do you mind if I sit here?" She points at a space on the sofa.

The woman gives a shrug and looks away.

"Thank you." There's a rustling of cellophane as Harriet lowers herself beside the woman, and I notice the wipe-clean cover over the cushions.

As Harriet retrieves the photo from her pocket, Marie gazes at her. How alien we both are here, but Harriet more so than me. The tall, willowy blonde must look exotic to this matriarch of a small, dark-haired family. Does she miss France, I wonder? Did ill health force her across the Channel, swapping her chic and vivid world for Planet Gloucestershire and a life of cultural bewilderment, dull food and frost?

Her eyes flick over the photo Harriet proffers before she goes back to her steady stare. Harriet reddens and writes in her notebook.

Monique Clarke enters the lounge, flashing the dark eyes that are so like her deceased daughter's. "Why are you bothering my mother?"

I explain the purpose of our call. Harriet stands up, seemingly grateful for the interruption and the chance to escape the older woman's scrutiny. "What about you, Mrs Clarke? Do you recognise him?"

Monique takes the photo from her outstretched hand,

studies the face and gives it back. "He has a dishonest face. A man who does not lift his mouth to smile hides many things. But I do not know him."

We hang about in the shop until Olivier returns from the cash and carry, but he doesn't recognise the photo either, which doesn't surprise me. Neither brother was much involved in the sister's life. Why should they know her killer? Does the same hold true for Alistair Hanson? My gut says the husband recognised Gerald's photograph. Is he hiding something?

When we're back in the car I ask Harriet what she makes of both house calls.

"There's nothing to make. They don't recognise him." Her tone is short and marks the end of another conversation. My young colleague still seems to be sulking about something.

CHAPTER TWENTY-FIVE

Pulling on her navy linen jacket, Superintendent Naomi Thomas walks out of her office. As she steps along the carpeted corridor, she unfastens her wooden beaded necklace. The piece is striking, perfect for her long neck and prominent cheekbones, but not appropriate for the sombre business ahead. She slips it into her briefcase, alongside her notes for the press conference. The notes are with her as a failsafe but she knows she won't need them. She'll be up to speed in front of the cameras. The new appeal is going to focus on Gerald Gittens-Gold and whether anyone has seen him since he left work on Monday afternoon. Hopefully her TV appearance will prompt other witnesses, besides the dog walker, to come forward to say they saw him by the cathedral that morning.

Progress, but on day five. The first serious lead has taken them nearly a week. Slower than Naomi would have wished. According to DCI Richards, Steph Lewis took the call from the dog walker but was vague about when the woman made contact. Naomi held the first press conference on Monday morning. Surely the witness would have got in touch on day one when the victim's image received wall-to-wall media coverage. The dog walker would have known then that she might have been one of the last people to see Sonia Hanson alive.

Naomi is losing patience with Steph, and not just because of this fumbled catch but also because of this latest business with Harriet Harris. Steph must learn to motivate her whole team, not just the old sweats she can banter with. They are not the officers Steph should be investing in. Naomi can see that Tony Smith – and Steph too, for that matter – has rough-diamond charisma, but neither of them is prepared to put in the homework. They lack the vision to realise that effortless charm takes effort.

She pushes through the swing doors into the stairwell and comes face to face with Jordan Woods. The detective constable moves aside to let her go down the stairs ahead of him. She thanks him by name and he smiles. Addressing staff by name is one of the range of motivational techniques that good leaders employ. But it's easy to remember Jordan, a key member of the team. Not the most creative of players but solid. After eight years in the force, he is the counter-balance to the youthful exuberance of Cally Lane and Harriet Harris. *Ah, yes, Harriet.* Her complaint is on Naomi's to do list. Most of the time, Harriet is the well-behaved kindergarten kid willing to do what she's told. But not today, apparently. According to Harriet, Steph Lewis has overdone the telling. Later this afternoon, Naomi will be redressing the balance. Off the record at this stage; no need to escalate the reprimand too soon. Steph will simply be reminded to empower her young detectives, encourage their initiative and support them.

Steph is a bright woman by all accounts. Good A levels, according to her personnel file – much better than hers. But, as Naomi has proved time and again, academic qualifications are just a stepping-stone, a get-you-in pack. Self-belief and determination count for far more. Does Harriet Harris possess those qualities? It would be refreshing to see another female officer flying through the ranks. At the moment Naomi is a one-off. But now that Harriet has spoken up for herself, is she the heir apparent or merely a loose cannon? Hard to tell yet. Naomi makes a mental note to keep a close watch on her development.

All in all, it isn't a bad team. The clear-up rate is good, but there's danger in complacency. Kevin and his inspectors, including Steph Lewis, should be inspiring their staff towards even higher results. Naomi has the same expectation of herself. Although West Gloucestershire provides better value for money than many forces, her masters expect her to deliver more and more for the same or less. It's what modern and effective policing is all about.

When she reaches the bottom of the stairs, Roy Keating, the press officer, is waiting for her. Kevin Richards is there too, pacing the floor of the foyer. He looks as if he's about to be fed to the lions. She really will send him on the next media relations course despite his protestations. Lose media goodwill and you've lost not only public support but also your career.

The Gittens-Gold angle might make the landscape of the Sonia Hanson case clearer, but she's prepared if the military man is dead too. She'll compile another briefing just in case; two briefings, one for the press and one for the staff. In the case of a political motive, it would be down to her to keep a lid on it, avoid escalation into an international incident. But for the moment she will concentrate on the general appeal for information about the missing man.

She shakes Roy's hand, pushes open the front door of police HQ and leads DCI Richards out to the waiting media.

CHAPTER TWENTY-SIX

Even to my nose the smell is more napalm than perfume, and as for my make-up, I'm going to need a tin opener to get it off again. It's been so long since I've been to a nightclub I've forgotten how to apply the camouflage.

I put the slice of Tony's cake, still in the serviette, on the kitchen table with a note: *Enjoy. Love Mum XXX PS I might be back late tonight.* But not too late, I hope. Home before broken vodka bottles and vomit hit Southgate Street.

Jake comes into the kitchen.

"I thought you were out," I say. He mostly is, far more than I would like.

"Is that cake?" In the next moment, he's munching, chocolate round his chops like the toddler he used to be. Sometimes I miss that version of him.

"You and Brad doing anything tonight?"

With his mouth full of cake, he shakes his head and says something that resembles, "Watching footie."

"Good. Right," I say, breathing out the relief of knowing he'll be safe, for another day at least.

He swallows the cake. "What have I done? You're looking at me weird."

"Nothing. I'm just... You and Brad are sensible, aren't you?"

"Where did that come from?"

"You remember you're still underage, right? No sneaking into clubs and getting arrested?" It wouldn't take much – one drink too many, one mouth of cheek to a community support officer and it becomes a crime. How far from there is the leap to having DNA taken and checked on our database? And a match I never want revealed.

"Seriously, Mum? You don't get arrested; you get chucked out, along with your mates, and end up having a better time at the kebab shack outside. Besides, why would Brad and I go clubbing and risk bumping into our mothers?"

"Terri and I hardly go anywhere except the King's Head."

"So where are you going tonight all dolled up?" He looks me up and down. The leather trousers are too hot for the time of year, but I've nothing else club-like. I instructed Cally and Harriet to blend in, so now that I'm going instead of Cally I have to do the same. At least the white cotton shirt might keep me cool.

"This is for work," I say.

Jake laughs. "You'd never go to work like that unless... You're not undercover, are you?" His eyes glitter. "You are, aren't you? Where does this top secret mission take place?"

"I can't say." I can, but the less he knows about Gloucester's nightclubs the better.

"Are you sure you're dressed right?"

"What's wrong with this?" I twist sideways to check my thighs. I reckon I look good for my age.

"If it's undercover, don't you need your Resistance rain-coat and French beret? And why haven't you got your team doing it instead? You're the boss, aren't you?"

"Sometimes it's good to muck in." Especially after a gypsy's warning from the Superintendent. Naomi Thomas was hovering by the office as I left. We had a 'what-are-you-working-on' chat in the corridor and she mentioned the importance of teamwork and motivating staff. I'm still wondering about the subtext of 'We senior officers have to set an example, don't we?' tossed over her shoulder as she clacked away on her flat but expensive sandals. It was almost as if someone had said something to her. Harriet? Unlikely. But to be on the safe side, I texted Harriet to say I'd join her tonight. Besides, it will give me an excuse to spy on Terri. Chances are she'll be out on the date she chose over going to the pub with me. He'd better be gorgeous or I'm going to feel seriously insulted.

"I'll get off then," I say.

"I wish you 'bonne chance' behind enemy lines," Jake says, picking icing off the serviette.

I sip deep into my lemonade. I ought to have arrested the barman; the prices are a crime, but I needed a drink. It's something to peer into while I avoid catching the attention of Tony Smith's birthday crowd. Harriet isn't here yet and there's no sign of Terri, but familiar faces in Taboo, the first club I enter, include Tony, his fiancée Nikki and an assort-ment of the usual suspects from CID and uniform. A bloke I recognise from Forensics slaps a tray of technicolour cocktails on their table. I shift further round the booth I'm in, out of sight.

Another glass lands next to mine and I look up as Harriet shuffles along the bench opposite. "Sorry I'm late."

I choke and feel lemonade-acid at the back of my throat. Her legs – that go on for days – are clad in leather trousers, and her blouse is white. Unlike mine, hers is lace and fitted under her slender bust line, but there's no ignoring the similarity between our outfits.

"Snap," I quip, even though I suddenly feel like mutton dressed as mutton.

She frowns, as if she hasn't a clue what I mean. She can't see the connection between us and I feel even shittier. "Who would you like me to start questioning first?" she shouts over the music.

I scour the room. Two wedge-shaped males in tight floral shirts stand on the edge of the dance area, giving off a predatory vibe; lions picking out antelope. I don't fancy questioning free-roaming testosterone without the safety net of a CID interview desk. This is going to be a long night. Then I remember that Julia, the receptionist at the Cross Care Centre, said Gerald always hangs around girls. She's never seen him in the company of other men. Before I can rule out the two men on these grounds, they deselect themselves by gyrating their way across the floor to a herd. Four women make space for them in their dancing group.

Two girls occupy a table close to us. One is squeezed into a woollen dress. As she reaches towards her drink, the neck-line moves down to reveal a greying bra strap. The other girl's calves bulge against the top of her platform-heeled boots.

"Come on," I say. We pick up our drinks and go over. "Can I ask where you got those boots?" I ask warmly – as warmly as I can with my throat still aching from the shock of seeing Harriet as my mini-me. Can I call someone who towers over me 'mini'?

"EBay," the girl says, bored and impervious to my attempted camaraderie.

"They look dead expensive. Mind if we join you?" Harriet says. She hooks her legs – those long, leather-clad legs – over a free stool. "We're supposed to be meeting some friends but they haven't turned up. Sonia and Gerald, do you know them?" She doesn't catch my eye and I wonder how long she's been practising her backstory. "Sonia is pretty and petite. Gerald's in his fifties, moustache and grey hair."

"No," says the other girl, also bored. There is a broad plastic belt pulled tight across her woollen dress. Maybe she's too hot for more than monosyllables.

"Gerald sometimes wears a straw hat," Harriet adds.

"Do you mean Titfer?" The girl's face comes to life. "The old guy?"

"That sounds like him," I say through gritted teeth. How many times am I going to have to say it: he's only fifty-bloody-six?

"Everyone knows Titfer. He doesn't smile much but he's dead nice for a chat," the plastic belt girl says.

"What do you chat about?" I ask.

Her eyes narrow. "What's it to you?"

"Take no notice of my mate. She's a nosy cow," Harriet says, deep in character and with too much relish. "Glad you know Titfer. Have you seen him with our other friend?"

"Titfer comes on his own, but you'd know that if you're his mate. You'll have to let us have that stool back now. We're expecting someone." She tries to tighten her belt. When the attempt fails, she settles for a firm yank of her hem.

We go back to our table where it's noticeably noisier. I lean across to make myself heard. "We need to drop the Sonia question and concentrate on Gerald."

Harriet folds her arms, the sulking from this afternoon making a reappearance. "I was just trying to speed things up. If we can establish a connection between them, we can get off early."

She's got a point. The place is filling up – which is good in one sense as new arrivals obscure the sightline to Tony's table, but she and I will never get round everyone even if we stay 'til dawn. There are no shortcuts in a police investigation, even when the detectives are dressed like an eighties pop duo.

We approach a forty-something woman who is shuffle-tapping to the music. Her thick bobbed hair, dark but overlaid with blonde highlights, is pushed off her face by a silver Alice band. Her black sleeveless t shirt is emblazoned with a white slogan, *Joy & Freedom*, the ampersand undulating over her left boob. Although she's alone, she looks at ease, as if she's part of the fixtures and fittings.

Smiling and adopting my modus operandi, Harriet says, "I just had to come over and say how much I like that top on you."

The woman's scarlet mouth returns the smile. "Thank you. It's one of my favourites."

"We're looking for a friend of ours. Perhaps you've seen him?"

My guess about her being a permanent fixture proves correct. "I know most of the regulars," she says. "I've been out with quite a few of them. What's his name?"

"Gerald, but some people call him Titfer."

"I know Titfer." She beams. "Sometimes when the pull's

169

a bit slow and I'm here on my own, he comes over for a dance. He's reliable like that. Such a waste. It's the story of my life. I'm sure you know what I mean." She looks at me. Her tone is conspiratorial. "It's easy to get on well with gay men. It's the straight ones we can't hang on to, can we?"

"Why do you think he's gay?" I say.

The woman laughs. "He must be. He's got more mince than the butchers, bless him."

"He's married to a woman," Harriet retorts, slipping out of character and showing her distaste of the woman's political incorrectness.

"I'm sorry. I just thought..." The woman stops smiling and turns to me. "You're not his wife, are you? I just assumed you were single like me."

Nothing like you. I smile and say nothing, but I see Harriet switch her gaze between the woman and me. *Two peas in a pod*, say her eyes.

Pissed off, I suggest we split up and cover more ground separately. Harriet's enthusiasm for this idea makes me wonder why she made a fuss about having to come without Cally. She and her leather trousers are so obviously at ease here.

On my own, I question other women – some in pairs, some single and one hen party. Quite a few remember seeing Titfer on previous nights out, but beyond saying he flirted with anything in a stiletto – age no obstacle and charming with it – they have nothing to say about him. Apparently, he didn't get off with anyone, not even a quick kiss or a fumble on the dance floor. The bride from the hen party – white netting on her head, L-plate round her neck and the wrong side of several Jägerbombs – thought she'd seen him leave with a red-haired woman once, but she couldn't be sure. The more she thought, the less certain she became, until she decided the woman was just being picked up by her dad who looked a bit like Gerald.

My last port is the bar. Harriet joins me and I get us both a cola.

"Thanks." She leans in close to my ear to be heard. "Are they worth a go?" She flicks a look at a striking middle-aged woman with a geometrically cut white bob and wearing a black velvet tunic. She sits on a stool beside a dark-haired girl in a red Regency jacket with puff sleeves. I'm no expert but they don't look like archetypal clubbers to me. Maybe they'll have something different to say. I give Harriet a thumbs up.

Well, we get that right.

"I know the silly little man," says the older woman when we ask her about Gerald.

We pull up bar stools alongside. I abandoned sitting at the tables after the first couple of interviews when no clubber said anything worth hanging around for, but someone who describes the charming Gerald Gittens-Gold as silly deserves hearing out.

"I told him my daughter and I were artists. He said he was too, a photographer. We wanted rid of him so I said I didn't class photography as art. But then he saw us as a challenge. He started on about the high level of artistic skill involved in enhancing an image or superimposing one image on another. He said it could be done across two different eras by combining old photos with new. Quite tedious he was. That was a few weeks ago. I've seen him in here since but he hasn't bothered me again. Has he spoken to you since then, Emma?"

"No, thank God," the younger woman replies. The dark

hair, pale skin and red velvet put me in mind of a fairy-tale heroine.

"Did he tell you about his time as an army photographer?" Harriet asks.

The older woman shakes her head. "He must have long since retired. As an artist, I'm a keen observer of people. He had no military bearing whatsoever. And always wearing a cravat. More Noel Coward than Field Marshal Montgomery."

"You should have asked him to model for you, Mum," Emma says. "A sort of out-of-the-box character."

"I haven't got enough in-the-box ones yet." The mother turns to me. "We're doing a series of sculptures for an exhibition entitled *After Hours*. We're visiting nightclubs to identify people typical of the genre. I don't suppose you'd sit for me, would you?"

"Me?" I twist my curls. "Surely you want someone younger. My colleague, I mean, my mate here maybe."

The woman barely looks at Harriet, instead keeping her gaze on me. Her white bob moves from side to side dismissively. "You fit the bill perfectly."

We're about to head off when there's a tap on my shoulder. Nikki, Tony's fiancée. We hug and I check my watch over her shoulder. Despite her unfathomable taste in men, she's a lovely woman, but Harriet and I need to trawl at least one more club before midnight.

"How's Tony enjoying his birthday?" Harriet asks after her turn to hug.

Nikki points to where Tony is still at his table. His arms

are over the shoulders of Jordan Woods on one side and Ned Smyth on the other. They sway in time to Jason Derolo, apparently singing along. Thank the lord for the blaring speakers so we're spared the sound of their unique interpretation.

The guy from Forensics leaves the table and comes up to Nikki. His colour is high, the hot weather clearly not suiting. I sympathise. My leather trousers are a mistake for several reasons. I glance at Harriet, looking as fresh as the bloody proverbial daisy.

"Just a half for me," he shouts to Nikki. When he spots me, he nods a hello. Then he sees Harriet and slides a hand through his hair. His gaze stays on my junior colleague a moment longer than necessary. Oblivious, she tells me she'll pop to the loo before we go.

"Seen anyone you like the look of?" I can't resist asking as he watches her walk away.

"Say again," he shouts. "Let's go over there."

I find myself following him to the other end of the bar.

"I'm just here for Tony," he says when we reach a quieter spot. "This isn't my scene. I prefer the relationship to outlive the hangover." The hand goes back through the hair. When was the last time he went to the barber's? There's curl at the back of his collar, and his stubble is too long to be designer and too scratchy to be called a beard. Something tells me his relationship preference might as yet be unfulfilled.

"I didn't know you and Harriet were mates," he says. So he knows her name. I'm struggling to recall his. Dave, is it? Chris?

"We're working," I explain. "A misper is known to come here."

"Any progress?" he asks.

"Not so far, but we haven't finished yet. More clubs to do." I glance at my watch again.

"Right." A look of disappointment flickers across his face and I feel like an overbearing guardian about to whisk Harriet away from this suitor.

Nikki comes across and hands him his beer.

"Have fun," she mouths at me and winks before she walks away.

Crap. Her wrong end of the stick is bound to reach Tony. I predict the innuendos coming my way at Monday's briefing.

Harriet makes her way back from the ladies, and falters when she sees me with a man. I try not to look too frantic as I wave her over.

"Hi, Harriet," he says, doing more hand-hair-combing.

"Neil," she replies.

Hearing his name on her lips seems to boil his skin an even darker red. "How's the murder case going?" His shoulder turns my way, blocking me out, as he directs his question to her.

I see an opportunity. "The investigation is stalling," I say. "Without the forensics on Sonia Hanson's computers, we're getting nowhere. Isn't that right, Harriet?" I stare at her and cock my head towards him.

"Yeah, it's a problem," she says, taking my cue.

"Come to my office next week. Both of you." Neil drinks deep into his beer. "I'll see what I can do."

"We need to establish a connection," Harriet says.

Neil splutters on his drink.

"The case, I mean. We've got to establish a link between the murdered journalist and our prime suspect, a relationship counsellor."

"I hope he's not guilty. We need more male marriage guidance counsellors," Neil says. He's still speaking directly to Harriet.

There's a lull in the music as the DJ gesticulates to a group of girls who've taken glassware onto the dance floor. Neil fills the gap, speeding up as he speaks. "It comes down to science, as most things do. It's a biological fact that men are more easily devastated by marital conflict. It's natural selection. Women's brains contain oxytocin. It keeps them calm so they can produce milk for their babies. The species wouldn't survive without it. As men it's our job to keep watch over the women and children, alert at all times. It's fight or flight adrenaline and stress all the way for us. It's fascinating stuff."

Harriet smiles. "Fascinating." She checks the time on her phone and asks me if we should make a move. Neil looks bereft until she says we'll be sure to pop by on Monday.

CHAPTER TWENTY-SEVEN

SATURDAY 7TH JULY

"Your phone's going."

I peer over my duvet.

Jake puts my ringing mobile on my bedside locker. "You left it in the hall. Thanks a lot for waking me up, Mum."

I accept the call as he grunts he's going back to bed and shuts the door.

"Steph?" It's Harriet and there's a weird question in her voice.

Despite a thumping headache I join the dots. I'm about to point out that the male voice she heard in the background was my son, but decide what the hell. Let her think I have a life.

"The DCI's called a briefing," she tells me. "We have to go to the station before we do the interviews with Gerald's counselling clients."

"Now? I'll be half an hour." How quickly can I get my migraine out of bed, showered, dressed and behind the wheel of my Golf?

"I can give you a lift."

"No need," I say quickly. With my head still thumping to the bass of the nightclub, I'm going to need that time alone in my car to practise being a functioning human.

There is a cavernous silence before she says, "See you in thirty minutes." She hangs up.

A thought dawns. Does she think I declined the lift because I'm not at home? She must be picturing me doubling-back to town to pick up a one-night stand after we went our separate ways last night. I should be so lucky.

In the bathroom, I splash cold water on my face and look in the mirror. A pair of panda eyes and a head of snakes stare back. With parted fingers, I pull taut the skin around my eyes. I'm out of wipes and the kohl isn't coming off with a wet flannel. It's going to need a full face cleanse and I'll be late for the briefing. Tongues will wag if Harriet shares her bad guess about my set up this morning.

Typical of the genre, the artist woman at the nightclub called me last night. I look in the mirror again. I've always thought of myself as the perennial thirty-five-year-old, but my reflection beckons a different future: withered hag with perfect nails. My clock is ticking. Maybe it is time to sign up to some sad singles club, hunt down a partner and join that exclusive club: The Couple. The ultimate stamp of success. Supper chez DCI Kevin Richards, where I'll discuss Le Creuset saucepans with his wife and still do the odd bit of policing while waiting for my jam to set.

Snapping out of my mood, I work on my face until it's clean, then apply a new layer of camouflage. After a breakfast of dry bread and two glasses of tap water, I head to work. Miraculously the water sees off the worst of my headache, and by the time I swipe into the police headquarters car park, I'm focussed on the case.

But my thoughts are still fuzzier than I need them to be. One clubber last night said something that nags in my brain, but I'm baffled why an Australian marriage guidance counsellor would want to murder a young mother of three. Because that's what Sonia is underneath it all. A prodigal daughter estranged from her family and a fiercely ambitious journalist, for sure, but scratch that away and what's left is a thirty-six-year-old pregnant wife and mother.

What is there if you chip away at Gerald Gittens-Gold? Remove the army, photography and counselling, and what's left? A friendly, fun-loving man who wears a straw trilby? What if the army couldn't be wiped away? His survival skills training might be so ingrained that operating behind enemy lines has become the only reality. The man could be on constant alert, spoiling for a fight, ready to execute an expert strangulation. But why Sonia? Is he so programmed to fear an enemy that a chance encounter outside the cathedral caused him to kill? But he worked in reconnaissance not open combat. He isn't a killing machine.

It has to be a different motive. Money? Blackmail? It's hard to cast Sonia as the blackmailer. As a journalist, if she'd discovered some sensation about Gerald, she wouldn't have blackmailed him. She'd have printed the story. The glory for her was in the scoop, not in financial gain. Besides, by the look of their house, she and her husband were already earning well.

So what else would make a man kill? Passion? A lovers' row? Had they been in a secret relationship unknown to both spouses? Was Gerald the father of Sonia's unborn baby? Am I about to reveal this cruellest secret of all and rip Alistair Hanson's world even further apart? DNA tests would answer that one, but they hardly seem necessary, as no one at the

178

nightclubs we went to last night recalled seeing Sonia there, let alone with Gerald. I can't imagine a more unlikely pair of lovers.

So is it down to journalism? Was Sonia about to use the pages of the *Gloucester Evening News* to expose him for something? But what scandal could be worth killing for? A war scandal? Was he part of some military atrocity in a distant land, hushed up at the time but about to be blown apart by a provincial pen pusher? I make a mental note to get Harriet to chase up her emails to the Australian Defence Department.

Incident Room – Saturday 7th July, 9.30 a.m.

I slide into the meeting between Cally and Harriet. Cally glances at me. At least I assume that's what she's doing. Her big brown eyes are hidden behind dark sunglasses, making her look even more like a supermodel than usual. Her skin is on the pale side this morning. It must have been one hell of a silver wedding party. Even out with her parents she's had a better Friday night than I did. And I was trawling nightclubs with her best mate, Harriet.

"As I was saying," Jordan Woods speaks from the front of the room, "all the 'Gloucester Reunited' pieces were quite tame. Sonia wrote about the mayor, both the current one and the one before, a few other town councillors, a couple of head teachers, a dinner lady, a hairdresser. The articles were mostly pictorial like this one." He clicks an image onto the whiteboard. Even in black and white, I recognise Councillor Vale's Hawaiian shirt in a family group photograph.

Jordan quotes from a photocopy of the same article. "Family man George Vale has been married to Thelma for thirty-six years. They have one son, Tim. Gloucester born and bred, George attended St Peter's County Primary School and Gloucester Secondary Modern. He was delighted when we reunited him with old school pals, Dennis Braddock and Len Gregory." Jordan clicks up the smiling image of the councillor flanked by two other middle-aged men and then moves on to a smaller, grainy picture of him as a boy in school cap and blazer. "All the features are like this one. No one had a bad word to say about anyone."

Staying perched on his desk, Kevin thanks Jordan and asks for updates from the detectives to whom I allocated research on Sonia's consumer affairs column.

DC Darren Ayres gets to his feet. "I looked into the last six months of Sonia's stories. Some of them were ongoing sagas. When Sonia wrote about a particular company, other dissatisfied customers would come forward and she'd write up their stories about the same company the following week. She did this to five firms. They are all national – a couple of double glazing outfits, a film processing company, a telecom giant, a package holiday firm. Because it was late yesterday afternoon when I tried to speak to them, their offices didn't answer the phone, but I got hold of the local complainants at home. They all said their complaints had been settled amicably. In each case, after Sonia's articles appeared, the companies were quick to offer generous compensation.

"It was the same with the one-off stories she wrote. The customers say the articles were just the right level of pressure needed for the companies to put things straight."

"So no outstanding grievances at all?" Kevin asks.

"Nothing that's any good to us. Two customers are still owed money by a building firm that Sonia had exposed for shoddy workmanship. Both directors were convicted shortly afterwards for fraud in an unrelated case and are currently doing time at Ford open prison."

Despite evidence of a hangover, Cally rises gracefully from her chair and gives her contribution. "I've looked through Sonia's theatre reviews for the last twelve months, about thirty in all. Most were quite bland, a bit twee about local amateur productions, but only what you'd expect."

To my right, Harriet folds her arms. "Come on, Cal," she huffs. "Amateur doesn't mean mediocre."

Cally smiles. "True, but Sonia only ever stuck the knife into the big names who appeared in Gloucester. She was scathing of a reality TV star in the Christmas panto and she rubbished a TV gardener's question time and a Channel Four comedian's stand-up show. But her reviews were small fry. Her editor is pretty sure none of her hatchet jobs got picked up by the nationals, so damage to celebrity egos would have been limited."

"Good work, thank you," Kevin says. "Before we move on from *Gloucester Evening News*, I've got another nugget for you. We ran the staff through the PNC. The editor, David Oakley, has form for aggravated assault."

"Nice one, boss," I say and offer to do the follow-up interview with Oakley. It seems unlikely he'd bump off one of his junior colleagues, but a history of violence needs looking into. "And there's another interview I want to do. We showed Gerald Gittens-Gold's photo to Sonia's husband and to her mother and brothers. The family had no recollection at all, but I think the husband might have known him. I'd like to put it to him again."

Kevin gives me a nod and makes a note.

Harriet's next with a concise summary of the interviews we conducted with the club-goers. I bet she's been up half the night preparing. Maybe she never went to bed. At twenty-four she wouldn't have had to worry about mascara clinging to the wrinkles.

"Tony, what have you got for us?" Kevin asks.

I hadn't noticed Tony Smith sitting with his head in his hands. I wonder what time he and Nikki left the club. He looks up but remains sitting. "I checked out Tracey Chiles, the witness who saw Gerald by the cathedral. When I called on her yesterday afternoon, I half-wondered if she hadn't bumped Sonia off herself. She's got a massive bandage round her hand. A cut from an umbrella spoke, she says. Bloody big prick, if you ask me."

Big prick. You said it, Tony. I glower at him, my heart thundering. "I'd already ruled her out yesterday morning. There was no need for the woman to be visited twice in one day." No need to snoop around that guesthouse. The last thing I need is Tony finding out it's where Jake's biological father stayed for his last ever bed and breakfast.

"I know that now. She seems sound. If you can call anyone sound who blow dries their pet terrier," he says.

Cally giggles. "Does she really?"

"Probably. I know she asks him the crossword clues. Barking in more ways than one." Tony turns to me. "That's why I didn't prioritise her call on Monday night. I could tell she wasn't all there. You didn't need to bollock me."

I think back to my comments at the briefing yesterday. "I didn't bollock you, just pointed out..."

"And it was his birthday," Harriet chips in. "You could have gone easy."

A light guffaw trips across the front row. I carry on before it reaches its half-life. "All I did was point out that an eyewitness had been overlooked. That's why I did the follow-up visit."

Since when did Harriet stick up for Tony Smith? And why now when my point is valid? It's only because Tracey Chiles phoned back three days later and got me on the line that we made a connection between our murder victim and our missing man.

The guffaw becomes a muttering. The vibe seems to be that I rained on Tony's birthday parade.

Kevin watches, frowning. "That'll do for now, folks," he says eventually. "Jordan and Cally, keep digging into Sonia Hanson's professional life. Go back further through her articles if you have to. Is there any mention anywhere about Gerald Gittens-Gold? But we can't yet rule out this being a family killing, so, Tony, see what else you can find out about Sonia's brothers.

"Steph and Harriet, you get off to see the Cross Care Centre clients you've arranged to interview. And play nice, you two."

I front it out by grinning, but can't help feeling his comment is directed at me more than Harriet, and that it's sincerely meant.

As the meeting breaks up, I turn to Harriet but she gets up without making eye contact. I find myself scurrying behind her long strides to the car park. So much for bonding over our night on the tiles.

CHAPTER TWENTY-EIGHT

Debbie Robinson looks at the photograph. "His funny smile took a bit of getting used to, but he's a nice man. I hope he turns up safe and sound."

Her son, a boy of about eight, is on the floor by her feet watching television and sucking on a carton of juice. "Are you sure I can't get you anything?" she adds.

"We're fine, thanks," Harriet says. Although we've barely exchanged a word since the briefing, we have agreed not to linger over the two interviews we've set up unless we smell something suspicious. Harriet needs the time this morning to track down Sally Parker and Tim Vale, the third pair of clients Gerald counselled on Monday before he disappeared. They haven't so far replied to her messages. When potential witnesses in a missing persons enquiry go to ground, I get jumpy.

Harriet slips the photo of Gittens-Gold back into her notebook. "How long has he been your counsellor?"

"A year, on and off. We saw his wife a couple of times, but we didn't like her. She kept banging on about how she and Gerald did things. Mr and Mrs Perfect. He's all right, though. Just sits and listens while I talk. It can't do any good, of course. He'd have had to be in touch with the spirit world to help me."

Harriet and I exchange a glance. Rosemary Davies, the manager at the Cross Care Centre, didn't mention that one of Gerald's clients was a widow. Is that why Debbie has insisted we conduct this interview with her child present, unable to be parted from what's left of her family for even a few minutes?

"I'm sorry," Harriet says softly. "When did your husband pass away?"

"He's not dead." Debbie lets out a cold laugh. "I meant we don't live in our marriage any more; we haunt it. We don't even row these days. There used to be some hum-dingers, screaming, throwing things against the wall. Then he gave up. He hid behind his newspaper and let me do the yelling. Now even I don't bother."

I'd have preferred to interview Mrs Robinson out of earshot of the child but decide that he probably isn't listening. He looks like Jake when he's glued to the screen. "I'm sorry we have to pry, but can you tell us what you and Mr Gittens-Gold talked about at your session on Monday?"

"Nothing much, seeing as Lyle, my husband, arrived late. Gerald let me talk on my own. Then he said something about my husband and me requiring a love map. We needed to be in each other's lives. I could have told him that. By the time Lyle arrived, there were only a few minutes of the session left. Gerald repeated the love map stuff to him and then we left." She sighed.

"What made you choose Gerald as your counsellor?"

"My friend Helen told me about the Cross Care Centre.

It worked for her marriage and she thought it could help us. But Lyle isn't taking it seriously." She sighs again and rubs her eyes. The dark circles below them suggest she isn't sleeping.

When we hear a key turn in the front door, the effect on Debbie is electric. Throwing off the mantle of fatigue, her eyes narrow.

As the lounge door opens, she snaps, "Your coffee's cold." The words leave her mouth like bullets.

"Sorry, love, I bumped into Jason. We had a chat." The man, in knee-length shorts and a crisp polo shirt, reaches out a hand to me.

"I'm Steph, a detective inspector, and this is DC Harris. We're investigating a missing person connected to the Cross Care Centre."

"Okay?" There's a slow question in his voice. We're used to wariness from interviewees as they plan what to say without incriminating themselves, but this sounds more like puzzlement.

His wife picks up on it too and gets to her feet. "That's typical of you. She means the marriage guidance place. You know, last Monday when you let me down. Oh but that doesn't really narrow it down for you, does it? It could have been any day of the week."

The man glances at his son. "Perhaps we could discuss this later."

"Discuss. Now there's a novel idea," Debbie sneers. "Don't both parties have to be in the same room to do that?"

"Perhaps we could call again at a more convenient time?" Harriet suggests. I feel as squirmy as she looks, not liking our roles as unwitting catalysts to a domestic.

No one is listening. Lyle Robinson says, "It went clear

out of my head when the boss called a meeting. I came as soon as I remembered."

"We've had that same appointment at the same time for weeks. How could you forget? The truth is you don't want to be part of this family. You take no interest whatsoever."

"That's rubbish. I do take an interest."

The boy leans forward to turn up the TV volume and his eyes don't leave the screen.

"All right then," Debbie says, outshouting Homer Simpson. "What's the name of Sam's teacher?"

"Don't start." The man looks wretched and then his face clears. "It's the school holidays soon. He'll have a new one in September."

"He's staying with Mrs Hargreaves. I told you. What year is he in?"

"Year Two?"

"Year Four in September. Who's my best friend?"

"I don't know." He shakes his head. "Sarah," he says, triumphant.

"Helen. I knew Sarah when we lived in Cheltenham six years ago. Here's an easier one: how old's Thumper?"

"How should I know how old the bloody rabbit is?"

I raise my eyebrows at Harriet. We get up and edge out of the room.

"He's two. Sam and I had a party for him. You said you'd come but you didn't."

"Thanks for your time," Harriet says, putting her business card on the phone stand. "If you think of anything unusual about your Monday session, give us a ring."

Lyle breaks off the argument to open the front door. "Nice to see you," he says, finding some hospitable charm on autopilot.

"Thanks for coming round." Debbie joins in the cordiality. "We'll give it some thought."

As we head up the drive we catch renewed bars of their argument through the open window of the hallway.

"It's typical of you."

"You're being unreasonable."

"You're selfish. I ground the beans fresh."

"I'll make some more. Let's drink it in the garden."

"We've no biscuits."

When we're back in the car, Harriet says, "Maybe Gerald did a runner to get away from them."

I laugh, but she's got a point. I'm knackered after only a few minutes of their marital ping-pong.

"Do you think they'll split up?" she asks.

"I haven't a scooby." The only marriage I've observed at close quarters is my parents'. They bicker, but spend all their free time together. I've never known one be late for a date with the other. My own relationships have not reached that level of union. There have been plenty of rows. Passion, you might call it, except passion can lead somewhere else entirely. My skin prickles as a memory threatens.

I'm about to pull out when I spot a bicycle in my wing mirror and at the last minute avoid a collision. Luckily Harriet doesn't notice the near miss as she's looking at her phone.

"I'm texting Sally Parker again," she says.

"Good idea," I say, glad to focus on the investigation instead of my past. We need to get hold of that third couple Gerald saw on Monday.

In the meantime, we head for couple number two, Charles and Angela Rice. Harriet puts the GL1 postcode into the sat nav. I ease off the handbrake and move into first gear. Almost immediately I have to touch the footbrake again. We stay in a queue of stop-start traffic for the two-mile journey. Unusual for a Saturday. I put the congestion down to folk being out in their air-conditioned cars rather than walking in the heat.

When we get into the residential area of the city centre, formidable three-storey Victorian semis line the route. The Rices live in Chancery Close, the next street along from Tracey Chiles's guesthouse in Cathedral Street. Our next potential witnesses live a stone's throw from where Sonia Hanson was murdered.

Charles answers the door. Despite the hollows beneath his eyes, the uncombed hair and the grey stubble peppering his face, I'd put him in his mid-thirties.

"My wife is upstairs," he says as he leads us into the lounge. "She's trying to get the baby down. She had a bad night. Teething."

His unkempt appearance makes sense; so does the state of the room. Calpol and gum gel on the coffee table. Packets of wet wipes and nappies on an armchair. On the floor is an empty Moses basket and a teated bottle of formula.

He scoops a pile of baby clothes off the sofa so we can sit.

"I remember those days," I say. "You have my sympathies."

He stares at me, sadness in his eyes. "Lots of people say that."

"How old is the baby?" Harriet asks.

"Six months."

"A tricky age," I say, still trying to sound compassionate.

"People say that too."

"We won't take up much of your time," Harriet says. "We'd like to ask about your meeting at the Cross Care

Centre on Monday, if you can remember. I'm sure it's been a tiring week."

Squeezing beside the nappies, he sits down in the armchair and stares into the distance. "I remember all right. It's the only time in the week when Angela leaves the house without Chloe. She gets her mother to babysit for that. Every week without fail."

"How did the meeting go?" Harriet asks.

"Same procedure every week. The counsellor, Gerald, welcomes us. Angela sets a timer on her phone. Gerald listens while we talk, or rather while I talk. Angela checks the time. After thirty minutes of our allotted forty-five, Angela says she has to go to feed the baby."

"How did Gerald seem this week?" I ask.

Charles looks at me. "How did *he* seem? I've no idea. I wasn't thinking about him. He smiled his tight-lipped smile, listened to me, then recommended a love map. He recommends it every week but I've never found out what it is because Angela always makes us leave before the end."

We hear footsteps on the stairs, then somewhere above us the baby starts wailing. The footsteps go back up.

Charles puts his head in his hands. "There are three people in my marriage these days." He looks at us, colouring. Perhaps he didn't mean to say that aloud. "She'll be ages getting her off again. Do you want a cup of tea? You might have a long wait."

"I think we'll leave you to it," Harriet says, looking at me. I nod in agreement. We'll learn nothing here. Gerald Gittens-Gold could have openly declared an intention to commit murder and neither Charles, mourning the loss of his wife's attention, nor Angela, wrapped up in motherhood, would have noticed.

As we're getting into the car, Harriet's phone goes. It's a call back from the third couple. Inwardly I groan, unsure I can face more marital discord right now. But I soon glean we have a two-day reprieve.

"Monday at eleven. Thank you, Mrs Parker. That's confirmed ... Sorry, Ms Parker ... I see ... That's not our concern ... Of course ... Bye for now." Harriet kills the call and explains that Sally Parker has a work deadline today, but will be happy to talk to us after the weekend. "She'll ask her partner, Tim, to attend, but he might have work. She says she's not his keeper. They're not even exclusive anymore."

After checking behind twice, I pull out of the line of parked cars. We're all on double-yellows; no residential spaces here. "Sounds like Gerald would have had a barrel of laughs with them too. Can't wait to meet them."

Harriet chuckles. "And I thought our job was stressful."

"Never thought a coachload of drunk and disorderlies would seem more appealing than three married couples."

"Only two are married. Not Ms Parker. She's clear on that."

"Fair point," I say evenly, but wonder whether Harriet is citing Sally Parker's pedantry or her own. I feel her gaze on me. Does she know what I'm thinking? I turn and smile.

"Thanks for letting me lead both interviews, by the way," she says.

Did I? It was unintentional, but I'm glad she thinks it. There's a chance Superintendent Thomas gave me the gypsy's warning about staff relations because of something Harriet said, so it's good to see Harriet warming up a bit.

"No problem," I say and add, "You did well."

There's an uncomfortable silence as we wait at the swing bridge traffic lights. It takes an age for two barges and a yacht to sail out of the quay. But I use the time wisely to think how to keep my young colleague on side.

"You can knock off now you've fixed that last interview. Enjoy the rest of your weekend."

"What about the deep dive into Sonia's journalism? And the other enquiry lines?"

"Neither of us are rostered on until earlies next week. Kevin takes staff downtime seriously, so do I. It's home time. Can I give you a lift to the station to get your car?"

"Er, well." She clears her throat. "Thanks, Steph. That would be great."

We lapse into silence again. I don't remember us being this awkward on our last case. "Any plans for the rest of the day?" I ask. "Will you make the most of this sunny spell?" I cringe for talking about the weather. When did I get so middle-aged?

"Are you watching the match?" she says, suddenly animated. "Kick off at three p.m. I think we can do it."

"Didn't know you were a footie fan?"

"Once every four years and only when we're winning."

I laugh. She sounds like Jake. For an unknown reason he fell out with football a couple of years ago, but has made friends with it again for this World Cup. His rugby team is watching today's England versus Sweden quarter final in the clubhouse. "Where are you watching?"

"At home. Too risky to go to a pub. Win or lose fans will go on the rampage, and I don't want to get caught up in that, even off duty. Besides, I've got audition pieces to learn. Gloucester Players are putting on *Cinderella*."

Ah, yes, the acting. "Who are you going to play?" With her pretty face she's bound to be Cinderella, although the legs are long enough for principal boy.

"Not sure yet. We've got another week of read-throughs. I'm learning a few audition pieces just in case."

Even in leisure she overeggs it. "I'm surprised you can fit it in with all the overtime you do," I say.

"Rehearsals are only twice a week, and I've got a spreadsheet anyway so no clashes."

My foot jinks on the accelerator but I don't laugh. Typical Harriet.

Harriet's phone goes and her good humour vanishes. She listens, takes notes, then ends the call. She puts a new postcode into the sat nav. "The Fire Service has received a call about someone jumping off the viewpoint at Sharpness. Severn Area Rescue are helping with the search."

I'm about to ask what a suicide and river rescue have to do with us, when she adds, "The witness calling it in described the jumper as elderly and wearing a straw hat."

CHAPTER TWENTY-NINE

The inshore lifeboat station at Sharpness is about fifteen miles south of the city. Poorly tarmacked approach roads run past farmers' fields, dotted with big wooden barns and the odd stone cottage. My sat nav decides it has no business directing me through the rural 1950s and packs up. My atlas isn't on the back seat because I took it indoors last week to give Jake a lesson on how to read a map if sat nav failed. Oh, the irony.

Before I lost phone coverage I loaded a webpage about the Severn Area Rescue Association fundraising open day last weekend. I follow directions to visitor parking for the event and end up jolting my car's suspension in a stony stubble field. I worry whether my tyres will survive, but the road I turned off wasn't much better. I park by a white van, the only other vehicle using the field today, and complete the rest of the instructions for arriving at the harbour: through a gap in the hedge, right along a track, down a hill. The webpage gives me other intel. SARA – the organisation is known by its acronym – is funded by donation, and Sharpness is one of the rescue stations they operate. I also know, because the phone call Harriet took explained, that it's the nearest lifeboat station to the viewpoint where a man was seen jumping into the water.

Round the bend, I emerge above the river. Steps to the harbour are decorated with bunting, probably left over from the open day, although several flags of St George suggest a World Cup vibe. My phone goes: Jordan Woods with an update.

"I'm at the viewpoint. There are a few picnickers, but none have been here long enough to have seen the jumper. There's a bit of an upmarket housing estate too. Uniform are going door to door. So far no one has owned up to making the call. They're not inclined to chat; England are leading one-nil." I hear the longing in his voice. Like many of my colleagues, he's a footie fan who's drawn the short straw on rostering.

"So no description so far of who called it in?" I ask.

"The 999 call to the Fire Service was from the call box at the picnic site. Forensics have cordoned it off to check for fingerprints. These days public booths don't get used much so we might get lucky. No witnesses yet to anyone seen in or near it. One pensioner buttonholed me, worried we're going to take it away. It's one of the few call boxes left in the county, apparently."

"Can our tech people isolate the call so we can hear the voice? It might give a few clues."

"We've already applied, but it will take time. According to the call handler, it sounded young, possibly a teenage boy."

Something feels off. What self-respecting youth uses a payphone when they're surgically attached to their mobile? Must have lost the signal like I did. But what was he doing out on an afternoon when the rest of his tribe are glued to the TV? I tell Jordan to see if he can speed up getting the recording. "And while you're on the door to door, ask the owners whether they have sheds or know of any barns or empty property. If the jumper is Gittens-Gold, he must have been hiding out somewhere since Monday night."

When we end the call, I realise I've reached the dark stone wall of the harbour. With the water, sun and bunting, the place has a seaside feel and I imagine coming back with a good book and an ice cream. All that's missing is the salty taste of the sea. The only smell I detect is a hint of fuel in the air. Parked cars line the promenade and I wonder how they got down. Even two pandas are here. Uniform must be walking the river bank as part of the search.

A hundred metres ahead is a warehouse with what looks like a whitewashed house adjoining it. When I get nearer I see a man at an upstairs window. Although he's no hope of reading it from this distance, I hold up my ID and he beckons me.

After knocking, I enter a kitchen where a transistor radio playing the football commentary competes with the hum of the old-fashioned fridge. I can't see an oven, but the tang of tomato suggests the microwave has been used recently. The room beyond is set out like a seminar room. I jump at the human shape on a large desk until I realise it's a Resusci-Annie mannequin for practising lifesaving skills. Three more are piled on the floor. Shame Harriet isn't with me; I'd love to see whether she would freak. But I crush the thought, remembering I'm trying to be nice. That's why I dropped her off before I came here, letting her have her afternoon at home with her theatre scripts and footie. Through the open door beyond, I glimpse into the space of what I incorrectly assumed was a warehouse, but is a boat berth. At the far end, wide-open doors lead into the river. Whatever boat usually docks here is out. One lifejacket lies on an otherwise empty rack, and a dry suit with built-in rubber boots hangs a on a hook like a seal skin.

"All right down there?" calls a voice, and I follow the sound up a staircase off the seminar room. It's narrow and creaky – not homely enough for a private dwelling, not solid enough for a public building. I'm reminded that SARA is self-funded. After they've paid for all the kit, there won't be much left over for refurbishments.

The man – well-preserved early fifties, clean-shaven and in a black polo shirt with a SARA logo – meets me on the landing. Showing my ID again, I introduce myself. He shakes my hand. "Pleased to meet you, Steph," he replies in a warm, local accent. "I'm John Turner. Come through to the ops room."

He leads me to a space no bigger than the seminar area, but much brighter. Large picture windows stretch across three walls, providing a perfect view up, down and across the river. Maps of the area, showing water levels, line the other wall. More charts cover a worktop, and a black transmitter picks up sound. Not football this time; more like the traffic on our police radios.

"We operate through three channels," he says when he sees me looking. "Channel zero is the Coastguard. The Mayday channel for all vessels in the UK is sixteen, and we use channel three five alpha for SARA internal comms."

"What time did you get the call about someone going into the river?" I ask.

"The Deputy Launch Authority paged me two hours ago. I live the furthest away, so by the time I got here, others

197

had already launched. The late arrival always takes charge of the ops room. In fact enough crew members arrived to launch a second asset." He chuckles. "Most of us were home watching football and easily reachable."

"That's dedication," I say and mean it. According to the webpage, SARA lifeboats are crewed entirely by volunteers. "Do you get a lot of call outs?"

He nods. "Increasingly they're shore-side searches for vulnerable people reported missing. This one's different because someone saw him go in. That gives us a starting point, but there are no guarantees. We don't know where the casualty is. RNLI Portishead is out too. They take over from us beyond the Severn Bridge."

"Would a body go that far?" I ask. If Gerald makes it into the Bristol Channel, he won't be alive. There's something deeply unsatisfying about the demise of the prime suspect in a murder case.

"We had a body last seen at Sharpness turn up two weeks later at Milford Haven."

Through one of the picture windows, I look out at a large sandbank in the centre of the river. If the current takes Gerald to one of those, there might be a chance. "How long will you search?"

"Until we're stood down, but the longer it goes on the more likely it is we will be recovering a body." He points at the sandbank. "Don't be fooled. When the tide comes in, water goes underneath and softens it. Not a safe refuge."

I thank him and turn to leave. Unless Gerald is found, my afternoon will be better spent at the viewpoint. Someone must have seen him go in the water or the person making the 999 call. I think of something. "Are there some searches that turn out to be false alarms?"

"Often a search will find nothing and we learn later the missing person has turned up safe and well." He smiles. "A happy ending for the family and a good training exercise for us."

"What about bogus calls?"

The smile vanishes. "Malicious calls are a problem. Not only the financial cost of launching an asset, but the unnecessary risk of harm to the crews. Do you think this is one of those?"

I raise my palms. "We assume it's genuine until we learn otherwise."

"So do we," he replies. "Every time." We shake hands again and I go downstairs.

I walk back along the quayside, still feeling something is off. I text Kevin and ask him to put pressure on the tech team to get the voice recording of the caller. This could be a kid's prank and nothing to do with Gittens-Gold and even less with Sonia Hanson. Suddenly there's banging behind me and I turn to see John Turner at his window, waving me back.

He meets me at the top of the stairs again. "SARA 4 crew has found something in the reeds down river. A hat. It's in a bit of a state but recognisable as a straw trilby."

CHAPTER THIRTY

SUNDAY 8TH JULY

"It was a classic set-piece: Maguire with a header off Young's corner," Jake says as he spirals gravy over his beef and veg, pausing the motion to fill up his Yorkshire pudding. He always floods his nan's deep-dish yorkies. I do too. Most meals I lace with ketchup, but my mum's roasts get the Bisto treatment. Jake and I are both happy to be Sunday-lunching at my parents' house.

Bradley takes the gravy boat from him. "And the second one was a header too. Alli on a cross from Lingard." There are six of us round the oak dining table, as Mum extended the invite to Terri and Bradley.

"We won because of Pickford, though," Jake says.

"Isn't he the goalie?" my mum asks. "Did he make a save?"

"Three." Still with the fork in his hand, Jake holds up three fingers. "He was kept too busy. Southgate needs to sort that. They won't get away with lax defending against Croatia."

Even though I smile, my stomach sinks. Why wasn't he

this animated on Wednesday morning after he'd watched the Colombia match the night before? Today he's reliving every shot. Last time he had no details. You could almost think he hadn't watched. And if he didn't watch, where were he and Bradley on Tuesday night?

Across the table, Terri has tuned out of the conversation to concentrate on her meal. Maybe I'll take her to one side later and ask her if the boys went out while they were supposed to be watching footie at hers. But there's something else I want to ask her about first. About the case. Even on my day off I can't switch off. As soon as this meal is over, I'll check my phone for news from the river. No sign of a body so far. The longer it stays unresolved the more cheated I feel. If Gerald Gittens-Gold killed Sonia Hanson, I want him found, dead or alive.

Mum watches me, cottoning on that I'm thinking about work. "I saw your superintendent's press conference on the local news. She's good, isn't she?" she says.

Good at bollocking detective inspectors. The dressing down she gave me still rankles. "Naomi Thomas can talk all right," I reply. "Like all senior officers she's well versed in the art of saying nothing at all. No doubt she'll be doing it all again tomorrow." When she'll disclose the Sharpness sighting.

Jake lets out a guffaw and coughs on a carrot.

"You're too much, Steph," Mum says.

"What else is there to say apart from, 'We are pursuing several lines of enquiry into the murder of Sonia Hanson. We are particularly anxious to hear from Gerald Gittens-Gold, who was last seen near Gloucester Cathedral, shortly before Sonia's death.'"

Bradley swallows a mouthful of roast potato. "Why is she holding another press conference if there's nothing to say?"

"Her appeal on Friday hasn't turned up any more sightings of Gittens-Gold. So I expect she wants to try on a Monday to 'capture a different demographic', as she might call it."

"Do you think Gittens-Gold really did it?" Brad asks.

Dad chews on a piece of beef. "The man disappeared at around the time of the murder. A witness saw him in the area. If it quacks like a duck... " He finishes chewing. "If I had my way, I'd make all counsellors disappear."

"That's harsh, Grandad."

"It's true, Jake. You give someone counselling and they become part and parcel of the whole victim industry we are so fond of these days."

"Pull yourself together, man!" Jake says, adopting a military tone.

Dad waves his fork in the air. "You can mock, but it's all over-analysis and open-toed sandals. Whatever happened to putting it all behind you and moving on?"

I glance at Terri, but she hasn't heard. She had a counsellor who helped with her PTSD after the gun blast left her deaf. Mum gives Dad a glare and he returns to his dinner. For a while the only sounds around the table are of cutlery chasing after peas and the swallowing of those captured.

I wait until Terri has finished eating and can look up to lip read, then I ask, "How are your aunt and uncle keeping?"

"Fine. Phil still has his motorbike and Jane has taken up baking. She's thinking of starting a cake business to make a bit of money."

"Good for her," my mum says. "If she needs some pointers on book-keeping, get her to text me."

"Do they still have the cuckoo clock?" I ask quickly, as I see the conversation drifting away from where I need it to be. I remember the clock being at Terri's aunt and uncle's house when I visited as a little kid.

Jake bursts out laughing. "That's random, Mum."

"I liked that clock," I say, ignoring him and looking at Terri. "Where did he get it?"

"The Black Forest when he was stationed on detachment with the Americans in south Germany."

"Did he get lots of souvenirs in his army days?" I ask the question I've been leading up to.

Terri takes a sip of water. "A wooden tray and coasters from Cyprus, champagne flutes from Rheindahlen camp, tea towels from the Falklands." Her eyes roll upwards as she hunts her memory for more examples. "Model of a Mayan monument from Belize, a cowboy hat from Calgary. When they downsized, most of it went in the loft."

"Does he talk about the army much?" I ask.

"Not the operational stuff, but he still has plenty to say about the places he toured. Not for nothing are army types known as 'When-I's."

"'When-I's?" Jake frowns.

"'When I' was in Aden, 'when I' was in Bosnia... Hong Kong... Gibraltar..." Terri grins and watches the chuckles around the table.

"And when you met your Uncle Phil's army comrades, they were the same?"

"His best mate died when I was a teenager, but I remember them reminiscing, and Johnnie had the same cuckoo clock."

"That's what I thought," I say and resume chewing my food. I'm guessing Phil and Johnnie were more typical ex-soldiers than Gerald. They talked about their travels and collected souvenirs, whereas Gerald regaled his neighbours with hard-core war stories. No detail on the places he went and, apart from a couple of photography certificates from Australia, no physical evidence in his bungalow that he's been anywhere. I get the same vibes I have about Jake's viewing of the England versus Colombia match. Maybe he was never there.

"It's not only army people who collect stuff," my mum says, and she sighs. She must be thinking about my late grandparents, whose house she spends her free time clearing. Nan died over a year ago but the cottage in the Forest of Dean is still crammed to the gills with junk. The latest find is a video camera on a tripod. When did my grandparents ever use that? Or the tin of snapped elastic bands in their kitchen drawer.

"Are you going to the Forest tomorrow?" I ask, knowing Monday is her day off.

"Just the afternoon," she says. "I'm doing training with Kelly in the morning."

"How's she getting on?" I ask and smile as Jake looks at his grandmother, waiting for the answer, his soft spot for the new hairdressing apprentice in evidence.

"It *was* going well," Mum replies, "but something has been bothering her for a couple of weeks. I think she's having to look after her little brother again." She puts down her cutlery and makes inverted commas in the air. "Her mother is 'unwell' again."

From what I can tell, Kelly's mum is as unwell as a newt every Friday and Saturday night. It sounds like her alcohol intake is sloshing into other days of the week.

"Anyway, let's not talk about work," Mum says brightly.

"While I was cooking, I heard on the radio they've pulled four boys from the cave in Thailand."

"Alive?" Bradley says. "Amazing."

"There are another seven still down there, but so far so good," Mum says as she stacks our plates. "Who's for trifle?"

Afterwards, Terri and I – full of dessert that's lusciously heavy on the sherry, and on the custard and cream too – do the washing up. It's like when we were kids and Terri came round for tea after school, except back then she liked to do the drying. These days she has to wash so I can stand to her left where she still has some residual hearing.

"How was your night out on Friday?" I ask. When she doesn't reply, I tap her arm so she's facing me.

"Fine," she says before I repeat the question. So she heard the first time?

"Was he nice?"

But she's gone back to the pots and still feigns not hearing. I'm sure she's pretending, because her face has coloured. I tap her again and wait until she looks at me. "It must have been good."

Even under her trademark thick foundation, her cheek colour turns noticeably higher. "It was a drink with a friend. Not a date." Her firmness puts me off asking anything else and we work in silence. It's another puzzle to solve: Sonia, Gerald, Jake and now Terri. Everywhere I look people have secrets. I could almost be jealous, except I have the biggest secret of all: even Jake doesn't know about his father.

"Do you ever think about school?" Terri asks eventually.

She knows the answer to that. I hope I've banished school from my thoughts forever after I had to spend this May thinking of little else when a case brought me face to face with my school rival, Amy Ashby.

"Do you ever wish we'd been nicer?" Terri asks.

"Nicer?"

"We thought we were Rizzo from *Grease,* didn't we? Two pink ladies who ruled the school."

"Let's face it, we had to be her; we'd no chance of fitting into Sandy's black satin jeans." I laugh.

But Terri doesn't. "Maybe we could have been kinder." She turns back to the sink.

I turn back to the draining board. The only person I had trouble with at school was Amy Ashby, and she deserved everything she got.

CHAPTER THIRTY-ONE

MONDAY 9TH JULY

The nearest I usually get to a man cave is my dad's garden shed, but today I go hard core with a visit to Digital Forensics in the basement of police HQ.

Sunlight seeps from small windows high on the wall but isn't sufficient to make up for the gloom of the ceiling lights being off. Harriet and I tread through a graveyard of stripped out computer carcasses to Neil Wright's workstation in the far corner. More death lurks on his desk – four cups of half-drunk coffee, a sheen of something white on the surface of one of them. Without the air con's valiant efforts, I dread to think what the stench in here would be.

"Hi, Harriet. It was a good night on Friday," is Neil's greeting. And just like that, I'm Hermione Granger in a cloak of invisibility. He can no more see me now than when he clocked Harriet at the nightclub. Stick a leggy blonde in a room and the rest of us vanish.

"It was a useful evening's work," Harriet replies.

Neil rubs his neck. "Of course. That's what I meant."

"Sonia Hanson's PC?" she prompts.

"Right, yes, absolutely." He points to a stack of papers behind his dirty mugs. "These are a list of documents on the home computer. I don't think there's anything dodgy, but you're the copper. She saved loads of articles she was writing. Some seem to be draft forms of others that look finished. Nothing hidden on the hard drive. No suspicious-looking deleted files. People don't realise that when they delete a file they are only deleting the directory reference to the file. The data is still there."

I roll my eyes. "No kidding."

"The printout is in alphabetical order. She doesn't seem to have been one for creating subject folders. The file names must have been enough for her to locate her work." He flicks through the papers, reading off a few document titles. "Clear Windows, Councillor Vale, *Oh What a Lovely War!*, Sandick Films, Szechwan. But Szechwan is empty. The file's been created but there's nothing in it. Like I said, quite a few stories seem incomplete."

"Is there one called Gittens-Gold?" Harriet asks. "One theory we're looking at is that Sonia Hanson uncovered a war crime in which he was implicated. He used to work under-cover for the Australian Army, parachuting into East Timor and Bougainville Island – wherever that is."

"It's a large, war-torn island east of Papua New Guinea," Neil says. "Did you know that mining its copper deposits wrecked an entire river system?"

"What about her internet searches?" I ask, killing his geography lesson.

"I've been through the web browser's history." He turns to Harriet again. "When you visit a website, the site tags the computer's cookie file."

"So I've heard," Harriet deadpans.

"Sonia Hanson was mad on alternative health sites and superfoods. I never knew there were so many websites devoted to beetroot."

"Really? Something you didn't know?" I mutter. I didn't know either, but I'm not surprised Sonia found them, given that she was a middle-class yummy mummy. "Anything else?"

He leans back in his wheelie chair and grips his chin like a college lecturer. "If I dissected a random sample of one thousand home computers, I'd predict one of three areas predominating: pornography, family history or social media. This PC was no exception."

"There's pornography on there? What kind?" My impatience is gone as a new lead beckons.

Neil shakes his head. "Social media, especially Facebook."

My teeth grind. I could have told him that.

"She was mad on it, tapped in schools and towns across the country and school reunion groups across the decades. Must have been a bit of a nostalgic."

The Sonia Hanson we know wasn't the sentimental type. It's more likely she was researching her Gloucester Reunited column. A couple of detective constables will have to go through her Facebook profile. Unlikely to lead anywhere, but it's a hoop, so we'll jump. I ask Neil what was on Sonia's work PC.

"Not much." He hands a thinner pile of paper to Harriet. "Those files look more polished. I get the impression that she did her researching and writing at home and only transferred things to the newspaper's PC when she was almost ready to file with her editor. A sizeable number of her emails were to send attachments between the two PCs."

"I'll go through it all, thanks," Harriet says. "Did you happen to see anything on either computer about the Cross Care Centre or marriage counselling?"

"Nothing springs to mind. Let me have a quick look." He reaches out for the papers, reddening as he grazes Harriet's fingertips.

"Our briefing with the DCI starts in ten minutes," I say, fed up with playing gooseberry. "We'll check out the marriage guidance angle ourselves."

"Marriage guidance." Neil toys with the words. Staying red in the face, he looks at Harriet. "Did you know happily married men and women have higher functioning immune systems and show greater proliferation of white blood cells when exposed to foreign bodies?"

"I'll bear it in mind," Harriet says.

He carries on speaking – blurting, rushing to get his thoughts out. "People who stay married live four years longer than people who don't. A spiralling divorce rate has implications for the survival of the species."

"Thank you, Charles Darwin," I say.

"It's true, and I'll tell you another thing. Since women have entered the workplace, there are now more women having affairs than men."

"Takes two to tango," Harriet snaps. And it's her turn to flush. It's the colour she goes when Tony Smith sails dangerously close to chauvinism.

"Let's move on," I say, playing the perfect boss by rescuing both of them from spontaneous combustion. If Superintendent Thomas could see me now... "Any forensics on the phone box at Sharpness?"

"Even in this day and age, public phones have traces of several individuals. We'll put any partial prints through the PNC, but it's doubtful."

"Soon would be good," I say.

His expression hardens. "This department meets the service-level agreement. If you've got a problem, we can take it to the Super."

"That's great, thanks," I say quickly. Last thing I need this week is a grumpy tech guy bleating to Thomas.

"What about the voice that made the emergency call?" Harriet asks. "Don't you have voice recognition software or something?"

Hearing from Harriet softens him up again. "We're still waiting for the recording of the triple-nine call to come through from Control. But we won't be able to identify the individual. At best we'll get some general characteristics of speech pattern, accent, age, gender."

"Can you chase it up, please?" I ask nicely. Something about the call bugs me. Too convenient. A big part of me thinks Gerald Gittens-Gold has done a John Stonehouse and faked his death. He could well have made the call himself.

Sidestepping the hardware on the floor, we thank Neil and head for the door. Harriet's long legs take the staircase back to civilisation two at a time and I follow, slowly, the heat outside Neil's air-conditioned cave not helping me.

At the top, she turns back to me. "Is Neil married?"

I stop mid-step. "Please don't tell me you're interested?"

Her cheeks go pink again, but whether it's embarrassment or indignation, I can't tell. "Just curious. He seems such an expert."

I catch her up. "Relationship experts are seldom married. They wouldn't think they had all the answers if they were.

That's what makes Gerald and Anna Gittens-Gold so weird."

CHAPTER THIRTY-TWO

Our briefing has been postponed until this afternoon because Kevin is at a hastily convened meeting to scope out an emergency exercise for a Novichok attack. A British woman from Salisbury died from exposure to the nerve agent yesterday. Many police forces are making plans just in case.

It's too early for our eleven a.m. interview with Sally Parker and Tim Vale. Sally lives in the hamlet of Klox, close to Frampton on Severn and built in a century that predates coffee shops, so I suggest we take a break in the police canteen.

But Harriet has other ideas. "The pantomime director has called an extra rehearsal tonight, so I need to get my script from home. It's on the way. We could sit outside in the communal courtyard. No one else much uses it. I can make coffee." She peers through her fringe and waits.

An invite to hers? Is this her way of apologising? If she said something to Superintendent Thomas about my management style, she damn well ought to. *Try working for*

*some of the old-guard detective inspectors, then you'll have
something to complain about, love.*

"That's kind," I say before I blurt what I'm thinking
through the silence.

We drive to the edge of Tufton, not far from my old
school but several streets from The Avenue, where my
parents live. Waveside Mews is the overpromising name of
the apartments built by the canal. This time of the year there
are more rusting lager cans and pushchair wheels than water.
However, the Tufton Tidiers anti-litter group do a good job
of keeping this section clear even if they can't provide rain to
cover the dried-up canal bed.

Harriet takes me straight into a courtyard that's
chequered by enthusiastic dandelions between the paving
stones. Grey, green and blue dustbins line up in the shade of
the building, odourless and wasp-free. A trick not managed at
the bin park at my place. I hate going down there, but I can't
make Jake do the bins any more. Not since his father died
there, even though he doesn't know it.

Harriet motions towards a set of garden furniture under
an awning – a coffee table, two chairs, a recliner, a sofa-
swing. The kind of stuff I admire in a garden centre, but
space and cost rule out any serious intention to buy. Opting
for a chair, I look up at the building – dark fascia, clean white
window frames, three storeys, small balconies to the top floor
windows. I'm seeing the apartments in the same light as the
summer furniture. The price tags here would be higher than
my Bell Tower home. Has the constable's salary overtaken
the inspector's? Maybe I should volunteer for the demotion
Superintendent Thomas was hinting at Friday.

"I'll get the kettle on," Harriet says.

Out of my handbag, I produce a sachet of green tea.

"Still can't get used to you not mainlining black coffee," she says, taking it.

She goes inside and then I see her moving about what must be the kitchen of a ground-floor flat. After bringing out the drinks, she pops back in for a plate of flapjacks she says are left over from her mother's last visit. As I take a bite, she studies me. My smile is genuine as the chewy sweetness melts in my mouth. Harriet relaxes into the sofa-swing. I'm unsure whether it's her mother's baking that's passed a test, or me.

We lapse into silence. Through an open window, the nagging cry of a too-hot baby reaches us, but it's far enough away not to give me flashbacks to sticky summers with Jake as a toddler.

When I catch Harriet looking at me, she slips her glance upwards. "Just a few flecks of cloud."

"It's been a good summer so far," I reply.

Harriet nods, but apparently out of small talk, eats her flapjack. I sit back in the cushioned chair, close my eyes and let my face and forearms soak up the morning warmth.

"Time for another?" Harriet asks eventually and I hand her another green teabag. "Sure I can't tempt you with rooibos?"

I pull a face. "What's the attraction of that stuff?"

"Bittersweet." Her gaze goes to the building, apparently making the same visual inspection I made earlier.

A lump forms in my throat as my detective skills finally kick in. Criminal compensation paid for this. Bittersweet isn't the drink; it's her home. Affordable because her dad, an off-duty copper intervening in a stabbing, was murdered.

———

When we get to our eleven a.m. interview in Klox, a man in paint-spattered overalls opens the door to the cottage. "Come through. I'm Tim." He leads us into a small parlour. Although the ceiling is low, it's cosy rather than cramped, the open staircase creating a sense of space. After the heat outside, the coolness of the thick walls is pleasant. Pink roses in a vase on a windowsill fill the air with a delicate scent.

"Sally's up in her study on the phone to her publisher. She'll be down any minute. Have a seat. Can I get you drinks?"

"We've just had one, thanks," I say, moving to the sofa. "We need to ask you both a few questions about your counselling sessions with Mr Gittens-Gold. In particular, the one last Monday."

"First and last session." A woman's voice calls from upstairs. A pair of shapely legs in ugly black slippers make their way down. "Tim didn't turn up. A problem at work apparently."

When the whole of her reaches us, I miss a breath. Brown eyes, freckles and shoulder-length auburn hair. At early to mid-forties, she's probably a few years older than her partner, but she's still beautiful. A stunner, as Tony Smith might say.

"I always said it was doubtful," Tim tells her. "You said you were okay with that."

"*Couples'* counselling. The clue's in the name. The truth is you don't want a relationship."

Here we go. I prepare to switch off as the exchange threatens to become a rerun of the Debbie and Lyle

Robinson argument we endured on Saturday, but Tim's comeback changes the dynamic.

"I've only ever been faithful."

The shine of anger leaves Sally's eyes, and her freckled face turns grey. "We never said we were exclusive. But for what it's worth I've been faithful too."

"Not for want of trying," Tim mutters. "The cat's not the only old stray you've taken in, from what I've heard."

Her eyes flash again, but although I'm expecting anger and a whip-hard reply, she stays silent. Is she afraid of her partner? Have we stumbled into an abusive relationship?

"What did you and Mr Gittens-Gold talk about?" Harriet asks, cutting through the atmosphere.

But if she meant the question to calm the woman, it doesn't work. Sally Parker looks even more anxious. "When? What do you mean?"

"At the counselling session?"

Sally's expression changes – relaxes. Harriet seems to have noticed too. She waits for an answer, frowning.

"I didn't stay," Sally says. "It was pointless without Tim."

"I can't turn down work," Tim protests.

"Ms Parker," Harriet says, drawing her attention before another argument starts, "it would help our enquiries if you could think back to that meeting, however brief. You may have been one of the last people to see Mr Gittens-Gold alive."

Sally's mouth gapes. Her pupils widen. "Alive?" she whispers.

"That's why they're here," Tim explains. "It was on the news. Didn't you see?"

"I've been device-free since Wednesday. Remember?" She looks at me. "My publisher wanted major changes to the translation I was doing. I've had a deadline, so I haven't seen any news."

"They think he drowned," Tim says.

Sally sinks onto the bottom step.

"Had you met him before Monday?" Harriet asks, apparently reading the spectrum of colour that crosses the woman's face from red to deathly white.

"Of course not," she replies too quickly and stands up. "And I hardly saw him on Monday. When I realised Tim wasn't coming, I left."

"So what did you talk about there?" Harriet asks.

"There?"

"While you were waiting for Tim?"

Sally hesitates as if deciding how to summarise what went on, but finally she says, "I didn't go in. The man opened the door just as I decided not to bother. I apologised and left."

"What did he say to that?" Good girl, Harriet, not letting go. There's something here; we both feel it.

"I... I don't remember. Nothing much, whatever it was."

"Had you paid for the session in advance?" I ask. "Did you request a refund or set a new date on your way out?" I make a mental note to speak to Julia, the Cross Care Centre receptionist, again. She'll tell me what kind of mood the bolting Ms Parker was in.

"I never thought of that," she says. "Perhaps they'll forward the bill."

"Except he may not have prepared the paperwork," Harriet says and we both look at Sally, gauging her reaction.

But before the silence forces her into answering, Tim wades in. "Surely you don't think my partner pushed a marriage guidance counsellor off a bridge to get out of paying a bill?"

Biting her lips, Sally looks his way. Grateful for his intervention or fearful? Something tells me there's more to this than an abandoned therapy session, but we'll have to come back when he isn't here to get any semblance of the truth out of Sally. We thank them both and leave.

CHAPTER THIRTY-THREE

At *Gloucester Evening News*, a young woman has replaced the homely, older receptionist who was here last time.

"Are you the police? Mr Oakley is expecting you. Would you like a coffee?" About the same age as Harriet, she gazes up at her as she speaks. I'm unclear whether the coffee offer extends to me, but I decline for both of us.

"Of course." The girl seems to notice me for the first time. "The newsroom's that way, madam."

I move on, trying not to fume. *Madam*. Amazing how a term of politeness can seem bloody insulting. The girl has made me feel a hundred years old.

The scene of cable-driven chaos that is the empty newsroom reminds me again of the CID office. I almost remark as much to Harriet but think better of it. Any such comparison would bring on another of her lectures on health and safety. Last week I heard her complaining to Tony Smith about overloading power sockets.

David Oakley enters from the back of the room with his

hand outstretched. "Officers, what can I do for the police this time?"

Harriet introduces herself and shakes his hand. "Where is everyone?"

"Out and about." He perches on a desk. In jeans, but they're not casual. An expensive brand, I'd say. "I task my team to search out the news, not rewrite what they see on Twitter."

His palms slip to the table top and he leans back in an open gesture, giving off amiable confidence. But I wonder what he's really thinking. Plenty of lowlifes I've nicked have refined how to hide their feelings. I don't have to wonder for long. When Harriet says we want to discuss his criminal record, his smile evaporates and he stands up.

"Come on, officer, that was years ago. Is this really necessary?"

Harriet ignores the question. "Assault occasioning actual bodily harm."

"Officer," Oakley says, using her job title again. I can't see why he's bothering. Notebook open, she recites details of the charge.

"It was five years ago in London. And it was a scuffle, not an assault. I was photographing some thug of a footballer who'd picked up a D list soap actress in a nightclub. He didn't want his girlfriend finding out so he went for my camera."

"And you tried to throttle him."

"The whole thing was blown out of all proportion. Even the courts worked that one out. I got off with a fine. It was obvious I was a journalist of impeccable character."

Harriet side-eyes me, having trouble putting 'journalist'

and 'impeccable' in the same sentence. Harsh. Reporters have their uses, but she's right to be sceptical of this one.

"You put your hands around another man's throat," she says.

"Officer, let's sit down." He points at a couple of wheelie chairs that seem to have stopped in transit between two desks. When Harriet doesn't move, he tries his luck with me. "Steph, isn't it? Come and have a seat."

"We're fine," I reply. "The trouble is that DC Harris and I have seen our fair share of scuffles. Most people start throwing punches or let fly with the odd kick. We don't come across many who go for strangulation."

"It was him or me. Self-defence, pure and simple."

"What about Sonia? Was that self-defence?"

Oakley reels back against the desk. "Come on, Steph. Do you seriously think I'm the sort of man who goes around bumping off my own staff? I'm a normal guy, a family man with a job, a mortgage and a Renault estate."

"You said yourself Sonia was ambitious. Was she just a bit too close on your heels for comfort?" I ask.

"Sonia Hanson may well have wanted my job, but she'd have to be made deputy editor first and that wasn't about to happen. She wasn't a threat to me. As far as I was concerned she was just another staff reporter, working her backside off to make a name for herself. She could be pushy and argumentative at times. That's no secret. She put a lot of people's backs up." He waves his hand in the general direction of two unoccupied desks. One with a pink water bottle on the corner, the other sporting a Gloucester Rugby sticker on the back of the monitor. "Sonia was resentful when Lauren started and she clashed with Gerry all the time. They had such different ways of working. Gerry is what you might call laid back. The same could not be said of Sonia." Another wave. This time to a desk with a newspaper open across the keyboard. "And she accused poor Roger, our retiring deputy, of being a doddery old fool. But that's the media industry for you. I bet you police have your own repartee that might seem odd to outsiders."

I think of the banter triangle that is me, Harriet and Tony Smith. Oakley is right, but 'odd' hardly covers it.

"Every workplace has its atmosphere," Oakley continues. "Especially when you're working to deadlines."

"In my experience, management and staff have differing views on atmosphere," Harriet says. I shoot her a look but she ignores me. "So if we interview your colleagues again, they'll paint you as a good boss, will they? Respect and harmony? No friction with Sonia Hanson?"

Oakley hesitates, eyes moving upward. Remembering something? Has Harriet's inelegant dig at bosses hit a nerve with Oakley as well as me? But a new glint crosses his face. "Tempers fray when we're under pressure, don't they?"

"Depends what you mean by temper," Harriet says.

"There must have been choice words in your office during the serial killer case." He's looking at me. "That was a nasty one."

Folk have been saying the same or similar to us ever since the mayhem of a couple of months ago, but there's something knowing in the way David Oakley has said it.

He goes on. "I was chatting only last night to the landlady of the Loch Lomond in Cathedral Street. You police had your work cut out, didn't you?"

My blood pulses hot and cold, but he can't *know*. One of the victims stayed at Tracey Chiles's guesthouse, but Tracey never discovered his connection to me. Oakley is fishing.

"I'm a newshound. When I find the witness in one case, it sometimes leads to another." He's still looking at me. And I'm still sweating ice.

Harriet's face clouds. "If you have information about what happened to Sonia, you need to tell us now." She's right. Our press office never revealed Tracey's name in connection with Sonia's murder or Gerald's disappearance, or the serial killer business back in May. How has Tracey's name come his way?

Oakley taps the side of his nose. "Newshound, like I said. I sniff out news." He looks at me. "And secrets."

When we get back to the car, Harriet frowns. "Do you think he had particular secrets in mind?"

"He's taking a punt, nothing more. Trying to make out he knows more than we do and hoping we'll let something slip." At least I think that's all it is, but I pray Tracey Chiles hasn't recalled to Oakley any chance remark Sean Farrell made while he was staying at the Loch Lomond Guesthouse before his death. Last thing I need is a journalist cottoning on to Sean's connection with me.

CHAPTER THIRTY-FOUR

Despite his earlier work-to-rule stroppiness, Neil Wright has hurried up the forensics from the phone box at Sharpness, and Kevin is outlining the report Neil has produced.

"The handset and keypad show traces of disinfectant," he says. "Someone wiped them. Does that sound like a teenage caller? Is hygiene the new trend, like waistlines below the underpants?"

Tony leans back, bringing the front legs of his chair off the floor. "So what are we thinking, boss? A caller with a cleaning fetish or a professional hitman?"

A few colleagues shake their heads and jeer.

"I'm serious," Tony says. "Gittens-Gold worked in Australian special forces. He's bound to have made enemies. If the Russians can take out defectors in Salisbury, a targeted assassination here isn't far-fetched. A professional could easily fake an emergency call and dress a murder up as suicide."

"Except we haven't found the body," I say. "The professional who faked the call could be Gerald himself."

"We should have a better idea about that soon," Kevin explains. "Forensics are now working on the triple-nine recording. As regards the body, it's a waiting game. The Coastguard is on the alert, but it could be up to a fortnight before there's a sighting, if ever.

"In the meantime, we continue to question his wife, colleagues, clients, friends and acquaintances. Harriet, can you chase up his service record with the Australians? It's a week since he was seen and we still don't know whether he's a victim or killer."

Or both. My mind races to the Clarke Brothers – ignoring their sister, Sonia, in life but avenging her in death – pitching her killer into the Severn and getting back before the cash and carry closes. These two cases are stretching my mental faculties to breaking point.

Kevin takes a pen to the whiteboard and writes *Gerald Gittens-Gold.* "Whether he's dead or sunning himself in Scarborough, he's a suspect in the Sonia Hanson murder. So, moving on, let's summarise where we've got to with that."

"Tracey Chiles," Tony says. "We only have one witness putting Gittens-Gold outside the cathedral at dawn on Monday. Is she telling the truth, mistaken or shifting the blame from herself?"

"Absolutely," Kevin says, jotting Tracey's name below Gerald's. "Have we even checked whether there's a connection between Ms Chiles and the murder victim?" He looks at Jordan and Cally. "Did Sonia write hotel reviews? See if she did the dirty on the Loch Lomond Guesthouse." Cally takes a note. "And pay Tracey Chiles another visit. Ask her to go over what she saw on Monday. Does what she says now match with her earlier statement? Any discrepancies? Sound out her background as well. See what slips out."

226

"I'll take that one," I offer. If anything's slipping out at Tracey's I want to be there to catch it.

"Thanks, Steph." Kevin stays poised at the board. "Who else are we looking at?"

"All the F and Fs," Jordan says. "Even though the location was public, it could still be a domestic."

Kevin starts a new column: *Family and Friends*. Below the heading, he puts *Alistair Hanson*.

Harriet flicks through her notes. "He doesn't have an alibi that can be corroborated. At the time of his wife's murder, he was home alone with three small children. He could easily have left them sleeping and followed her to the cathedral."

"Anything on ANPR to show his car out and about that morning?"

Cally answers Kevin's question. "No match. And the cathedral is a CCTV blank, so that's no help. The few pedestrians seen heading along Chancery Close between four and six a.m. are picked up again fifteen or twenty minutes later when they appear on the railway station concourse."

"Is Tracey Chiles on camera?" Tony asks.

Reading from her notes, Cally says, "A slight figure in an olive green hoodie with a small black dog is captured on the north side of Cathedral Street at five fifteen a.m. and returns up the south side at six thirty."

"Over an hour? Plenty of time for murder."

"That's true, Tony," Kevin replies, "but she said herself she dawdled on the green to let the dog play."

"Wouldn't you get your excuses in early if you'd committed murder?" Tony says. "The dog walker is one to watch."

To cut off his return to Tracey Chiles, I ask Cally a

different question. "Any CCTV footage of a man in a straw hat?"

Cally shakes her head. "Nothing. No one matching Gittens-Gold's description with or without a hat."

"So Tracey Chiles lied about seeing him," Tony exclaims.

"Not necessarily," Harriet says. "If Gerald is ex-army and had murder in mind, he'd know how to move around without detection."

"I suppose so." Tony spins around to look at her. "Given what's happened in Salisbury, I'd say anything's possible."

"Alien abduction," Jordan quips.

A few colleagues laugh.

Tapping the board, Kevin gets our attention. "Let's get back to the probable." He adds *Olivier* and *Jerome* to his list and brackets them with the surname *Clarke*.

Yes, they lost a lot – a successful Quayside antique business reduced to a convenience store in a dwindling parade of shops – but unless something happened to reignite the feud, I don't buy Sonia's brothers strangling her four years after their falling out. Besides, someone else was more directly responsible for their change in circumstance. I tell Kevin to put another name on the list.

As he writes *Carl Bryant*, he asks what we know about Sonia's ex-fiancé.

"He certainly holds a grudge," I say. "When Sonia dumped him, he took it out on her family by upping the rent on their retail unit to unaffordable. And his alibi for Monday is shaky." I glance at Harriet for clarification.

"He claimed to have spent the night with a married woman," she says. "The lucky lady did eventually corroborate his story. But by the time I got her name, he could have got to her first to set up a fake."

Kevin sighs. "Probably a nugatory exercise, but carry out background checks on the woman. Start by asking her husband if they were together on Sunday night/Monday morning. A mistress can't be in two places at once. But be discreet. Carl Bryant is a big cockerel in these parts. No sense ruffling feathers unless it's necessary."

"What about Sonia's mother?" Cally says. "I gather there was no love lost there."

Kevin hesitates, apparently not convinced about putting Monique Clarke on the board.

"The French are a passionate lot," Tony says, as if that's justification.

"I don't think our Gallic cousins are known for murdering their young," Kev says, but he puts Sonia's mother up. "Who else?"

Sonia's grandmother, Marie Fournier? A woman who spits when her granddaughter's name is mentioned. Her fury could have led to an attack on Sonia, but the woman couldn't walk further than the lavatory and would never have reached the cathedral. I wonder whether in her years in England she's ever been there. Perhaps ill health and the language barrier have limited her to the flat, the shop and family weddings. And Sonia made sure that there was one less of those to attend.

Before we answer Kevin's question, PC Izzy Barton enters, this time without knocking. I anticipate the open door bestowing a breeze on us, but my expectation isn't met and we continue to roast. However, it turns out a reprieve from the heat is only moments away, as Izzy tells Kevin that Alistair Hanson is downstairs waiting to speak to Harriet and me.

———

I take my seat next to Harriet and opposite Alistair, a man with the life sucked out of him. Round shoulders, deep shadows below his eyes. Seldom have I been face-to-face in an interview room with a lawyer of such humility.

"I've left Edith with my mother. She wouldn't go to nursery today. She screamed so much that I couldn't get her in the car. I don't like leaving her like that."

"If you say what you want to tell us, we won't keep you," I say.

"It's the photograph you showed me. It was after you said he was a counsellor, it came back to me. I wasn't going to mention it because it would mean airing dirty laundry in public. It would seem disloyal." He pauses, breathing jerkily.

"We will treat anything you tell us in the strictest confidence." There's tenderness in my voice and it's not an act. I've a nose for criminals; this man doesn't have the smell.

"The hours we wasted arguing," he is saying. "If only I'd known we had so little time left. I used to moan that she didn't spend enough time with the children, too ambitious, in too much of a hurry. I said we needed professional help, marriage guidance. I actually told her to slow down. There was no rush. I said she had years ahead of her." He chokes on his words.

Harriet lays down the photo of Gerald Gittens-Gold we showed him on Friday. "Are you saying that this man was your counsellor?"

"Not him. We went once about six weeks ago to the Cross Care Centre. We saw a woman. She was dreadful. I thought counsellors were supposed to listen. She never stopped talking. She banged on about her own marvellous husband. It was Gerald this. Gerald that. It was nothing about us. I was really angry."

"Was Sonia angry too?" I ask, but think I already know after all I've heard about Sonia's volatility. Alistair's answer is therefore unexpected.

"Sonia responds, responded, to situations in one of two ways. She either blew her top or she saw a potential story. On this occasion, she put her journalist head on. She actually started interviewing the woman, asking her about her past. She tried to persuade her to be in her Gloucester Reunited column. The woman wasn't keen but Sonia was like a dog with a bone. It was as if she'd forgotten I was there. The counselling was a complete waste of time. At the end of the session, the woman gave us some exercises to do. She didn't know anything about us, so how could she prescribe therapy?

"Afterwards Sonia was eager to go back. She booked us in for the following month, but I knew it was only because she wanted to interview the woman for her precious newspaper. It wasn't to help our relationship."

"Did you go back?"

"Our rows increased. Sonia could be very stubborn. I ripped up the exercise worksheet and demanded we cancel the next appointment. To my surprise she agreed but said she'd go in person to cancel. I think she wanted to see the woman again for her column, so I went with her to make sure she really did cancel. I needn't have bothered because appointments are cancelled at reception, and it was the woman's day off anyway. While we were there, that man came in." He touches the photograph. "As he passed by the reception desk, he said hello in a friendly way. I was about to reply but then it dawned on me he was probably talking to the receptionist. That's why I didn't mention it sooner. There wasn't really any connection with Sonia. We only saw him fleetingly."

"Can you be sure it was the same man?"

"I remember the tight mouth and the straw hat."

"And you're absolutely sure you hadn't met him before?"

He shakes his head.

"Had Sonia met him before?"

"I don't think so," he says slowly. He doesn't seem sure.

I encourage him to think. "This is very important. Did she react in any way when she saw him?"

"Not at the time but she was excited afterwards. Like she'd got a story. She scrolled on her phone screen as soon as we got in the car. I should have taken more interest."

"Can you remember the date you saw him? If we have a date our techies might be able to match it with the searches that Sonia made that day on her phone and laptop," Harriet says. *Good one, detective constable. I would never have thought of that.*

"I can check my work diary. I took an hour off to go to Cross Care with Sonia to cancel our booking. I'll ring you when I've found the date, if you think it will help."

As we escort Alistair out of the station, our front desk officer calls out to Harriet that she has a phone call from Australia.

CHAPTER THIRTY-FIVE

The same two cars are parked on Maple Gardens as last week and I squeeze my Golf in between again.

Harriet unfastens her seatbelt. "In what order do we give Anna the news?" she asks. "First, we could tell her we've made no progress with the missing person's enquiry. No one's seen hide nor hair of her husband since four p.m. on Monday, apart from two sightings: the one at Sharpness that uniform broke to her, and the other that implicates him in a murder."

"Poor cow." My voice sounds hollow. The little I know of Anna suggests she'll thrive on her tragedies.

"Then we could round off by telling her that the Australian Register of Births, Deaths and Marriages shows that the name 'Gittens-Gold' doesn't exist, but a certain army photographer, Sgt Gerald Gittens of the Royal Australian Corps of Signals, died aged thirty in 1992."

Harriet's phone call from a diligent official down under, working in the small hours, made it clear that Anna has been married to a dead man for twenty-five years.

"I still can't believe it," Harriet says as we go up the short driveway.

"I can. I didn't buy all that Boys' Own stuff. It's the difference between a vasectomy and the SAS." Taking a moment, I smile at Harriet's bafflement. We stop walking so I've time to explain. "Men wear their vasectomies like a badge of office. If you meet a man who's had one, within a very few minutes he will tell you about it. If you meet a man who's been in the SAS, you'll never know. Take it from me, anyone who claims to be in the SAS – or undercover for the Australian Army – is having you on. Real heroes don't talk about it." I stop speaking, lost in an eighteen-year-old memory. Some men who haven't had the snip lie that they have. Some men don't get consent either way. Some men...

"So are we sure now the fake Gittens-Gold hasn't drowned?"

Snapping away from my thoughts, I walk up to the door of the bungalow. "He's gone to ground. Somehow Sonia Hanson found out about his fake ID and was going to run the story. He killed her and did a bunk, but anyone who's managed to live a fantasy life for over twenty-five years is going to be hard to track."

Harriet rings the bell. "I'm not looking forward to this."

"Any news?" Anna asks, answering the door and gripping its edge, possibly poised to lapse into a swoon if Harriet's response deems it necessary.

"Our enquiries are still ongoing, but we've had no concrete sightings," I say, giving her no scope for theatrics, not yet anyway.

She looks at me as if I'm something she's trodden in. As we enter the hall and pass the photos of her starring roles in school productions, I can't help feeling she'd rather talk to

234

Harriet alone. Perhaps she's recognised a fellow thespian; one who will enjoy the drama. We follow her into the lounge, breathing in a hint of old tobacco. The thought that Gerald is hiding in the kitchen crosses my mind, but I dismiss it. We've made enough noise in the street to get the neighbours on the alert. If the local action man had reappeared, the curtain twitchers would have been in touch.

"Sit there," Anna instructs. Her mouth bestows a mechanical smile on me, but her eyes look over my shoulder. I'm left in no doubt that she views me as her social inferior. My mum used to complain sometimes about Amy Ashby's mother and others like her on the school run, who kept their eyes on the look-out for someone better to talk to. Now I know how she felt. "Nice sofa," I say. "Real leather?"

"Naturally," Anna replies with the same fixed smile and turns her attention to Harriet. "What's the matter with you people? Gloucester's a small city. Someone must know what's happened to Gerald."

"We interviewed all the clients he saw on that Monday," she replies. "They couldn't shed any light on where your husband went after four p.m."

"Well, they wouldn't, would they?" she scoffs. "Couples in counselling are too wrapped up in themselves to notice what's happening to anyone else. As it was a Monday, he would have seen the Robinsons and the Rices, and the new people, the Parkers. If you spoke to them, it would have been pointless," she says crossly, her previous insistence on confidentiality vanishing with each word. "I used to counsel Debbie Robinson myself. Her marriage was dying before her eyes. The husband has completely disengaged. He can't even be bothered to argue any more.

"I haven't met the Rices, but from what Gerald has told

me of their case history, they're suffering from classic new baby syndrome. It's no coincidence that half of all divorces occur in the first seven years, when the children come along."

She gazes haughtily out of the window. "Counselling is all about common problems: apathy for the marriage, being jealous of the children, or leading separate lives like the Parkers. Tim Vale didn't even turn up for their first session." She turns back to Harriet, peering down her nose. "I'm afraid that interviewing the clients won't have advanced your enquiry one iota. Nor will dredging the river. As I told the police women who came on Saturday, Gerald isn't the type to throw himself into the river. He must have had an accident, lost his memory. You should have officers searching the city."

"If he's still in Gloucester," I say idly. My thoughts catch on something I can't process.

"Where else?" Anna demands.

"Australia?" I say, lobbing out one of Tony Smith's wilder theories.

"Don't be ridiculous. Do you know how much it costs to fly there? Have you actually checked our joint account? Has Gerald withdrawn any money?"

"He hasn't used his credit cards since last Sunday and there are no large transactions before that," Harriet says.

"Precisely. He's injured, or worse." She rocks on her sofa.

"There is another possibility," Harriet says slowly. "Does the name Sonia Hanson mean anything?"

Anna gives a shrug, even though we passed a recent *Gloucester Evening News* on the hall stand.

"She's been front page news for the past week," Harriet prompts.

Anna's voice softens. "The journalist, of course. Tragic.

You'll forgive me if I only have a vague grasp of the details. I've been scouring the newspaper for news of Gerald. I can think of little else."

"You knew her professionally, too," Harriet adds. "She attended the Cross Care Centre a few weeks ago."

"That's why the face looked familiar. I did notice her photograph in the newspaper and saw the headline. Her poor husband must be beside himself. He'll be thinking how futile their rows were. The sad thing is their marriage was doomed. They couldn't have stayed the course."

"You counselled them on just one occasion," I say, wondering how this woman can make a pronouncement on the marriage of a couple she barely knew.

Perhaps sensing my disbelief, Anna launches into a lengthy explanation. "Marital discord is founded on four basic arguments. They had them all going on." She stretches out a finger on her chair arm. "Number one: she wanted another baby, and he wasn't ready. Number two: he wanted more sex than she did. Three: he didn't do enough round the house. And number four, the biggest problem of all: religion. As a French woman she wanted to raise the children Roman Catholic; he was Church of Scotland."

"They told you all this?" Harriet asks. I hear her scepticism. Neither Sonia's husband nor her mother mentioned their faith to us.

"They didn't have to. A good counsellor picks up the clues from what they don't say. I gave them some listening exercises. They didn't open up. Thirty-somethings often don't. Youngsters are so much easier to work with." She meets Harriet's bemused gaze. "Your generation understands that there's no shame in counselling. Recently I bumped into one girl I used to counsel. Cheri I think she was called, or was it Demi?" She shrugs. "Anyway, she said how much I'd helped. Didn't care who heard. You wouldn't get an older person doing that."

Harriet takes her revenge for the stereotyping with a simple statement. "One line of enquiry suggests that Gerald murdered Sonia Hanson."

Anna seems to stop breathing, her mouth gaping, gold bridgework flashing.

"Never." When it finally comes, the one word has the gravitas of a BAFTA winner. "Why on earth would he? Gerald is a pacifist. He wouldn't even go to my self-defence class with me."

"A pacifist in the Australian Special Forces?" I ask.

"He was a photographer, an artist. He did reconnaissance work."

"He didn't even do that. According to Australian army records, Gerald Gittens died in 1992."

———

"What is the meaning of this?" She really did say that. We confirm it to each other in the car afterwards. In my ten years and Harriet's three in the Force, no witness has ever actually said that. For the rest of the interview, Anna steadfastly refused to accept the evidence of the Australian authorities. She fetched out Gerald's birth certificate. Birth registered in Subiaco, Western Australia, Surname: GITTENS-GOLD, Other Names: Gerald Brian. Harriet pointed out that it was very likely to be the genuine certificate for the long deceased Gerald Gittens. The Forensics team would be able to show that the hyphenated 'GOLD' had been added later.

With a flounce of her shoulders, Anna pulled herself together and adamantly reassured us she would have noticed if she'd been living with a phoney for twenty-five years. She proudly pointed to their black and white wedding photograph on the lounge wall. What more proof did we need? Harriet looked mildly surprised when I asked if we could borrow it and then more surprised by Anna's reluctance to let the photo go. I let her keep the photo in exchange for taking a snap of it on my phone. She wasn't happy about that either, but couldn't argue when I said knowing more about his early background might help us find where an injured, disoriented Gerald would seek aid.

"I don't like her," Harriet says as we pull into the station car park.

"Steady. Your impartiality halo is slipping."

"One thing she said really got to me."

"Only one thing? What was that?"

"I can't put my finger on it. I wish I could."

You and me both. Something she said about Tim Vale and Sally Parker is still bugging me, but I can't work out what.

"I can see why the couples we interviewed had wanted to be counselled by Gerald and not by her," Harriet says. "She didn't know anything about the Hansons' family life. I bet she was wrong about the housework and the..."

"Sex life," I supply.

"Maybe Sonia's news story wasn't about Gerald at all. Nothing to do with his army background. What if she wanted to expose Anna's shoddy counselling techniques in her consumer column?"

"It's possible, but that would have meant admitting publicly that she and Alistair were having marriage problems. Would she have gone to those lengths for a good story?"

"We may never know," Harriet replies. "I've started going through all the incomplete files that Neil Wright lifted off her PCs. There's nothing so far, not even a sentence relating to Gerald or Anna Gittens-Gold."

I switch on my mobile to check for messages as we walk towards police HQ. *Bingo.* Jordan has sent news of a phone call from Alistair Hanson. He's provided the date of their counselling session and the date they went to cancel the second one.

"Perhaps we should dig into Anna's private life," Harriet suggests. "Despite her denials, she could have known her husband was an imposter right back when they met in Australia."

"Worth a go," I say, damping my forehead with a tissue. Still no let up from the heat, but I know somewhere that will be cooler. "Anna told us last week they met while she was a student. See if you can find any of her old Australian university tutors even though they'll be fossils by now. And go back to Maple Gardens and knock on a few doors. We asked them about Gerald, but see what the neighbours have got to say about Anna." I remember my earlier thought about Gerald hiding out at home. "And check they haven't seen anyone else but Anna in her bungalow this week."

"Sure, Steph. Where will you be if I discover anything?" Her face is neutral but it's code for: what are you doing while I do all the work?

"Now that we have Alistair's dates, I'm going to ask Neil Wright for the internet searches Sonia made immediately after she and Alistair visited the Cross Care Centre. It's a long shot, but we might just get an inkling of what she was working on." The somewhere cooler is Neil's air-conditioned IT cave.

As we part in the foyer, I lob over my shoulder, "Unless you'd rather go and see Neil?"

Harriet doesn't reply.

CHAPTER THIRTY-SIX

Neil Wright checks the time on his screen. Harriet – and Steph – will be here any second. Good job Steph texted first. Neil doesn't like surprises. Their meeting this morning was planned, so he'd left home with a decent shave and wearing his best Def Leppard t-shirt, but he didn't expect a return visit in the late afternoon. He sniffs his armpits. No time to go to the gents in case he misses her, them. From his bottom drawer, he retrieves the unopened Lynx body spray Nan gave him for Christmas. He's been saving it, just in case. After a grapple with the lid, he shoves the aerosol up his shirt. As the ice-cold droplets connect with his perspiring chest, he takes a sharp breath. He sniffs again but can't smell anything. He gives the canister another lengthy squirt and stuffs it back in the drawer.

The morning meeting went well. He showed his professionalism, and not just in forensic science. The ultimate Renaissance Man, he chatted knowledgably about immunodeficiency and social interaction. He could tell Harriet was impressed. Perhaps this next visit will provide an opportunity for another chat. He's read some fascinating stuff in his *National Geographic* and he knows she'll be interested.

Wheeling back from his desk, he plans his strategy to get her on her own at the end of the meeting. Like playing chess – he'll first remove the black knight: "Steph, you don't mind if DC – er –Harriet and I have a private word, do you?" Then intercept the white queen: "Harriet, can we speak?" Perhaps he won't have to say anything. She'll dawdle behind anyway, willing him to make his move. And make his move he will. He'll come right out and ask her. His birthday will make a good first date. Only a few weeks to wait. Yes, checkmate; he'll seize the moment and sweep her off her feet.

Steph comes in first, hair damp on her forehead, but otherwise still looking cool in her white shirt and loose black trousers. But it's not just the leather jacket she had in tow this morning that she's ditched. He looks over her shoulder. Where's Harriet? His insides deflate, like a balloon that's turned up at the wrong party.

Steph puts her hands on her hips. "Am I made of UPVC all of a sudden?"

"Unplasticised Polyvinyl Chloride," Neil replies automatically. "Why?"

"Because you're looking right through me." Waving her arms with a flourish, she steps further into the room. "Everywhere I go today, I get ignored, so either I'm a typical older woman in the workplace or I've turned into a window."

"Sorry." He feels himself reddening. "I just... Where's..."

"On other enquiries, so you'll have to make do with me."

Retreating to home territory to pull himself together, Neil wheels to his desk and agitates the mouse next to his keyboard. "What can I do?"

"If I give you dates and times, can you see the internet searches Sonia Hanson was doing?"

He rubs his chin in contemplation, his fingers finding a tuft of hair he missed on his shave. As the hard disks have been copied, he can conduct a variety of analyses. For once, the CID boys didn't mess about with the computers first. They aren't supposed to, but they all fancy themselves as IT literates these days. Their amateur hacking comprises booting up the system and reading the deleted emails. Incriminating old data can be lost from the swap file when they switch on. It takes a skilled professional to make a copy of the hard disk before hitting the on-switch. But he's got lucky this time, with all protocols correctly followed.

"Anyone home?" She tilts her head, scrutinising him.

"Just thinking." The coppers who brought in Sonia's kit told him that she always used the same workstation at her office, but he didn't take their word for it. *Gloucester Evening News* has a firewall server, so there was a record of which workstation visited which internet site and at what time. There was no challenge; he wasn't pitched against a cunning computer genius. The web browser's history was intact. As he told Steph and Harriet this morning, he could see at a glance which pages had been downloaded most recently – a recipe for Pumpkin Seed Patties at healthkids.com, the National Union of Journalists home page, and various social media pages. He doubts the web-caching servers inside the newspaper's firewall will have been purged. A first year computer science student could handle this case. Nothing to get his teeth into. No signs of encryption. Why would there be? Sonia Hanson used her computer like every other technophobic journalist, creating a jumble of saved and deleted files and clogging up the Inbox with read emails.

"It's two dates," Steph explains. "On both computers and her phone. And has a separate work phone been brought in?"

Neil explains there isn't much on the work phone – a few calls to and from local businesses and texts to set up interviews. "She seems to have operated the phones like she did her laptops: the meat of her work done on her home devices, then completed articles were transferred to work."

He pushes aside the mouse, bored. Forensics won't be the key to this case. If it gets solved at all, Steph Lewis and the rest of the plods will be in line for the glory. And Harriet, of course. She'll be there, too.

"Anything else?" Steph asks. "Something amusing?"

Neil stops smiling and returns to his screen. "I've got the analysis of the triple-nine call at Sharpness. Want to hear?"

She comes closer, then backs to an empty workstation where she perches. Neil wonders if he's overdone the aftershave. Perhaps it's just as well Harriet isn't here. After loading the file, he presses play on the recording.

"Smart guy in a straw hat has jumped off the jetty ... Can't see him in the water ... That's all I know." It's the burr of a recently broken voice, speaking in a local accent.

"So not a fifty-something Australian faking his own death," Steph concludes. "Or has the pitch been manipulated?"

"Our tests suggest not. And there are no clicks or breaks. It's one continuous piece of speech, i.e. not spliced together from separate recordings."

"Was it definitely live?"

"The caller could have played a recorded message down the line, but our analysis of the background detects sounds consistent with the area." He types into his computer to replay the recoding with the voice removed. They listen to birdsong and more distant heavy machinery, probably from the cement factory half a mile down river. Something that sounds like a light plane flies over, getting louder on its approach, then fading away.

Steph asks him to play it though twice more. "I was hoping for traffic noise," she says afterwards. "A police appeal for a passing motorist might have led to an eyewitness who could describe the caller in the phone box. Does he say anything else?"

Neil explains how the boy rang off without giving his name. "The control operator was able to see his location. Apparently, she was sceptical about it being genuine, but it was a quiet afternoon with the accident-prone public staying in to watch the big match, so she dispatched a fire appliance to check it out."

Steph takes out her note book. Neil stretches to see the word *HOAX* appear. She underlines it and adds a question mark.

"Do you think it was a teenage boy having a laugh?" Neil asks. "He'd seen something about the missing man on a news alert and decided to have fun?"

She shrugs. "Except fun-loving lads operate in packs. None of the families at the picnic area report seeing a group of teenagers."

Neil agrees. Nor was there any recent rubbish by the phone box to speak of crisp-guzzling and cola-glugging teens, and the recording picked up no sniggers from the boy's mates listening in.

Steph slaps her knees. "Anyway, I'm parking the missing Gerald for now. How soon can you look at those timelines on the Sonia Hanson case?"

"Give me half an hour."

Steph gapes. "You can get her internet search details to me today?"

"Two dates, four devices, a check on the workplace fire-wall." Neil tots up the time in his head. "I'm going home at five, so by then."

Slipping off the desk, she jabs a thumbs-up his way. "Neil, I could kiss you." She steps over a broken monitor on the floor and heads to the door.

Neil breathes away the heat surge his body is feeling and watches her leave. Tidy for a woman of her age. What is she: five years older than him? Maybe nearer eight. But still... potential.

CHAPTER THIRTY-SEVEN

TUESDAY 10TH JULY

The news headlines on the hour with me, Dale Green. The final four boys and their football coach have been rescued after eighteen days trapped in a cave in Thailand.

Running late, I smile at the good news before slugging down tap water and grabbing my car keys. It has been a short night, but long enough for me to suffer a recurring dream. Anna Gittens-Gold's metallic teeth were gnashing at a toffee apple, the sugary coating dripping through her fingers. Jerome Clarke came along in a sports car belonging to Carl Bryant and announced it was an Adam's apple. Anna spat it out and Jerome dropped a box of groceries on it.

When I wasn't dreaming, I was thinking about work. True to his word, Neil called me back to his IT cave before I left the station last night with the information he promised. He was in a funny mood, kept looking at me in the way Tracey Chiles's dog eyes its blanket. Talk about going off at tangents. The quotes from *National Geographic* came thick and stupid. What the mating rituals of dolphins had to do with a marriage counsellor possibly murdering Sonia Hanson never became clear. The only thing that stopped me clouting some sense into him was that his delving into Sonia's searches had thrown up results.

After her first marriage guidance meeting with Anna on 31 May, Sonia had used her home PC to search reunion sites for 'Anna Gittens-Gold', but she hadn't made any hits. Neil said he hadn't noticed the name when he first examined the PC because Sonia had a habit of flooding social media sites with countless names, presumably whenever she met anyone new. No doubt, it was a journalist's lust for gossip, usually unsatisfied. But after 20 June, when she and Alistair had gone back to the Cross Care Centre to cancel their next appointment and they'd bumped into Gerald, she'd tried the same searches again. She'd been more persistent this time, with various combinations and spellings of the name such as 'Ann Gittens-Gold', 'Annabel Gold', and 'Anna Gittens'. She'd also given the same unsuccessful search treatment to Gerald. This was also not in itself remarkable. She could have worked out without too much difficulty that the man they'd bumped into at the counselling centre was Anna's husband. Sonia was known to be very thorough, going the extra mile for any story. It seems just as likely that she would work this hard only to find that there wasn't a story after all.

Thoughts of whether any of this is relevant to her murder plagued me throughout the night and clung uncomfortably to the remnants of my toffee apple dream. Since my headaches started a couple of months ago, I've got used to not sleeping well, but this was unrest on a new scale.

Half an hour ago, when I got up after the fitful night, I was on time, but I got distracted playing on my phone. I discovered that the St Michael logo was removed from the main Marks and Spencer label in April 2000 to be incorporated elsewhere in the packaging as a quality mark. After finding that out, I went down an underwear-related internet rabbit hole. Inconclusive, but for my money, April 2000 is a long while ago. Yet I'm blowed if I know why I'm seeing a relevance to my current cases. And now I'm late.

And the weather today. Dry morning, plenty of sunshine and a high of twenty-eight.

As I scramble for the front door, Jake sticks his head out of his bedroom. Fluffy haired, sleep in his eyes. I pause a moment to take in my man-boy, but can't delay as we have a briefing at eight thirty a.m. "Love you, see you tonight."

"I'm going out tonight."

That puts my brakes on. Impeccable timing: drop kick the announcement when Mum's too short of time to make the tackle. When I step back level with his door, he draws inside, but thinks better of it and puts his head out again. "Round to Brad's."

How many Tuesdays is that? And didn't Thursday figure last week too? Plus most of the weekend. They've been mates forever but haven't lived in each other's pockets like this since primary school. "So if I check with Terri, she'll confirm that, will she?"

"Mum, I'm not one of your suspects." He lets go of the door and folds his arms. There are hairs on his chest that weren't there last time I saw him in his boxers. Eighteen in November. Old enough to vote, to marry, to serve time in an adult prison.

"Everything's all right, isn't it?" I ask. "You'd tell me, wouldn't you?"

"Have I ever let you down?"

My mind goes to the humdinger of a bollocking when I caught him smoking in the cow meadow.

"I was thirteen," he says, guessing what I'm thinking. "What was your excuse?"

I'll always regret telling him I didn't quit until I was twenty-five. "What about football club?" I counter. "You never did explain." When he was fifteen, he walked out of training four days before a league match and never went back. No amount of cajoling from me, the coach and his grandad would make him give any reason other than the one he offers now.

"I lost interest, that's all. I prefer rugby." This time the door closes. It's not exactly with a slam, but it's emphatic. Discussion closed. He won't be out for round two.

Whether it's the argument or my bad night's sleep, I can't tell, but suddenly a full-blown migraine hits and forces me to the kitchen for another drink. When I hold up the glass, twin streams of water flow from the cold tap and the glass forms into two. Can't drive if I'm seeing double. Or go into the briefing. Headaches have been a taboo subject since May when, with my career on the line, I blurted out that I needed a brain scan.

Head throbbing, I sit at the kitchen table and scroll my phone, hoping to latch on to a good excuse for skipping the incident room. Any excuse, frankly. I need a reason to stay away and keep my headache under wraps.

CHAPTER THIRTY-EIGHT

I'm tempted to sit opposite two lads in baseball caps. If they're anything like Jake, they'll be good for a laugh. But the carriage is almost empty and it wouldn't be British to do anything other than claim four seats for myself and spend the fifty-minute train journey in silence.

Out of the window are fields, sheep, the odd horse, more sheep, a few villages. The air con in the train is working and my headache eases now the atmosphere isn't so stuffy. We pull into a station and I vaguely take in the place name to check it isn't my stop. As the travelling motion starts again, a plastic bottle skitters past my foot. I recall the can of pop that had joined the stagnant coffee mugs on Neil's desk last night and I go back over what he told me.

Sonia's online searching finally became remarkable on 21 June when she added another search term: *St Maur's Convent School*. While Neil proudly recounted the step-by-step way Sonia would have identified the school's location, I switched off, scrolling my phone for something that started nagging. And I found it in the snaps I took in Anna's hallway the first time I interviewed her. I photographed the framed images of school theatre productions. One was entitled *More St Maur's, 1983.* According to Neil, Sonia's searching pinpointed two matches for a school by that name. One is in Weybridge, Surrey. The other is in a village, fifty miles north of Gloucester. Sonia had scoured social media for old pupils from both, concentrating on the mid-1980s, and she visited the schools' websites.

Despite Neil's detailed investigations – the minutiae of which he would have gladly imparted if I hadn't cut him short – he wasn't able to follow the thread of any kind of resolution to the searches. So when I was racking my headache for an excuse not to attend this morning's briefing, his inconclusive evidence came to the rescue and I looked at the websites of both schools. I found no mention of Anna on either. Hardly surprising, as the oldest pages I found dated from 2014, but I had the excuse I needed to miss this morning's briefing. As a detective inspector on a misper case, I've dispatched myself to visit the nearer of the two St Maur's schools. An exploratory trip to the Weybridge school will have to wait for budget approval from Kevin and might prove unnecessary, as I suspect that beneath Anna Gittens-Gold's clipped home counties accent lurk the distinctive vowels of the West Midlands.

A woman takes the seat opposite me. Stick thin, platform boots, a mauve woollen scarf over a short white dress, gloves, one hand clasping an iPhone. I'm in cotton trousers and sandals. She sees me looking and smiles. "Are you going anywhere nice?"

"Cheston. And you?" I say, glad of the company. After

my recent spats with Jake and Harriet, it will be good to prove to myself I can still converse with young'uns. I'd put this woman at pushing thirty, but still nearer to Harriet's age than I am.

"I'm going to see my boyfriend. He doesn't know I'm coming." She rubs a tube of lip-gloss over her mouth.

I envy her spontaneity. To jump on a train for fun and wear gloves in July.

"I try to have a day for myself a couple of times a week," she says.

She's got the balance right. Did Sonia Hanson ever take time out for herself? Her husband doesn't think so. He paints a picture of work, sleep and work again.

When the train enters a tunnel, the girl admires her scant eyebrows reflected in the darkened window.

Sonia was only a few years older than this woman and yet she was a lifetime apart. Was Sonia ever a carefree girl, paying Alistair a surprise visit in their courting days?

"I can't wait to see his face," the woman says. "He was a bit funny with me last time after I told him about the kids, but they stay at my mum's most of the time." She fetches earbuds out of a pocket. "I told him I'd never bring them with me. Have you ever been with kids on a train?"

Terri and I took Jake and Bradley to the pantomime at the Bristol Hippodrome once. The journey was a laugh, with a dozen rounds of 'I Spy' and 'Spot the Christmas Lights' out of the window. Brad won every game.

The girl doesn't wait for my answer. "It will be better when my fella can come down here, but he's still tagged at the moment." She plugs in the earbuds.

When the train pulls into Cheston, I leave her applying

more lip gloss and nodding along to whatever music is playing into her head.

———

The taxi speeds away and I wonder if he's dropped me onto a ploughed field as I negotiate the thick clumps of dried mud on the private road up to the convent school. Then the building comes into view, scaffolding along the right-hand side, and, to the left, a separate roofless construction. Instinct alone guides me to the main entrance. There are no signs, but the architecture, beneath the scaffolding, screams boarding school. Solid grey stone walls, multi-paned windows and white gables.

The door is open wide and apparently unattended. An odd lapse in child protection procedures, I would have thought. Inside, savoury kitchen smells assail my nostrils. In my day, school catering meant boiled cabbage and beef gravy, but this gives off notes of garlic and melted cheese. My stomach rumbles and I recall I skipped breakfast.

The whitewashed vestibule is narrow, with several closed doors in front of me. Because of their odd shapes and sizes, I imagine them leading to cupboards rather than classrooms.

A woman comes through one door. Before it swings shut, I make out a surprisingly substantial office.

"Are you lost, love?" she says. "Sister Agnes is addressing the staff in the chapel at the moment. Are you their guest speaker or here about the building works?"

I show my ID and the woman introduces herself as Bernie, the school secretary. She's mid-fifties, comfortably plump – what I might expect a school secretary to look like, except her tightly permed hair is dyed purple. I mentally slap my wrist. As I'm rapidly moving into the older woman category myself, I shouldn't stereotype those already in it.

She sees my expression. "Term finished last week. It's only teachers in for training so we're in civvies. Hence the kaftan." She looks down at her loose-fitting tunic. Distracted by the hair, I hadn't noticed.

I explain I'm making routine investigations into a Gloucestershire case with possible links to this area and ask whether the school still has records of pupils in the 1970s and 80s.

"Not another one? My, we are popular all of a sudden. It's lucky we've moved our archives downstairs because of the building work." Before I can ask what she means by another one, Bernie disappears behind a different door.

After a few minutes, she returns with a cardboard box of beige foolscap booklets. "These are the attendance registers for seventy-eight to eighty," she explains. "The nearest empty space where you can work is the junior library. If you'd like to follow me."

Still holding the box and declining my offer of help, she leads the way into a short corridor. At the end, she pushes another swing door with her shoulder. After taking the weight of the door from her, I step through. In contrast to the grey tiled floors of the hallway, the library has a warm, sea green carpet. The walls are a brilliant turquoise, and the bookshelves are sleek and modern.

Bernie sets the box down on a table. "You make a start and I'll fetch the registers for the next decade."

"Can I help carry?"

"Visitors can't go into the temporary archive store because the builders have left equipment there. Health and Safety, and all that." She rolls her eyes.

After she's gone I pull a book off the shelf marked *Quick Reference*. Volume one of a thirty-year-old children's encyclopaedia. The shelf below is the start of the fiction section. *Little Women*, *Mallory Towers* and *Chalet School*. I'm no expert, but I reckon the private school fees haven't paid the salary of a chartered librarian for at least twenty years despite the swanky bookcases. It's like they've upholstered a Rolls Royce but filled it up with cooking oil.

I get the door when Bernie returns with a second box.

"Thanks, I'd better not chip the paintwork. It's only just been decorated. The whole school's being refurbished. New headmistress. She's good news, is Sister Agnes. I just hope she's left enough in the kitty for new library books. Some of this lot were here when our Ciara was a pupil," she says.

I smile, pleased I'm not the only one who's noticed.

I lower myself onto a wooden chair that is the same turquoise as the walls. It's bright, inviting and comfortable – for an eight-year-old. The tops of my legs press against my stomach as I sit sideways, my knees too high to fit under the table.

"Sorry I had to put you in here. They're plastering the senior library today," Bernie says.

She returns twice more until I have four boxes for the years 1978 to 1989. There are twelve registers for each year. The girls in the photographs in Anna's hallway were teenagers. If Anna was one of them, she'd have been at the senior school at the time, so I start with the third form for 1978. There's only one possibility, an Anna Wilkinson. It takes me a good half hour, but I find several more potential matches in forms further up the school. In the fourth form are Ann Cartwright, Anna Forbes-Martin and Annie Weston. The fifth form register features Annabel Foster and

Ann Jones. The sixth form is home to the frighteningly named Anna De Courtney Evans-Phipps. I wonder if I've struck lucky, but this Anna would be in her sixties now. Too old to be Anna Gittens-Gold unless she's been as theatrical about her age as she has been about everything else.

CHAPTER THIRTY-NINE

Sally Parker slams a mug of coffee in front of Tim. "You're never here."

"I've come this lunch-time, haven't I?" he says, unbuckling the bib of his overalls.

"Why's that then? Run out of paint, have you?"

"I came so we could have a proper talk, when you're not on a deadline."

Sally sneers. "So you do remember my work. I was beginning to wonder. When was the last time you asked about my projects?"

"I do my best." He grips the spoon in the mug and stirs it slowly, with resignation. "I have to work, pay my way. You'd have something to complain about if I didn't."

Sally pulls out the second chair, scraping it loudly on the kitchen floor. "I have to work too, but I still find time for us. Why can't you turn up once in a while? Four times I told you about our counselling session last week, four times, and you still didn't come."

"I know. I'm sorry." Tim lays the spoon on the table. Sally fetches a cloth to wipe up the trail of coffee it has made.

"You could try putting reminders in my overall pockets," he says and hazards a grin.

"So you think that would help, would it? Do I need to issue a written invitation just to request a conversation with you?"

"I'll make time for us tonight, that's a promise. Why don't you take me to one of those nightclubs you like?"

A flash of something crosses her face. Anger? He isn't sure.

"Nothing doing on a Tuesday," she says. "Besides, I've finished with all that." Looking away, she draws her hand through her pony tail. Her long, red hair was the first thing that attracted him. He liked the fiery temper that went with it too. Still does.

"Let's go out to dinner then," he says.

"You'll be back in time?" She sounds eager, but sceptical.

"Sure. I'll need a few minutes when I get here to have a shower and get the gloss paint out of my fingernails."

"It will be too late to get a table after that."

"Just give me twenty minutes."

"I know your twenty minutes. By the time you're ready and we've driven somewhere, we'll be very late."

"Let's eat here then. Cook something together."

She lets out a bitter laugh. "Like that would ever happen. You can't cook. Are we at all compatible?"

"There've been good times."

Sally shrugs and tries drinking her coffee but recoils as it burns her mouth. Tim draws no satisfaction from the mishap. "We're going to get engaged, aren't we?"

"Does it count when you don't set a date?" she snaps.

He rests his hand over her wrist. "Just let me get the business on its feet, then we'll have time again."

She shakes off his hand. "What if I can't wait that long?"

"Don't say that," he replies. "You should be careful what you wish for."

The strange look in her eyes is back. This time Tim wonders if it's fear but doesn't know why.

"I don't wish for it," she says quietly. "I'm telling you what I think."

"So let me start putting things right tonight. I admi̱ might be better if you cook, but I'll bring the wine. S̱ thing nice. How about it?"

He takes her wrist again and this time she doesṉ him off.

CHAPTER FORTY

...rough the St. Maur's register for 1979. Anna
...joined the third form. Miss De Courtney
...as dropped off the top end. I wonder what
...levels – university or marriage to a rich
...er ambitions not quite work out the
...hudder. Thoughts of what became of
...a beauty therapy business touch a
...e Courtney E-P has lived a happy

...names appear every year but in the
...to check the names for the third form
...e are two possibilities for the intake in
...d Ann Harrod. Checking the third
...xt six years brings up a further crop
...ndering what to do next when it
...check all the registers for all the
...y another Ann/Annie/Anna joined
...Needles in haystacks are looking

"Supply drop!" Bernie comes in with a tray of tea and biscuits.

"Thanks. I could do with a break. Did you know there were nearly thirty pupils here in the eighties with the Christian name Annie or Anna, or else Ann with or without the 'e'?"

"It was a popular name back them. It's still quite fashionable now. Who are you looking for? I've been here since eighty-two. I might remember."

"You were a pupil here?" I ask, not sure I'd fancy returning to my school as a member of staff. My years at Charlton Hall High School for Girls were rocky at times. Thank God I had Terri there with me.

"Not a pupil," Bernie explains. "I was their youngest school secretary ever. I should have joined a convent proper with all the time I've spent here. But I wouldn't have been able to marry my Patrick and have our Ciara, so it's just as well I didn't. Life is for the living after all. Who is it you're after, love?"

I smile. If I dyed my hair purple, would I get as wise? I explain that the married name of the pupil I'd like to trace is Anna Gittens-Gold."

"But you don't know the maiden name, and telling me what she looks like probably won't help. She's bound to have changed since I knew her."

"She's tall, so she might have stood out in the early eighties."

"The other girl who came asking to see the school archives wanted to know about Annie Bones."

"What other girl?"

"Said she was a journalist wri▊▊g a story about school plays, wanted to know about the ▊▊▊ of school revues, and what they'd done since, to see whether any of them had gone into show business and all that. She said it could be good publicity for the school. Sister Agnes was all for it."

A journalist? My brain leaps a gear. "Did you get her name?"

"I can't remember, love. Sister Agnes took her straight through to her office to look through school magazines, so I didn't issue a temporary pass. She came a couple of weeks ago. Quite pushy she was, I recall."

Ice melts down my spine. The description fits Sonia Hanson. How close did I come to never finding out? It's astonishing yet depressingly typical that fifty miles beyond the *Gloucester Evening News* catchment, Sonia's photograph and murder are unknown. This woman is clearly unaware her recent journalist visitor is now dead. Without Alistair Hanson giving me the date that he and Sonia met Anna at the Cross Care Centre and without Neil's computer know-how to interrogate Sonia's internet activity that day, I would never have made the connection to St Maur's Convent.

"What else did the journalist want to know?" I ask.

"She asked me if I could remember any Anns from the early eighties who'd been in the school shows. I mentioned Annie Bones, who starred in the school play every year."

Hand shaking, I scroll my phone for the image I took of Anna and Gerald's wedding photo. "This was taken in the nineties. I don't suppose..."

Bernie removes her spectacles and peers closely. "She seems to have changed a lot since she left school, but it could be her. The nose is big enough, but she must have had her teeth fixed. Her teeth were terrible at school. And she's put on weight, because she was never that curvy. Bones by name and bones by nature. Never expected her to get married."

"If this is the same woman, she's very slender now. Maybe she put on weight for her wedding. Most people I know go on slimming diets before the big day," I quip, thinking of the stories my mum tells me of brides-to-be at her salon, armed with wedding preparation plans. Weight loss is top of most lists.

Bernie is still studying my phone. "Her husband must be tall. She only comes up to his chin."

Witnesses who know Gerald put him at five ten max. "Maybe the photographer had him standing on a step," I suggest. "What sort of a girl was Annie Bones?"

"Dreadful. The nuns teach the girls to see the best in everyone and I know I should, too, but Annie made that virtue hard work. She was so full of herself. Tried to run everyone else's life. Made pronouncements on everything."

"You seem to remember her well after all this time."

"We get one or two girls like her in most years, but she sticks in my mind as one of the worst."

"Did she do well academically?"

"Not really, although she was a bit of a technology boffin, always fiddling with gadgets, taking photographs with a fancy camera, listening to a transistor radio she'd built. For a convent girl in the early eighties she was decidedly odd. I'm afraid she was a bit of a laughing stock. After her mother died – suddenly, an electric shock, all very tragic – people tried to be sympathetic, but she was someone it was hard to have sympathy for."

"When did she leave the school?"

"She'll be in here somewhere." She picks up one of the registers. "Here you are. Annie Bones, sixth form, eighty-five to six."

I stare at the name in neat fountain pen, at a loss for what to ask next. I'm sure that the visiting journalist was Sonia Hanson, but how does this old register entry explain Gerald as her killer? Did Gerald even know Anna when she was at school? Why was Sonia interested in school plays? Did it have something to do with her theatre review column? These school plays are ancient history. I scroll my phone for the rest of the photographs from Anna's hallway. I spot a bandy-legged girl in a chorus-line from 1984, and the same girl as Snow White from the following year. What does any of this have to do with Sonia, or for that matter with Gerald?

"So I'm guessing Annie Bones did her last school play in the summer of eighty-five when she was in the lower sixth?" That would tally with the most recent photo in Anna's hall that I snapped on my phone.

"Sister Agnes got me to dig out the old school magazines for the other lady. We found a photo and review of the spring show in eighty-six. Annie Bones was in it. She was magnificent, apparently. Our Ciara was a baby so I didn't go, but I don't think it would have been my cup of tea. They always used to do a musical but, for some reason, they chose a heavy German play that year.

"Any chance you can remember which play?" My heart reaches top speed. Something's nagging so hard, my headache's coming back.

"I'll get the magazine. It should have the title."

While she goes back to the archives, I flick through the registers, forcing my way through my latest migraine. I've noticed each form lists the teacher's name. Maybe Gerald was Mr Chips before his days as Rambo, but there's no name resembling Gittens-Gold. I catch sight of the name Sally Parker for a pupil in a third form class in 1985, the year

Annie Bones was in the upper sixth. No doubt coincidence; Parker is a common enough surname.

When Bernie lays the magazine open in front of me, I see the playwright is Bertolt Brecht and the play's title is *The Good Woman of Szechwan*. Significant, I'm sure, though I haven't the foggiest why.

CHAPTER FORTY-ONE

The journey back passes in a miasma of headache and nonsensical thoughts. I try to phone Terri from the train for her drama-teacher take on Bertolt Brecht – no idea what I need to know but hope a chat will churn up something – but her phone is off. Unlike St Maur's and other private schools, Glevum Academy hasn't yet broken up for the summer. I send a rambling text she can pick up when she's not in the classroom.

Back at the flat, I slug three of my dodgy, over-the-internet painkillers and get in my car. I'm not seeing double, but when I check my reflection in the mirror, I know I won't get away with it. This morning I worried my appearance would remind my colleagues I need a brain scan; now I look full-lobotomy post-operative. Skin the colour of a St Maur's school register and eyes as dead as their encyclopaedias. I've got ninety minutes until the briefing. Only one thing for it. I don't want to, but the fix has to be quick.

"Sit down before you fall down," Mum says, leading me to a comfy chair in the waiting area. "I'll make you a cuppa."

Apart from a toddler on her mother's lap, having what may be her first haircut, there are no customers. Two stylists – Hayley and Travis – are beyond the open door of the store-room, working along shelves of products with an iPad.

"Where is everyone?" I ask Mum.

"Too hot. No one wants a new hair-do when they're going to sweat it out of shape as soon as they step outside. At least it gives us a chance for a stocktake."

While she operates the drinks machine, I close my eyes and take in the welcoming fragrances of the salon. It's the olfactory soundtrack of my life. I've been coming here forever – for haircuts edgier than anyone else at primary school, for a consolatory manicure when Marty Pearson dumped me in year 8, for a sophisticated up-do at the sixth form ball, for a pep-me-up wash and blow dry after a no-sleep forty-eight hours with newborn Jake.

Mum puts the mug of green tea in front of me and I thank her for remembering.

She taps her head. "I've got the tea and coffee preferences of a hundred clients up here, so I can certainly remember my daughter's." Her glance moves to my hair. "I know your styling preferences too, but given how quiet we are, how about we experiment a bit?" She peers at my face. "If you're well enough."

"I'm pushed for time," I say quickly. Mum's a great stylist, but my days of flicks and layers are long gone. "But I'd like a head massage." Despite my initial doubts, I've discovered Mum's wet massages are one of the few things that can see off a migraine.

"I knew as soon as you walked in you had a headache.

You need to get back to that hospital and demand a second opinion."

"They wouldn't have signed me off if there was a problem," I lie – the only signing off has been by me and that was more of a bolt than a self-discharge. "Today is just heat and work stress."

We go over to the basins. Pressing a lever, she raises my legs on the vinyl chair. I lie back into the stream of warm water as she sprays my head. The scent of coconut shampoo and the firm movement of her fingers are calming. I feel the knots in my scalp untangling already.

"By work stress, I suppose you mean the murder," Mum says.

"Among other things." And the more the murder entwines with the Gittens-Gold misper, the stressier it becomes.

"Poor family. Her husband will have his work cut out looking after three tinies. And how will her mother cope with the loss of her child?"

"The sad thing is mother and daughter were estranged. Hadn't spoken for four years."

Mum's grip on my head loosens. "A mother doesn't stop loving a daughter no matter what." This is dangerous ground. Throughout the years of teaching me beauty treatment techniques and showing me how to work a profit and loss account, she never dreamt I would get pregnant, chuck in my chance of owning my own salon and then join the police.

She restarts the massage and changes the subject. "Actually, now you're here, perhaps you can speak to Kelly."

"Your apprentice?"

"Her little brother is still giving her aggro and she's

worried. I suggested that a stern talking-to by a police officer might get him back on the straight and narrow."

"Wouldn't it be better coming from one in uniform?"

"I don't know that sort of police officer; I know you. Let me give her a ring. With us being so quiet I sent her home early, but you could have a word on the phone. Arrange a time to see the lad."

"Does it have to be today, or even this week? I'm going to be needed on two major enquiries for some time unless we get a breakthrough, and we've nothing much on either case so far."

"Don't be a donkey, Steph. Kelly's a good kid."

Calling me a donkey is the closest my mum gets to anger, but she only unleashes her equine expletive when she's seriously pissed off. She must be concerned about the girl. "Okay, give me her number," I say. "I'm not promising, but I'll aim to call by Monday."

"Perfect. But before the weekend if you can. It sounds like the brother is running wild."

When she's finished the massage, I manage – with difficulty – to dissuade her from using a hairdryer, pointing out that my ponytail will dry by the time I've walked through the hot town.

"Where have you parked?" she asks.

"Quay Street." Finding myself without change for a car park, I sought out a free space near the river.

"I'll walk with you," Mum says. "There's a pound shop down there where I should be able to get England banners."

"So you're a footie fan now we're doing well?"

"Purely business," she says, drying her hands and dropping the towel into a laundry basket. "I'm hoping some paraphernalia in the window might attract walk-ins."

"Cunning," I say.

"No harm in following the zeitgeist."

We both laugh, and she tells Hayley and Travis she'll help with the stocktake when she gets back.

By unspoken agreement, we avoid the cathedral forecourt, although it's no longer cordoned off, and skirt the far side of the playground. It's busier than when I visited last week with Harriet and Ned Smyth. The hot afternoon has brought out crabby toddlers and put-upon grandmas. I spot the same father and son in red football shirts. The boy licks a blue ice-cream. The father tilts his head in my direction, and that's more of an acknowledgement than I would have expected.

"Shouldn't that one be in school?" Mum mutters.

"I don't think he goes much."

The child bites the head off his ice-cream, drops the cone and heaves himself up the slide.

"I suppose the seagulls will eat it." Mum tuts. "Better than a toffee apple stick at least."

The mention of toffee apple prickles the skin under my drying ponytail. I try to recall my dream, but nothing comes to mind.

When we reach the Cross streets, Mum stops. "Now do I go to Marks and Sparks before the tea-time queue in the food hall, or grab what's left of the football stuff first before they run out? Retailers won't have expected England to reach the semi-finals."

My neck prickles again. Marks and Spencer. I think of the logo search I carried out on my phone this morning. It's something else that's nagging.

Mum decides on the food shop first and leaves me alone with my muddled thoughts.

272

CHAPTER FORTY-TWO

INCIDENT ROOM – TUESDAY 10TH JULY, 4.00 P.M.

I needn't have worried about looking like the odd zombie out. My colleagues also appear dead from the neck up. And their bodies below aren't much better – slouching shoulders, sprawling legs, damp patches at the underarms, sleeves rolled, top three buttons undone.

Only Harriet, standing at the front to give her briefing, is still crisp in a pale green polo shirt and matching cotton trousers. The archetypal cool cucumber. On days like this, her inexperience shows. She still thinks we are making progress. Those of us older and wiser can't be arsed.

After she's summarised everything that her most recent phone call with her contact in Canberra has revealed about the real Gerald Gittens, Tony raises the possibility of tracking the imposter to Australia.

"Gittens-Gold could have skipped the UK on another false passport." He lets out a languid breath, clearly going through the motions of the line of enquiry he's tried before. "A cold-blooded killer would have more than one fake identity. He's been duping his wife for years, so he's good at covering his tracks."

"If she was duped," I mutter.

"What's that?" Kevin asks, but even the boss sounds lethargic. He stands in front of his laptop, but leans heavily against the desk.

"Nothing." Although I got Bernie to make a photocopy of the St Maur's theatre article, the link I've found between Anna Gittens-Gold and Sonia Hanson is too tenuous to mention. Anna's appearance in a school play thirty years ago bears the same name as an empty file on Sonia's computer. *Szechwan*. A theatre connection? Is someone playing a part?

Why can't people be what they were supposed to be? Why does a carefree woman applying her lip-gloss on a train have to be a feckless mother involved with a convicted criminal? What makes black-robed Goths feed the ducks with wholemeal bread? And why does an up-and-coming school entrepreneur wear a nun's habit? If Sister Agnes, the head teacher at St Maur's, hadn't seen the PR value of a journalist's visit, would she have given Sonia the school magazines? If people stuck to their intended roles, would Sonia still be alive?

Harriet turns out not to be the only young'un with fire in her belly despite the already fiery heat in the room. Cally and Jordan give us an animated double act on what more they've found out about Sonia's colleagues at the newspaper. Laidback Gerry Donnelly wasn't always so easy-going. In his youth he'd been on a watch list for football hooliganism. Shiny-haired Lauren Chambers was banned from a social media platform last year for inappropriate content. Apparently there was too much flesh on show in her photo feed.

Tony slouches a little less in his chair when Cally explains that.

"Not the murdering kind, though," I say. "Neither Gerry nor Lauren has to kill to get their own way." Things happen for people like them. "Besides, their editor said Sonia wasn't in the running for the deputy editor job, so what motive would Gary or Lauren have to kill her?"

At least Sonia died before she got turned down. Disillusioned ambition would have been hard to bear. She had been a ferret of a journalist, popping up everywhere, rubbing everyone up the wrong way, sometimes digging where there was nothing to find. She could have been on a wild goose chase to St Maur's. Finding out about Anna's school play might have still been a complete dead end for whatever story she was hoping to write. According to the school secretary, Sonia hadn't jumped for joy or shouted Eureka during her visit to the convent. Was she just a woman in the workplace clutching at straws – or at the greasy pole to promotion because she knew her boss wouldn't give her a leg up?

Who resented her ambition more – her boss or her husband? Alistair Hanson, lawyer cum househusband? Sally Parker, Gerald's counselling client and girlfriend of the workaholic Tim Vale, would have sympathised with Alistair. I keep coming back to Sally Parker, and not just because I saw her namesake in a St Maur's register. There's something else I can't fathom. Where does a disgruntled woman at her first counselling session fit into Sonia's murder or Gerald's disappearance? Sally resents her partner's ambition. While he's building his decorating business, he's never around for her. Did Alistair Hanson feel the same? Was he frustrated by an ambitious wife who ignored her domestic responsibilities? But her death has only made things worse. The precious little time she spent at home has gone now. If he got angry enough, he might not have been thinking that logically. Did he finally snap when she spent one late night too many at the newspaper office?

My eyes startle open as I become aware that Tony is talking now, from his seat – no sweating it out front for him. My phone pulses in my pocket. Two texts, both from Mum.

Kelly's been in touch. Can you call me?

And just to be clear, the follow-up reads: *asap.*

"I did more background checks on Sonia's brothers," Tony says. "I found a woman who was at school with them. Apparently Jerome Clarke had a temper."

"Did he now?" Kevin wafts his papers close to his face.

"Had a reputation for it. He even started a fight in the playground with his older brother."

"Olivier?"

Tony nods. "Keeping it in the family. If there was sibling violence then, what's to say it didn't extend to the sister after she cost them their antique business? If it's all right with you, boss, I'd like to pay them a visit tomorrow."

Kevin agrees, but is Tony right? Do passion and dishonour go hand in hand – hand around neck? "Just because Jerome Clarke was handy with his fists at school, it doesn't mean he'd strangle a woman," I say.

"Doesn't rule him out either," Tony counters.

"Ten minutes ago your money was on Gerald doing a Lord Lucan."

"I'm capable of pursuing more than one line of enquiry."

He's barely capable of tying shoe laces, but I don't take the bait.

No one else has anything to say, perhaps figuring the room is full of as much hot air as it can take. Kevin allocates tomorrow's tasks. I'm saddled with another trip to the Cross Care Centre to see if another round with the manager, Rosemary Davies, will shake out new nuggets about Gerald. Old ground and wrong enquiry. I'd rather be opening new lines on Sonia Hanson. Maybe something will break early tomorrow and plans will change. Here's hoping.

The second that Kevin closes his laptop, Harriet's out of her seat.

"In a rush?" I ask.

"Rehearsal." She strides to the door way faster than the room thermometer should allow.

"I thought that was Thursdays."

"Tuesdays and Thursdays." And she's gone.

I sit back, smiling. Connection made. Maybe one mystery has been solved today.

CHAPTER FORTY-THREE

Jake's bedroom door closes with the gentlest click, but my mum-antenna picks it up. Moving more quietly than his usual teenage gangliness allows, he goes into the hall.

I meet him at the front door with my arms folded. "Going out already?"

Startled, he takes a step back. I'm sure he's toying with a retreat to his room. But he brazens it out. "I said so this morning, remember."

"I'm not senile."

"Yeah. Sorry. Can I – er – go?" He makes to get past me but thinks better of it when I don't step aside.

"What time will you be back?"

"Ten. Maybe eleven."

"On a college night?"

"It's two weeks to the end of term," he says tetchily. "They'll repeat the stuff in September."

"Make it ten thirty. Humour a mother who thinks every day of education is important." I suppress another smile. It's not exactly a lie – I like having good A levels in my back pocket – but school hardly prepared me for the real world.

"I'll try but..." He responds slowly, his eyes looking upwards as if searching his brain for a plausible excuse. "Brad and I want to devote enough time to our project."

"What project would that be? One the teachers are going to repeat in September?"

"No... well... yes. But the thing is..." His speech speeds up as he latches onto a backstory. "Brad's really into it. He's a stickler for putting in the time."

"Brad's a stickler?" That may come as a surprise to his mother, Terri. She'll be thrilled.

"Yeah. Brad..." He rubs his hair and looks at the front door longingly.

I go in for the close. "Who do you really mean – Brad or the director?"

The small amount of acne at his temples – not normally detectable on his handsome face – glows red.

"You know, the director of the pantomime for which you and Brad are rehearsing."

His expression sets for a denial but veers into surprise. "How did you find out?"

"I'm a detective." When Harriet mentioned her rehearsals were Tuesdays and Thursdays, I joined the dots on Jake's mysterious disappearances. The sense of relief was a wonder drug and my headache vanished as soon as I realised Jake wasn't hanging round street corners. "Why the secrecy?"

"That really is down to Brad. Because Terri's a drama teacher, he doesn't want her to know until he's got a part. He wants to prepare for the auditions without her help."

"Why the sudden interest in treading the boards?"

A puzzled frown appears, but his colour has returned to normal.

"It's a theatrical term," I explain. "You'll get to know several now you're a luvvie."

There's an eye roll but he doesn't bite.

"So go on then, why the sudden interest in drama?"

"It looks good on personal statements for uni applications. Admissions tutors want rounded candidates. I need to show I'm not just a knuckle-headed sports guy."

"What part in the panto do you want?"

"Brad and I are going to try out for two rugby-playing ugly sisters."

Really going against type, then. "Good for you." I step aside. "Say hi to Harriet. One of my colleagues is auditioning."

"Oh, right. The older cast don't mix with us much. So is eleven all right now you know? The director really is a stickler. She goes over every scene until we're perfect."

Nodding, I open the door. So he and Harriet, in the same theatre club, haven't made the connection to me. Not surprising if Harriet is as circumspect about her job as I am. Terri and I learnt early on to fabricate bios when we're out socially. Tell a stranger you're a teacher and they'll ask for help with their offspring's maths homework. Mention you're a police officer and they'll demand you tackle vandalism in their neighbourhood. Terri and I both say we're army officers. No one responds with: "I'm thinking of invading Libya, what armoured tanks do you advise?" The conversation tends to move on. Funny how that line has worked differently for the fake Gerald.

———

Keeping Hamish indoors all day is torture for them both. Tracey knows dogs have a sense of smell forty times better than humans, but didn't realise he'd be able to scent a bitch through three brick walls. His whining only stopped for a while after she fed him and he fell asleep. But adding an extra feed to his diet isn't a long-term solution. Combined with restricted access to walks, it will damage his health.

Automatically, she reaches for her fleece, but the afternoon is too hot for woollies. Pity, though. The dark green shows less dirt and blood than her polo shirt, and that's almost as grubby as her bandage. After eight days, the deep scratch must have healed. She'll see to it when she gets back, but her eardrums will explode if she doesn't get Hamish outside now.

When she picks up his lead, he shoots across the kitchen floor and leaps at her. A wee fella he might be, but there are springs in his legs, and his snout connects with her nether regions. She grasps his collar and forces him to the ground. The lead has a calming effect and he walks sensibly through the house, his claws tapping on the hall tiles.

Once the door is open, she pulls back with her full weight, anticipating his next move. In a lunge, he hits the connecting fence to next door, his throat pressed against his collar. She scoops him into her arms. It's not easy to keep hold as she negotiates the front gate, but she manages and turns right, away from the bitch's lair.

When she gets to Potter Street, she puts him down. To her relief, he trots beside her and they move towards the pedestrian crossing. Her plan is a walk along the towpath near Quay Street, where there will be plenty of people about at this time of day. After her recent encounters, Tracey is done with secluded places. He'll have to stay on the lead, but at least he'll feel grass under his paws – or what passes for grass in this drought. The summer has been relentless. At times she's found herself missing Scotland despite the midges.

"Mrs Chiles?" a voice calls out.

She halts abruptly. Hamish circles, looking up.

Across the road, a man is waving. "Can I have a word?"

It can't be, can it? Is nowhere safe? She lifts Hamish and, staggering, retraces their steps. Him again? The shock makes it hard to catch her breath and she has to put the dog on the ground. Hamish seems to remember what's waiting near home and sets off at speed. Tracey sprints behind, hanging onto the lead for life.

When they turn into Cathedral Street, she glances back and nearly dies. The man is still in view, following them at a distance. She grabs Hamish, bolts along the street and through the gate, ignoring his yelps. One-handedly, she gets the key to the lock and by some miracle doesn't drop it.

After letting Hamish down inside, she slams the door. Double lock, chain, two bolts. Panting, she sits with her back pressed against it.

A few minutes later, the bell rings and Hamish's deafening barks bounce off the tiled floor.

CHAPTER FORTY-FOUR

The benefit of being a professional French translator is that Sally can refer to the source language for the best recipes. Boeuf Bourguignon, Tim's favourite. But with no time to marinade, she's had to go for a version that's *simple et rapide*. As she adds the chopped bacon to the pan of browned beef, the salty aroma makes her stomach growl.

Typical Tim. No thought. A grandiose gesture of mid-week supper together that leaves her with no time to prepare. Such a contrast to Gerald. The meals they shared were planned to the minute, dates and times decided by him a week in advance. Sally took it as evidence that he wasn't a free agent; any absences from home would have to be explained to a wife. But it hadn't stopped her. At her age, it felt good to have options. Although Tim didn't *know* – only suspected – she was seeing someone else, the suspicion revived his interest for a while and even prompted mention of an engagement. Until it waned and he put his business first again. But tonight could make up for that. Maybe. She adds the chopped onions and carrots before turning down the heat. If he gets here by 7.30 p.m., she'll believe he meant what he said.

In the sink the potatoes are waiting to be peeled, but when she picks up the knife, her annoyance returns. How many root vegetables has she scrubbed for a man and still no ring on her finger? There have been near misses over the years. Better bets than Tim, much better than Gerald. Crossly, she takes the knife to a potato and gouges out a thick layer of skin.

Looking back over the last few weeks, she'd have to say Gerald was the bigger player. What else could she call it but leading her on? The chat-up in the club – which comprised on his part asking questions and straining against the deafening music for her answers. Of course, she knows now that listening was his day job. Perhaps he only ever saw her as a chance to practise his counselling skills.

Back at the hob, she folds in flour and stirs. She dabs her forehead with paper towel, knowing she's luckier than most this month as the thick cottage walls keep out the heatwave, but the sizzling pan makes the kitchen hot, and her annoyance at Tim and Gerald has warmed to anger.

On the counter is the supermarket plonk she grabbed when she went into Gloucester earlier to get the ingredients. After dousing the beef mixture in the thin red liquid, she adds a spoonful of honey to sweeten the acidic bouquet it's giving off.

She snatches another potato out of the sink. With Gerald out of the picture, she and Tim can get back on track, but there's frustration she'll never find out why the older man left in the middle of their last meal together. She holds up the potato, recalling that it was the last time she made Gratin Dauphinois. The melted gruyère was sumptuous in her mouth and he listened while she talked about becoming a translator from the early promise she'd shown in languages at her private school to getting a first at Exeter. But the open, engaged face opposite her changed. The blue eyes flickered shut, the moustached mouth twisted. Pulling back from the coffee table, he said he was awfully sorry but he'd remembered something he had to do. The food was delicious, thank you. He'd be in touch. Just her luck. Two men in her life: one always arrives late and the other leaves abruptly never to return.

There's a knock at the back door that startles her and sends Fool shooting into the kitchen through the cat flap. Early? Tim is early! Her body stiffens as her annoyance is back. Trust him to turn over a new leaf when the Boeuf Bourguignon is a good two hours from ready and she hasn't started cooking the potatoes or even prepared the red cabbage. Doesn't he know French cuisine doesn't materialise by magic wand? He could at least use the key she gave him, or has he lost it? Wouldn't surprise her.

Then she smiles. When has he ever started an evening together at six? This is a supreme effort on his part. Proof that he means what he says. The night bodes well. She's glad she's already showered and shaved her legs. In her head she does a hasty replan of the menu. Baked potatoes – most of them are still in their jackets – and a salad she can prepare while they talk in the kitchen. Quickly she tips the potatoes into a sieve and gets out a baking tray. She'll dry them off after she's let him in and put them straight in the oven.

"Just a minute," she calls.

Although it's a bit soon, she tips her plate of sliced mushrooms into the pan on the hob and roots through the cupboards for a big enough casserole dish.

"I'm coming," she shouts when he knocks again. Keeping him waiting is no bad thing.

After transferring the contents of the pan to the dish, she turns on the oven and puts it in. The food can look after itself on a low heat, while she and Tim build up a high heat upstairs.

She scoops up the cat and bolts the cat flap. "And you can stay outside; we don't need an audience."

Still smiling, she opens the door.

CHAPTER FORTY-FIVE

Tim Vale rings the bell. Through the solid oak door, he hears it chime like a grandfather clock. The sound is the biggest thing about this cottage. Everything else is tiny and, to Tim, poky. It's what comes of spending his days wallpapering five-bed houses; he's got a taste for space. It's one reason he's held off suggesting they move in together. But he'll have to broach it soon. After tonight.

As he presses the bell again, he goes over in his mind the speech he has prepared. It's only short and there's still no ring to go with it, but he means it this time. The engagement he suggested a couple of months ago, when he got wind of another bloke on the scene, was – he realises now – just to mark his territory. Today is for love.

Should he have knocked off early, headed into town to buy a ring? But as he chimes the bell again, he knows that would have been a bad move. Sally is the kind of independent woman who would want to choose her own engagement ring. But he's not completely empty-handed. The cava he got from Sainsbury's should show he's trying.

When she still doesn't answer, he feels rattled. Now what's he done wrong? Why keep him waiting when she was the one insisting he shouldn't be late? A smile creeps over his face. Maybe she's upstairs, putting on make-up while wearing nothing but her underwear. New underwear – black probably, or red to match her hair.

Something rubs his legs. He looks down as the cat mewls then stalks away. So she's shut him out. Another sign that's promising. He remembers something. Tapping himself down, he searches for the pocket he's put his van keys in and finds them in his jacket. It's too hot for jackets and, as someone who works in overalls, he feels awkward. But he wants to please her, and if the first impression goes well, he won't be wearing it for long.

When she still hasn't answered after another half minute, he searches his keyring for her key. He's had it since she got him to feed that cat while she was at a translators' conference. The decision not to give it back and her not requesting it seemed significant at the time, but when he tested the waters by continuing to ring the bell whenever he visited, she never asked why he hadn't used his key. He figured its use was a one off.

But now, after a few jinks in the sturdy lock, he gets it to work and the door creeps open.

The sofa has its back to him and beyond it the coffee table is dressed for dinner. Two place settings, red napkins in tall-stemmed wine glasses, white candles. No sign of Sally through the open kitchen door, although the cooking smells are divine. His guess was right; she's upstairs. She must have known he'd get the message when she didn't come down and he'd use his key.

Still holding the cava, he takes the stairs two at a time. They can drink it from the bottle, an aperitif. In bed.

The bathroom door is open. She's not in there but his groin swells as he breathes in the scent of the still damp atmosphere. Nor is she in the bedroom, although a short, black dress is laid out on the bed, red sandals on the floor nearby. She must be in the kitchen after all.

But when he goes back down and checks properly, she isn't there. Something in the oven gives off rich notes of wine and onion. Half-peeled potatoes balance in a sieve over the sink. A bulb of garlic and an unopened packet of cheese are on a chopping board beside a block of runny butter and a plastic bottle of milk. She must have popped out for an ingredient, but given the remoteness of the village, a pop means a 20-minute drive to Tufton Retail Park. Should he put the milk and butter in the fridge? Best not interfere. No point in winding her up when the evening is looking promising.

His mood changes when he sees the wine and flowers on the other worktop. He's sure the wine has the same posh label as the empty bottle he found in her recycling bin. Knowing her secret tipple was chardonnay, he'd tackled her about her unusual choice. It was rare for them to have a confrontation that he initiated, but it led to her angry admission she was seeing someone else.

So has the other man been here tonight? Pink carnations still wrapped in paper suggest a visitor. Is Sally telling him something? Spicy red wine and flowers – like a metaphor in those bloody French books she reads. Despite Tim's overtures at lunchtime, she's chosen the other man. They've left out his gifts and made themselves scarce until Tim gets the message.

His father said it all along. For months, Tim ignored him,

but wise old Councillor Vale knows life. "A woman who objects to a man's business ventures is not worth a fig," he said. Tim should have listened. His father's marriage to his mother is thirty-six years solid, and his business sold for a packet when he retired. Tim storms to the front door.

Then he stops. Why should he scarper? Let Sally and her crock of a boyfriend look him in the eye and say it. Tim decides he's going to find the nearest thing to a sports channel on her TV, sprawl on the sofa and wait. If he didn't know now that he would be driving home instead of staying the night, he'd open the fancy red and guzzle the lot.

But when he steps round the sofa he sees her lying on it. On her back, both legs twisted at awkward angles. One black slipper still on; the other on the floor. Her neck is a vivid purple and her eyes stare out, unblinking.

CHAPTER FORTY-SIX

In our separate cars, Harriet and I arrive in Klox at the same time. A uniformed officer stands by a cordon in the lane and directs us to the parking area, a recreation ground with a well-kept cricket pitch. We keep off the green, although I doubt this hamlet will hear the sound of leather on willow for a while, now murder has shattered their notion of quaint village life.

We don't enter the cordon, but Siobhan Evans, after stripping off her forensic gear, comes out to the car park. This initial briefing with our pathologist is short and comes with the familiar prologue: "I'll know more when we've examined the body at the lab." The upshot is that Sally Parker has been strangled and, like Sonia Hanson, it appears to be with bare hands.

"Same killer?" Harriet asks.

"Can't possibly say at this stage."

"About what time?"

"The body can't answer that, but my loose guestimate is after five thirty."

"How loose?"

"It depends how good her oven is." Siobhan waits for us to frown, then carries on. "The casserole was just starting to dry out. We got it out at eight fifteen, so I reckon the most it had been on was two and a half hours. Of course, I can't be sure it was the victim who made the meal, but if it was her, she was likely alive and prepping Boeuf Bourguignon at five thirty."

Harriet looks out to the road where an ambulance has its doors open. Tim Vale sits just inside with a foil blanket over his shoulders. "Maybe he didn't like stew."

"We've swabbed him," Siobhan says, "taken samples from under the fingernails and bagged his clothing. My med school days of dealing with the living are prehistoric, but I'd diagnose deep shock. A hospital bed for the night would be better than a police cell."

"Has he said anything?"

"Over and over he says he wishes he'd got here earlier. He had the presence of mind to phone the emergency services, but he's been less coherent since."

When Siobhan has nothing more for us, we head over and climb into the ambulance to sit opposite the suspect. He raises his head. At this time of the summer's evening, there's enough light to see his eyes are red-rimmed and his skin is bleached.

His head dips again and he whispers, "I should have got here earlier. She wanted me to. She always wanted me to."

"What time did you get here?"

Harriet's gentle tones coax a reply. "Seven thirty. I went to my place after work for a shower and to get changed." The foil blanket slips and he looks down at the temporary outfit he's wearing. Grey joggers and a navy hoodie – goodness knows who's provided them. More suited to a lazy winter's night in front of the fire, but he doesn't look too hot. In fact he's shivering.

As he's responding to her, I let Harriet continue leading the questions. "And you used your own key to enter?"

He gives a hollow chuckle and nods.

"Was anything out of place when you walked in?"

"Apart from my fiancée... like... that." He chokes back tears.

Harriet, no stranger to losing a loved one to murder, presses on. "We're sorry for your loss. If you can talk us through exactly what you saw, what you did, we can set about catching whoever did this to her."

"I should have got here earlier," he replies, rocking back and forth. Whether he's a traumatised man or an accomplished actor, I don't yet know.

"How soon after arriving did you phone the police?" I ask. We need to see whether his version tallies with any comings and goings the neighbours observed.

"A few minutes. I didn't see her straight away. I looked for her upstairs first, and in the kitchen, but she wasn't... The wine." His head shots up and he stares at me. "It was him, wasn't it? The one in the newspaper who's done a runner."

I cock an eyebrow at Harriet. Does he mean Gerald? If Tim Vale is going to frame someone, maybe start with someone who's not dead or hiding in Australia. "Can you explain that remark?"

"Sally had been seeing someone. She wouldn't tell me who, but when I asked around, people said they'd seen her with an older man in a hat. Last week she told me they were finished, but it's his wine in the kitchen. You can check for prints, can't you?"

Our crime scene investigators will be inside dusting every surface. We might get lucky if this was an impetuous killing, but if it was planned – possibly by Tim – the killer will have cleaned up.

"What makes you think the wine was brought into the cottage tonight?"

"Sally only buys white unless she's cooking – there's an empty bottle of red on the window sill. It's bound to be in the casserole, but another red is on the side." Tears prick his eyes. "When I arrived, I thought she was cooking for me, but I was wrong. The meal was for him, and look how he repaid her."

"Because of the unopened bottle?" Harriet steers him back on track.

"When I found a bottle with the same fancy label in the recycling a few weeks back, we had a row. It's when she told me another guy had been for dinner. Nothing happened between them, she said, but what business was it of mine as we weren't exclusive." He stares at me again. "This is my fault, isn't it?"

I wait, curious to see what's coming. He doesn't hold back.

"It was after that night I mentioned getting engaged. Tonight was going to be about making it official. What if he couldn't take no for an answer? If I hadn't mentioned engagement, she wouldn't have dumped him and he wouldn't have... done that." He looks out of the ambulance towards the cottage. Despite it still being light, all the house lights are on and a forensic-suited figure moves at an upstairs window. Police do-not-cross tape adorns the hawthorn hedge. "I should have got here sooner... sooner." He folds into sobs and we conclude the interview.

CHAPTER FORTY-SEVEN

WEDNESDAY 11TH JULY

The local and national headlines this hour. West Gloucester-shire Police have opened a murder enquiry following the discovery of a body at a property in Klox yesterday evening. Final preparations are underway for the start of tomorrow's four-day visit by US president Donald Trump. Football fans are converging on Moscow ahead of tonight's World Cup semi-final clash between England and Croatia.

Despite working on the new case late into the evening, I am wide awake again at first light. Instead of my thoughts going to Sally Parker, I'm chewing over St Maur's Convent and why Sonia Hanson showed an interest in school theatre productions from thirty-odd years ago. Is that empty file *Szechwan* on Sonia's computer of key importance or an idle fancy that never developed? I tried phoning Terri at ten last night but she didn't pick up. I send another text about the Brecht play of that name now, hoping she'll see it before she sets off for school.

No sooner have I put the phone down, than it pings. A

295

reply, great. Terri might be able to straighten out my thinking.

But the text is from Mum. *If you're up, ring me.*

Damn. I forgot to follow up the text she sent during yesterday's briefing.

She answers as soon as I've finished dialling and gets to the point without a greeting. "Can you come to the salon before work? Kelly's here with her brother. You need to hear this."

There are three reasons I should demur: Sally Parker, Sonia Hanson and Gerald-Gittens-Gold, but I tell her I'll be right over. Hopefully whatever's the matter won't take long.

———

The salon window is adorned with plastic England flags and cut-outs of some of the squad. The flimsiness of the cardboard suggests Mum had to scrape the pound shop barrel to find anything still in stock.

They're not open yet but Mum is looking out for me and unlocks the door. Inside, a junior stylist is wiping down the reception desk and two kids sit in the waiting area. I recognise the girl as Kelly even though I don't think I've seen her without make-up before. Younger, prettier than usual, more like her seventeen years, but, clasping her knees, she also looks vulnerable and on edge.

Beside her is a boy of about twelve. His school shirt is ironed, but a dark stain decorates the hem. His small brown eyes are a match for Kelly's. He appears both young and old, like an extra in *Bugsy Malone*. I imagine him looking the same at sixty.

Mum squats on the low table in front of them. "Can you explain, Dominic? Tell Steph what Kelly told me."

"It's Dommo," he mutters. The voice is more child than teen.

"Just tell her." Kelly nudges his arm. "Tell her what you hid in your bedroom."

The boy's brown eyes harden. "I just found it. It was all burnt anyway. Nobody wanted it."

"Wanted what?" I ask.

"A bag. Me and me mates found a fire by the towpath. We didn't start it. We watched it for a while. I went back after school. The fire must have gone out before everything got burnt up. The bag was a bit melted and all black but..." He looks at Kelly.

"Go on," she says.

"There was a purse with money inside. I didn't spend it or anything. Just put it under my bed."

He reminds me of Jake at this age. If he'd found a bag in a pile of ash where the dossers hang out, he would also have been daft enough to bring it home.

"Do you want me to hand it in at the police station for you? Is that it?" I ask.

"I... Dunno."

"Tell her what else," Kelly says.

Dommo shrugs and looks at the bowl of oranges on the reception desk. It's always there, looking fresh, although I've never seen any get eaten.

When he doesn't speak, Kelly fills in more detail. "There was soot at the bottom of his sheet. That's when I looked under the bed and I found the bag and the purse. It was all black and flaky but I made out the name on the driving licence." She faces me. "*Mrs Sonia Hanson*. That's the woman who was murdered, isn't it?"

An avalanche of thoughts overtake and I don't know what to ask next. Could the murder of a thirty-six-year-old journalist have been orchestrated by a young boy? I remember the youthful voice on the 999 call about the man on the jetty. Is this scruffy kid responsible?

With a supreme effort to conceal my suspicions, I say gently, "Were you in Sharpness on Saturday?"

"Where's that?" he asks his sister.

"Dommo was home all day. In the morning I stood over him while he learnt his spellings, and after a sandwich he watched footie on TV." She flushes a little. "We don't go out much."

My suspicions subside. His bare arms carry no tan. The indoor alibi Kelly has given him would seem to stack up. But I have to make sure. Squatting beside my mother, I say, "You won't be in any trouble if you say yes; have you ever phoned the emergency services?"

Dommo and Kelly exchange a worried glance. "The ambulance lady said he did the right thing," she says. "You can die of alcohol poisoning."

My mother puts her hand on Kelly's wrist. "Steph's not talking about that time with your mum, love. Has Dommo called more recently?"

Dommo shakes his head. So does Kelly.

"Where's the bag now?" I ask.

"Still in his bedroom," she says. "With the other stuff."

"What other stuff?" I say slowly, turning to Dommo.

He squirms under my gaze. "There were some other things in the fire. I kept them."

"You should see the state of his carpet under the bed. I doubt I'll ever get the stains out," Kelly says.

"And you kept everything?" I'm struggling to catch my breath, imagining an infuriated Kelly putting Dommo's cache in the dustbin before coming here and picturing myself in a sweaty race against time to intercept the council bin collectors.

"It's all under his bed," she says. "I thought we shouldn't mess up forensics."

I smile. Even overwhelmed teenage girls have time to watch *CSI*. "Can you show me?"

"What, now?" Kelly says. "There isn't another bus for twenty minutes. It will make Dommo late for school again."

"Your mum still ill?" My mother asks gently.

"Well, you know. She can't drive." Kelly blinks fast.

"We'll go in my car," I suggest. "Afterwards I'll drop Dommo at school and you back here."

As we go to my car in Quay Street at a slow, teenage lollop, I text Kevin with apologies. I'm going to be late to another briefing, but I assure him I'll be worth the wait.

CHAPTER FORTY-EIGHT

After collecting the burnt handbag from Dommo's surprisingly tidy bedroom – thanks no doubt to young Kelly's cleaning efforts – I sign it in at the station as evidence and ask for it to be fast-tracked to Forensics.

Harriet is out front in full flow when I slip in the back row of the briefing. Her restless stance, balancing from one foot to the other, says she's bursting to tell us something but is making a supreme effort to give her story a beginning, middle and end.

"According to Tim Vale, the first red wine bottle appeared in Sally's recycling about two weeks ago. We only had his word and, if he's telling the truth, a hazy memory that the label on it was the same as on the bottle left in Sally's kitchen last night." She beams at us. "However, you won't believe how lucky I got with the bottle found in Sally Parker's kitchen yesterday."

In the row in front of me, Tony puts his head in his hands as his shoulders shake. He's obviously come up with a punchline too dirty to share.

"Tim was right about it being a fancy make," Harriet continues. "The first off-licence I tried claimed it as theirs. They are the only wine shop for thirty miles that sells it. And because of the price – thirty-five quid – they don't sell many. The manager checked his till rolls and found only two recent sales: one in June and one yesterday. He keeps the CCTV for a month." She turns to Kevin, who loads an image onto the big screen.

It's a still from the shop. Along the bottom is the date and time code: 14.6.2018 16:30. Front and centre, paying cash over the counter: with a straw hat and grey moustache, a dead ringer for another image we hold. I glance at our incident board. The soft focus portrait of Gerald Gittens-Gold radiates respectability. Cameras and lies.

Harriet waits for the excitement around the briefing room to die down before asking her killer question. "Who do you think was caught on CCTV buying the second bottle yesterday?"

"Tracey Chiles?" Tony calls out, generating a few titters. And I hold my breath in case Kevin asks me about the follow-up visit I have so far avoided making. But the guessing game moves on.

"Carl Bryant," Jordan offers.

Tony has another go. "Joking aside, is it one of the Clarkes? I plan to call at their shop after this and see what shakes out. They could be..."

Kevin holds up his hand, putting Tony on pause. "You'd better tell him, Harriet."

"Is it Tim Vale, trying a double bluff?" Cally butts in. "Sally's partner is the one who drew our attention to the wine."

That seems like a decent guess, but Harriet's poker face

still gives nothing away, so I lob in another name as something still nags about the Brecht play performed at St Maur's. "Gerald's wife, Anna."

Harriet shakes her head. You're all wrong." She waves at Kevin with a flourish.

Like a magician's assistant, Kevin loads another still. Apart from a different date and time code: 10.7.2018 11:30, it's a carbon copy of the previous still. Handing over cash is Gerald Gittens-Gold.

There are gasps around the room, the loudest being from me. Although I was convinced his suicide was faked, I never thought he was still strolling the streets of Gloucester. I thought he'd either absconded or – in my wildest imaginings – Anna had buried him under the patio.

"Have you interviewed the assistant who served him?" I ask.

"It was the manager's nineteen-year-old son on both occasions, but the lad can't recall the customer at all. Given he spent the entire time I was talking to him scrolling YouTube, I believe him. Uniform are asking neighbouring retailers, but despite the media coverage, no one seems to have noticed a misper in their midst. And not only a misper, but quite probably a double murderer."

With another flourish, Harriet takes her seat. Kevin moves to the front of the room.

"We need to find this man urgently. Throw the net wider and interview more premises' owners. Capture every piece of city centre CCTV for yesterday. Where has this guy been, where is he likely to go now?

"Tony and Harriet, question his neighbours again. Are they sure they haven't seen him or anyone else apart from the wife entering and exiting his bungalow? Then call on her.

Give her the joyous news she's not a widow any more. See how she reacts."

"I'll take that one, Kev," I say. That nagging feeling makes me need to study her response face to face.

But Kevin shakes his head. "I want you to go to the Cross Care Centre. The manager said Sally Parker met Gerald at one counselling session, but is that the truth?"

It's a fair line of enquiry and I make a note, adding *nightclub*. It's almost certain Sally first met him out clubbing, and I may need to head back to the land of throbbing bass tonight for confirmation.

Most of us pack away our stuff, but the front row, which include Jordan, are still waiting for instructions.

Kevin gives them now. "Until Siobhan Evans has done the post mortem on Sally Parker and can say with some confidence it's the same killer, we have to treat Sonia Hanson as a separate enquiry. Revisit all her email correspondence and examine traffic on the newspaper website. Follow up negative comments and seek out anyone with an axe to grind against the newspaper in general or Sonia in particular."

He tells us to reconvene at one thirty p.m. The determined set of his expression says he's expecting us to come with answers.

CHAPTER FORTY-NINE

Before I do as I'm told, I return to the Forensics bunker to chivvy Neil about Sonia's handbag. Well aware the sweet talk would be better coming from Harriet, I set my face to my best approximation of charm as I open the door.

But he's already made a start. The bag and its contents are laid out in separate evidence bags and he's typing his inventory notes.

He stands up, rubbing his hair. "Tests aren't done yet, sorry."

Why the apology? Has Naomi Thomas had a quiet word with him too? The woman is on a fruitless mission if she's hoping to bring about behaviour change in Forensics. Why would they care what a management-speaky superintendent says? Let's face it, they call the shots on most cases.

But keeping to my end of the civility rules Thomas has laid down, I say, "That's fine. I didn't expect results yet. Just checking things are moving." I approach the exhibits desk. "But can you tell me anything at all about this lot?"

"We'll be as quick as we can, I promise," he says, hand-combing his hair again. "But part of the handbag burnt away, so contents at that end are cinders. Not sure we have the budget for reconstruction."

The exhibit bag he lifts contains lumpy black ash. I take it from him and press against the see-through cover. I'm no scientist, but I used to be a young mum. My best guess at the frazzled contents of Sonia's handbag are wet wipes, plasters and a box of raisins.

Neil picks up a clutch of other evidence bags. "Her purse survived more or less intact. The lab will test for prints, but as the kid who found it had his paws all over, I'm not hopeful." He spreads them out on the desk so I can see into each bag: a black zip wallet; a twenty-pound note; a handful of coins; three cards – for Severnside gym, National Union of Journalists, Costa loyalty. A squirrel keyring on the zipper has melted and fused against the wallet like a piece of miniature roadkill. The membership cards are curled and browned at the edges. When was the last time she used the gym? I imagine the card was pristine before the fire.

"We'll get it analysed, but this looks like the rim of a straw hat." He holds up a packet containing a crescent of yellow fibre.

My gut churns uneasily as I rein in my thoughts. It's got Gittens-Gold stamped all over it, but, if he is the killer, why would his hat be found in a pile of his victim's belongings? Besides, his hat – fully intact – was found floating in the river at Sharpness. Two hats? An elaborate attempt by a third party to frame the missing man? Or did Sonia have one of her kids' hats in her bag? I wince sadly, picturing little Edith in a boater and pigtails.

I reach for the exhibit that most interested me when I collected the bag from Dommo. Even through the protective cover it still stinks of smoke. A notebook, or what's left of it. The fire ate away the bottom half, but the spiral binding is still there and there's a line of symbols on the page that's been folded to the top, as if it was the last page Sonia wrote on.

"Can we get this translated?" I ask. "Could be an Eastern language. Hindi or something."

Neil grins. Even before he opens his mouth, I anticipate something smug is coming out. "Not Hindi. Shorthand, or stenography to give it the scientific name. Many forms exist; the most well-known in the UK was developed by Sir Isaac Pitman in 1837. It's based on phonetics and—"

"So we need someone who can read Pitman shorthand," I cut in, steering him back to the task in hand.

His face remains smug, skin a shiny pink through his day-old shadow. "Oh, this isn't Pitman, although it was invented by a Pitman teacher, James Hill, in 1968. This is Teeline. I'm not surprised it's in her notebook. Teeline is what trainee journalists learn. It's an alphabet-based—"

"That's great," I snap. But to keep him on side, I soften my tone. "Well done. It's good that you know it too."

"Not me. The only code I know is JavaScript." He laughs. "That's a programming language for website..."

I stop listening, weighing up which journalist I can get to translate. The only ones I know are connected to the case.

"...anyway. I sent Mum a photo of the page and she told me straight away." He stops speaking and looks at me, eyes wide, apparently waiting for something.

"I don't quite follow," I say, knowing he'll love it if I act dumb.

The smile goes wider and smugger. "My mother is a retired P.A. Her secretarial college taught Teeline." He sits at his computer. "She says it represents a single word. I'll get up her email." After tapping a few keys, he spells out the word in Sonia's notebook. "S-Z-E-C-H-W-A-N." He glances up. "It's a province in southwest China. There are several spellings..."

Blood thunders in my ears and threatens a migraine. So not just an empty file name on her computer, but probably also the last word she ever wrote. "What about these other exhibits?" I have to shut him up. If he fills my head with his interpretation of the word, I'll lose track of my own unravelling thoughts. This is momentous, I know it, but I'll have to ponder when Neil Wright isn't downloading a geography lecture into my earhole.

The next packet he turns to contains a hair scrunchie. "The few strands of hair caught up are dark. A DNA test is possible, but can you justify the budget?"

Untouched by the fire, the circle of elasticated material is patterned with white bunnies on a pink background. My eyes water. The little girl – Edith – will never again have her hair combed and tied by her mother. "No need," I reply quietly and move onto the final packet.

A clump of grey fibres. My heart rate rockets. In her last moments, did Sonia put up enough of a fight to pull out her attacker's hair? The colouring is a shade darker than the photo we have of Gerald Gittens-Gold, but it's probably down to the scorching. Is this the proof we need?

But Neil is laughing. Smugly. Again. "There might be skin cells where it's been peeled off, but the hair is synthetic. If this was real, it would likely have burnt to coke or ash, whereas this stuff has become a sticky ball. I knew as soon as I got a whiff. The smell is plastic not protein. It's the polymers..."

My phone pings, offering an escape. "I have to read this." He barely pauses for air.

The text is from Terri: *I did Brecht at uni but not that play. All I know is...*

As Neil throws out "...acrylic" and "...nylon", I read on. For a play she doesn't know well, drama teacher Terri knows a lot. My head fills with crazy possibilities. But I'd never be able to prove it. Already on dodgy ground with Superintendent Thomas, can I risk blowing my credibility with Kevin as well? How can I tell him the key to this murder is Bertolt Brecht?

"Am I boring you?" Neil stands in front of me, arms folded.

"No," I say, coming to a decision. "Right now, you are the least boring person I know." As I scroll my phone, I catch him stroking his hair and stretching his neck. His skin colour resembles red cabbage, but I've no time to interpret what it means. "I'm going to send you a photo," I explain. "I'd like you to tell me everything you can about it."

"Right-o." He launches into his wheelie chair and has to grip the edge of the desk to stop himself overshooting. He pulls up to his screen and opens my email, but his face falls. "It looks like a photo of a photo. Not sure what you think I can find."

I place my hand beside his mouse. "Work your magic," I say softly. "I'm relying on you to think of something. I'll call you in an hour."

I dash from the room before he can hedge on the timescale.

CHAPTER FIFTY

As soon as I set foot in the Cross Care Centre, Rosemary Davies swoops. She rushes out of her glass office, leaving another woman inside. Despite Kevin's orders, it's not her I've come to see. I conceal my irritation with a smile.

"I've prepared a statement," she says.

For one ludicrous instant, I think she's confessing. Who is she owning up for – Gerald, her staff member, or his client, Sally Parker?

"If you'd like to come this way," she continues, ushering me to the office.

In crisp linen, the other woman has similar dress sense to Davies. She rises from her sofa and introduces herself as the Cross Care Centre solicitor.

Even an old and bold copper like me gets fluttery when caught unawares by a lawyer. I sit down and pick my words carefully. "What would you like to tell me?"

"The charity has called me in," she says, "to represent their interests at this tragic time. The centre manager has something to say." She turns to Rosemary Davies.

Of course, Cross Care is charity funded and I should have guessed they'd get legalled-up. My experience of altruism is that it comes in hob-nailed boots.

Davies clears her throat. "My statement, which I have already issued to *Gloucester Evening News*, expresses my shock and sadness at the death of our one-time client, Sally Parker." She speaks formally and I'm guessing she's practised at the mirror in the staff loos. "However, I must make clear that Ms Parker visited here on just one occasion and then only briefly some days ago. Our thoughts are with her loved ones." As something of an afterthought, perhaps because she remembers who this version of her statement is aimed at, she adds, "We think also of you, the police, as you search for the person responsible."

"And you're sure Sally Parker visited here only once, on Monday the second of July?" Despite her condescending tone, I believe Davies's statement, but I can't let her off without probing.

After a nod from the solicitor, she answers, "She made no other bookings. I didn't personally see her that day, but other staff have said she turned up on time for her appointment and then left soon after she was called through."

"By 'other staff', you mean your front desk receptionists?"

"Among others, yes. Apparently Ms Parker had distinctive red hair, so her presence was noted."

"But it wasn't noted on other occasions?"

"Not that anyone recalls. Sally Parker's association with this centre was fleeting."

Both women sit forward like tennis players waiting for my return of serve, but I'm playing a different game.

"Well, thank you. If I can just get Sally's one visit confirmed by one of your receptionists, I'll be on my way."

"If Ms West sits in that should be fine..." Rosemary Davies tails off, looking at the solicitor.

"It won't be a formal interview," I say quickly, looking at the lawyer. "I don't know about you, but I try to avoid unnecessary paperwork." A crazy punt, I realise afterwards – what lawyer doesn't love paperwork – but it throws Ms West off guard enough for me to leave the office before she responds.

The queues in the foyer are longer than on my first visit here. Two women in the line at Julia Paget's counter are taking selfies and I suspect they're on a ghoul trip. With the Cross Care Centre linked in the media to two major crimes, the city's scandal-hungry have found themselves in need of urgent counselling.

"Sorry, folks, I've got an emergency," I tell the line and feel them bristle as I step up to the desk.

Julia recognises me immediately. "Steph, how can I help?" My admiration for the woman increases; she's remembered I don't use the 'Inspector Lewis' tag.

Despite what I said to Davies, I don't intend to ask about Sally Parker. My questions to Julia will follow a different tack. I lower my voice, keeping my enquiry discreet. Much as I'd love to stir the pot for Davies and her lawyer, I'm not going to feed the five thousand queuing behind me.

"Can I ask you about the Centre website?" I ask. "You mentioned Gerald took the photographs. Did he rent a studio?"

She smiles. "That was a fun morning." Well versed in the need for confidentiality, she also speaks quietly despite her obvious enthusiasm. "We closed for an hour and he set up here. Mrs Davies told us to dress up, so we came in our best frocks and plenty of slap."

"And you did the whole thing in an hour?"

311

"Yes. It was very professional." She smiles again. "I loved my photo, so did my mum. We got a copy framed for her kitchen."

"Did everyone who works here have their photo taken that day?"

"He'd already done Anna's at home, plus his own with a fancy timer. There was a bug going round so a couple of people were off sick. Gerald brought his camera stuff in again to take theirs about a week later. We all got done eventually. Mrs Davies was thrilled with the results, and the website designer was impressed, apparently."

"That's great to know. Thanks for your help," I say and add, "I've seen the website and I'm not surprised your mum framed the photo. You're very photogenic." Why this attractive, efficient woman has to trawl round nightclubs and dance with losers is beyond me.

Armed with new knowledge and a fire in my guts, I return to my car. It's time I showed Julia and everyone else just what a nonentity Gerald Gittens-Gold really is.

CHAPTER FIFTY-ONE

INCIDENT ROOM – WEDNESDAY 11TH JULY, 1.30 P.M.

Stiff in my seat, with my heels touching the cardboard box underneath, I keep my powder dry while everyone else reports their morning's progress.

Tony called on the Clarkes, but they stuck by their cash and carry alibi for the time of their sister's murder, and when Sally Parker was murdered yesterday evening, Olivier was delivering a cabinet to a customer. However, Jerome was home alone. This weak alibi is enough to convince Tony that the pair of them are 'well dodgy' and likely prospects for both murders, even though his idea of motive for the second murder is dodgier: "Ms Parker was a translator. French connection, innit?"

Harriet paid a visit to Anna Gittens-Gold, but the woman was shocked and disbelieving of the evidence that Gerald was still alive and probably the killer of not one, but two women. "To be honest, she was beside herself," Harriet tells us, "too upset to answer questions, but her neighbours confirmed they haven't seen any sign of Gerald. I don't think he's been back to the bungalow."

As I listen to Jordan and Cally talk about Sonia's email correspondence over the last two years, I sit even stiffer. It will be my turn soon. Do I have enough? After visiting the Cross Care Centre, I went back to Neil and he confirmed what I thought. Except he didn't use the word 'confirmed'. Instead he said, "I think you're right. You're a great detective." He rubbed his neck. "But I've had to send the image to the central lab in Birmingham to be sure. They have better equipment, though even for them it's hard when it's a photo of a photo." I thanked him and signed out some exhibits that currently reside in the box under my chair.

"Steph, what have you got?" Kevin asks. All eyes are on me.

Heart pulsing a new headache between my temples, I pick up the box under my chair, walk to the front of the room and, as calmly and rationally as I can, I tell my colleagues the most batshit crazy theory they have ever heard.

Afterwards, I remain standing, taking in the silence and the frozen expressions. The young detectives on the front row risk a relay of raised eyebrows between themselves and manage not to laugh. DCI Kevin's face is the stoniest, staring through me. When the mailbox on his laptop pings, he goes straight to it, clearly grateful for the distraction.

Tony shakes his head and is the first to speak. "You're wasting your time, Steph. The killer is stacking pot noodles in Hucton." He looks at the box I've placed by my feet. "Even after showing us your stage props, I'm not buying your drama."

"It's Hucton now is it? Sure it's not Australia?" I fire back, recalling his earlier assertion that Gerald Gittens-Gold had headed to his homeland.

"Take the mick while you can. I've got evidence."

"What evidence?" I say, suppressing my nerves. My theory is barking mad. If Tony has evidence, he could be right. My doubts go into overdrive.

"I've put in a request for the CCTV from the cash and carry. We've only the Clarke brothers' word they were there. I'm expecting them to be conspicuous by their absence when we roll the tapes. And even you have to accept they had motive. A grudge brewing for four years is a powerful thing."

"You're clutching," I say.

"Not as much as you are."

"Yeah, but—"

"What do you think, Harriet? Is Steph's idea a step too far, like Tony says?" Kevin's questions cut off our argument. With his laptop open in his arms, he has gone to stand at the back.

Slowly, Harriet gets to her feet. Her cheeks bulging with colour, she looks first at Kevin, then at me, and then at Tony, who has twisted round in his chair to watch. There is an easy twinkle in his eye.

She hesitates, swallows hard and makes her choice.

"You are absolutely right, Tony."

"Well said," Tony whoops.

My seat is too far away to effect a graceful sinking into it, so I stand my ground at the front, my shaky ground. I knew she was pissed off, but I never thought she'd betray me in open forum.

But Harriet has more to say. Ignoring the heat from my glare, she faces Tony. "Right at the start of all this, you said there was no crime scene in the Gittens-Gold missing persons case. I'd say you were spot on."

She smiles at me and nods. Slowly, I smile back, as I realise I've misjudged her.

315

"Yeah, so..." Tony falters. "What's that got to do with Sonia's brothers?"

Kevin holds up his laptop. "No connection whatever. The CCTV at the cash and carry just came through. Both Clarke brothers had starring roles on the Monday morning."

"Tracey Chiles, then," Tony says, slipping easily between theories. "There's something off there."

Ignoring him, Kevin looks at Harriet and me. "As you two seem to be in agreement, you can bring in your suspect and conduct the interview together."

CHAPTER FIFTY-TWO

I enter the interview room, sit next to Harriet and place the cardboard box under my chair.

I launch into my first question. "Did you never want children?"

Across the table, Anna Gittens-Gold turns to her lawyer, a young, dark-haired man in a sharp suit.

"Unless you can demonstrate relevance, inspector," he says, "I advise my client not to answer."

"I don't mean to offend you, Anna," I say, doing my best to sound as if I'm on her side. "I'm trying to establish an important point about your relationship, about what kind of husband Gerald might have been."

Her eyes feign sadness and she looks down. "I've been married twenty-five years. No children have come along."

I drop my fishing trip for the moment and let Harriet take over.

"Going back to the day of Gerald's disappearance, you said you hadn't seen him since he left for work that morning."

"That's right. He kissed me goodbye after breakfast."

"But you saw him again that evening, didn't you?"

"Of course I didn't. He didn't come home from work on Monday. I've been through this countless times."

"But you must have done." Harriet fixes her with a stare that has her turning to her solicitor.

"My client has stated that she has not seen her husband since the early morning of Monday the second of July."

"But that's not entirely true, is it? We know that Gerald had three counselling sessions that afternoon with the Parkers, Robinsons and Rices. If you didn't see Gerald that evening, how is it that you were able to tell us everything that was said in those sessions?"

After an angry glare at Harriet, she smiles and a plausible explanation crosses her gold bridgework. "I don't *know* what was said. How could I? But I can make a pretty good guess. I used to counsel one of the couples, the Robinsons. And Gerald had discussed the Rices with me. We always share our treatment plans with each other. Counsellors often rely on colleagues for advice. It's called being professional."

"What about Sally Parker?" Harriet asks.

"I'm afraid you've lost me."

"She was Gerald's first client that day."

"What of her?"

Even before Sally was murdered, I knew she was important to this case, so did Harriet, but we couldn't work out why. On the way to this interview, we put the reason together. Harriet explains it now.

"It was Sally and Tim's first counselling session at the Cross Care Centre, but you knew all about it."

Anna hesitates but only briefly. "Not really. Gerald must have shown me the case notes sometime before Monday.

Nothing remarkable about that. As I've just told you, we shared client information."

"But you didn't see Gerald later?" Harriet asks.

"Absolutely not."

"Then how did you know that Sally Parker's partner, Tim Vale, didn't turn up for Gerald's counselling session that afternoon?"

Anna folds down her mouth and shrugs. "What on earth makes you think I knew that? How could I?"

Harriet is already flicking through her notes. "We interviewed you on Monday the ninth, a week after Gerald's disappearance. You were forthcoming about all of Gerald's clients, even about Tim's no-show."

Anna inhales sharply but recovers her composure. "I didn't *know*. I simply guessed as much from the case notes."

"You saw Gerald that afternoon, didn't you?" Harriet says.

"What is the matter with you people? I did not see Gerald, but I'm at a loss for how to convince you."

"I believe you," I say and pause for her dramatic sigh of relief. Then I ask, "How tall is Gerald?"

The change of subject catches her by surprise. "Average height," she replies cautiously.

I check my notes. "When you reported him missing, you told our colleague, PC Barton, your husband was five feet ten. How tall are you?"

"Well, really." She nods at Harriet. "In my stocking feet, about her height."

"I'm just over five feet eight," Harriet says. "Would you stand up please and take off your shoes."

"Well, really," she says again. Her solicitor shrugs.

Harriet slips off her own pumps and moves round the

table to stand next to her. Reluctantly, Anna unbuckles her high-heeled sandals and stands up. I look from the top of one head to the other.

"Thank you. You can sit down again. Even without your shoes you're taller than DC Harris."

When Anna bends to put her shoes on, Harriet stops her. "May I look at them?"

As if protecting a baby, Anna cradles a sandal in her arms.

Harriet holds out her hand. "Please. Just for a moment." Anna places the shoe on the desk. Without lifting it, Harriet peers inside. "Size seven. You can put them on again now, thank you."

I ask the next question. "I'm just wondering why Gerald is so much taller than you on your wedding photograph."

"What on earth? It was twenty-five years ago, but as far as I can recall, the photographer positioned us like that. It's traditional for the groom to be taller than the bride."

"It's a lovely picture. You make a handsome couple."

Anna says nothing, but the compliment puts pride back in her eyes.

"It's not your picture, though, is it? Whose bodies did you borrow?" I lean across the table.

CHAPTER FIFTY-THREE

The vacuum cleaner hose sucks against a cushion in the breakfast room. The noise sends Hamish stalking off.

"Sorry, son," Tracey calls after him. "You be away to your bed 'til I'm done." Though she's not sure why she's bothering. The room hasn't been used since the last guest left, and the next one has made it clear he won't be here for home comforts.

Yesterday, as her heart hammered and Hamish barked, he talked through the locked front door, raising his voice to make her hear. It was in the public interest, he said. He was sure she – as a local hotelier – took her community responsibilities seriously. The city's safety was at stake. She could help.

She remained silent, sitting with her back against the door and hoping he would go away, but his business card dropped through the letterbox and she had to force it out of Hamish's jaws before it was gone. Changing his approach, he asked to book a room for the night. She could name her price, he said; whatever she thought it was worth to answer his questions and give him desk space to write up and file. She stood up and peered through the spyhole. As she suspected, it was the same man who came to her door on Sunday with questions about what she witnessed at the cathedral. Mistaking him for a prospective paying guest, she'd said more than she should have done. Would she never be rid of him?

Reading the business card, she came to a decision. Told him there were no vacancies until today and quoted an outlandish room rate. The fact that he haggled went some way to convincing her he was genuine. They agreed terms and he went away. Afterwards, a flick through the back copies of *Gloucester Evening News,* piled by her back door for recycling, confirmed his identity.

Despite expecting him, she jumps when he rings the bell now. She closes the breakfast room door on the vacuum cleaner and lets him in.

CHAPTER FIFTY-FOUR

"Detective Inspector Lewis, may I remind you that my client has come here of her own free will. Although you believe her husband is implicated in a murder, you have no evidence to suggest that my client was in any way involved. Indeed, she was herself duped by her husband for many years," the solicitor says.

My gut says he's a lawyer going through the usual motions. Whether he's got sufficient range to deal with the scenario I'm about to depict is doubtful. "We've sent the wedding photograph off to our experts in Birmingham, and I'll bet my pension, they're going to tell us that the faces have been superimposed on another photograph. I've got a colleague in Forensics who knows about everything. He's written it down for me." I read from the notes I took during Neil's most recent lecture. "Biometrics is 'the identification of a person based on his or her physiological or behavioural characteristics'."

"Please be explicit," the solicitor says. "What is your point?"

"Facial recognition. Our experts take measurements of the characteristics a person can't alter – the distance across the eye sockets, the cheekbones, the sides of the mouth. I'll make another bet – my annual salary – that they'll tell us there's something very odd about the bride and groom's faces."

"How dare you!" Anna huffs.

"Conjecture. You do not have the findings of any such tests." The solicitor sweeps the table clear of his papers and puts them in his briefcase. "I advise my client to answer no further questions."

"I have other evidence, which I'll come to in a minute." My foot taps against the cardboard box under my chair and I carry on speaking to Anna. "You knew Gerald was a fake, didn't you? What was it like living a lie for twenty-five years?"

"Inspector Lewis. I must ask you to stop goading my client."

"The real Gerald Gittens died in 1992. It was a nice touch adding Gold to his surname. It took us a bit longer to track down the fraud. And then there was the posthumous promotion. The real Gerald died an army sergeant but was reborn a full colonel."

Anna blots away a tear with her handkerchief. "How unkind. I didn't know any of this. I'm still coming to terms with what my husband didn't tell me."

"But he's not the only one with a colourful past, is he?" I lift the cardboard box onto my knees and delve inside. "For the benefit of the tape, I am handing DC Harris a cutting from a publication entitled *St Maur's Review of the Year, 1985–86*."

Taking the photocopy Bernie made, Harriet picks up the

commentary. "I am going to describe the photograph on page twelve. It depicts a stage set. On the left-hand side is a girl in a pillbox hat and an embroidered tunic, carrying a yoke with buckets on each end. In the centre are three girls in sunvisors, flowing robes and open-toed sandals. To the right is a man in a pinstriped suit, thick moustache and trilby hat. The caption reads: 'Players from left to right – Helen Carter as Wang the Water Carrier, Ann Harrod, Catherine Prior and Joan Baker as the Gods, and Annie Bones as Shui Ta'."

"What do you think of that, Annie?" I ask.

She blows her nose. "Annie? My name is Anna."

"But you used to be called Annie when you were at school. Do you remember Bernie, the school secretary at St. Maur's? She's still there and remembers you very well. I'm sure she'd have no trouble recognising you again."

Harriet points to the photograph on the photocopy. "That was you in the trilby hat, wasn't it?"

Anna glances pleadingly at the solicitor. He gives a succinct nod as he fastens the briefcase, clearly wanting to get this over now he's packed up his notes.

"What of it? It was years ago," she answers.

"It was your finest hour and yet there's no photograph of it among your other framed photographs and certificates in your house," I say.

"Isn't there?" She sounds suitably vague.

"Come on, Annie. DC Harris and I have seen the meticulous display of all your achievements from school shows to photography trophies."

"The trophies are Gerald's."

"The convent says you were an expert photographer yourself. Why didn't you study it at college?"

"I chose electronic communications."

"In the eighties? Wasn't that still the age of two paper cups and a length of string?"

"I didn't go straight into further education. I wanted some life experience."

"After all the school fees she'd paid, your mother couldn't afford to send you to college, could she? She'd always hoped you'd marry a rich husband and not need to bother with further education, but no man seemed interested."

"You've no right to delve into my family background." A note of nervousness has crept into her voice.

"But then your mother died. Electric shock. You must have been devastated that you weren't there to check the wiring on her iron before she used it. The convent says you were a bit of a technical wizard."

Anna gives another pleading look to her lawyer.

"Please explain what raking over my client's past grief has to do with her husband's disappearance," he says.

I ignore him. "You inherited your mother's house and then you sold it. It wasn't a fortune, but it was enough to pay for a trip to Australia. And it really was the chance of a lifetime."

"This is disgraceful." Anna mops fresh tears.

"We know you've lied. Being the wife of a high-achieving army officer wasn't quite enough for you. You were determined to give yourself graduate status. You knew your flair for technology was your only credible chance. You were no academic at school, so the pretence of a degree in history or biology wouldn't stand up for five minutes."

"Where is this nonsense coming from? I came here to answer your questions about Gerald." Her face buckles as she mentions his name and she dabs the hanky over her tears.

"We know your qualifications are bogus. You told DC

Harris you went to a private university in Brisbane. You certainly researched your cover story. There is indeed one such institution. The only problem is they've never heard of you, even under your maiden name. In any case, they didn't offer communications courses until ninety-seven. And quite how you could have studied in Queensland and met an army photographer based three thousand miles away in Subiaco, Western Australia, is beyond me."

Anna and the solicitor put their heads together and whisper. The man nods.

Anna takes a breath. "I met Gerald when I was travelling in Western Australia. I admit I may have embellished my qualifications, but it has no bearing on my competences."

I tip up the cardboard box, and spill the contents onto the table. "Do you recognise any of these?"

"They..." She falters but quickly regains her composure. "They look like bags of charcoal."

"They've certainly been in a fire. Someone tried to get rid of them but it didn't quite work. For the benefit of the tape, I am holding up three evidence bags. One contains a voice-operated tape recorder. The second contains a clump of grey fibre, believed to be part of a toupee or a false moustache. The third holds the remains of a reporter's notebook. Whose are they, Anna?"

"I haven't the faintest idea."

"As a technical expert yourself, you'll understand that these items can still reveal a lot about their owner. There's a tape still in the recorder. What do you think our techies will be able to retrieve from it? How about Sonia Hanson's voice, dictating her last story? And you never know our luck, the second bag might have a smattering of DNA."

"Why are you telling me this?"

327

"There are bound to be a few skin cells on there from when Gerald peeled off his moustache. We might even find strands of real hair inside the toupee. What do you think?"

"Inspector Lewis, this has gone far enough. You know as well as I do the chances of lifting DNA from that lot are minimal. You are leading my client."

Harriet reaches for the evidence bag containing Sonia's notebook.

"This makes fascinating reading. I learnt a bit of shorthand once. What do you think the draft headline on the last page might be? Something about you, perhaps?"

"You're bluffing. Why would a woman I barely know write about me?" Anna says with apparent confidence.

I study her face. She's good. Amateur groups like the Gloucester Players must be on the look-out for acting ability like this. She is the old hand who delivers her lines even when the scenery is crashing down. We still have work to do.

"How much shorthand do you actually know, detective constable?" the solicitor asks, managing to keep up with the action.

But for her part, Harriet is more than keeping up; she's a step ahead. A side step ahead, which she takes to wrong-foot Anna.

"What size shoe does your husband take?" she asks.

"I really don't see... An eight I think."

Harriet turns to me. "What size men's shoes did you find in the wardrobe at Mrs Gittens-Gold's house?"

"Did you have a warrant to search my house?" Anna says in her crystal clear playhouse tones.

"You gave us permission, remember?" Harriet answers. "You said we wouldn't find Gerald in the broom cupboard."

"And I was right, wasn't I?" she responds defiantly.

"Gerald has been missing for over a week, so why are we discussing his footwear? If you must know, he takes a seven or an eight, depending on the style of the shoe."

"Gerald's shoes in the bungalow were size seven – the same as yours," I explain. "You were a perfectly matching couple. Two sides of the same coin, wouldn't you say, DC Harris?"

"Gerald's a heavy smoker, isn't he?" Harriet says, changing tack again.

"I wouldn't call it heavy."

"Your bungalow has a distinctive tang."

"How dare..." Anna begins, glaring first at Harriet, then at me. "Smoking is Gerald's only vice. I think it's a filthy habit, but he has many other admirable qualities. At least I thought he did." She sniffs.

"We'd like your consent to undergo a medical examination," I say and wait to be shot down.

"Whatever for?" the solicitor asks, predictably.

"Mrs Gittens-Gold claims to be a non-smoker. We believe an examination will prove otherwise."

To my surprise, my ridiculous punt forces a concession. "I have the odd drag now and again, but I'm not addicted," Anna says.

"I bet you eat meat, too. You're the only vegan I know who has a leather sofa," I say and drown out her protests with more observations. "Gerald is in his mid-fifties, a lover of red wine and red meat, and yet he's as slim as a twenty year old. You are the clean living one, a vegan, into self-defence. How has Gerald managed to keep his figure?"

"He's a fit man, a soldier. At least I thought he was a soldier. That's what he told me."

"Want to know what I think?" I say, folding my arms. "I think it came down to arrogance."

"Now you really are going off piste, inspector," Anna drawls, growing in confidence. "Gerald isn't an arrogant man. Ask anyone."

"I was talking about your arrogance. You couldn't bear for your perfect husband to have a middle-aged paunch, or a bit of a stoop to create the illusion of greater differences between your heights."

Anna lets out a noisy breath. She and the solicitor stare at me in apparent bewilderment.

I meet her gaze and say slowly, "Let's give up the pretence, shall we? You are Gerald Gittens-Gold."

CHAPTER FIFTY-FIVE

Anna's golden teeth loom large as she gapes. "Why are you doing this to me? You're making it up to hurt me. You've no evidence."

"When you were in Australia you somehow came across the birth certificate of a deceased army photographer. You stayed in Australia long enough to perfect a masculine voice and to build your story. You came back, moved to Gloucestershire and reinvented yourself as Mr and Mrs Gerald Gittens-Gold."

Anna buries her face in her handkerchief.

"I don't know how you managed it, but you played both roles for twenty-five years. You fooled all your colleagues and clients. No one had an inkling. Then you got bored and went off to nightclubs in search of a new audience to impress. But I have to tell you that you were less successful there than you thought. Drunk to their eyeballs they might be, but young clubbers recognise a bloke on the pull when they see one. They didn't quite buy Gerald and laughed behind his back."

Anna shields her eyes behind her hands and issues a series of loud sobs. "I didn't know Gerald went to nightclubs. There's obviously a lot I don't know about my husband. Your questions are cruel. Haven't I been humiliated enough?"

But I've plenty more humiliation to deliver. "We didn't find Gerald's teeth with Sonia's burnt handbag, so you must have ditched them somewhere else. It's a shame decent actors' mouthpieces weren't around when you started this. All those years ago you couldn't risk giving him a broad grin because your distinctive dentistry would have given the game away. By the time you got a set of false teeth for him, all his acquaintances were used to his tight-lipped smile. "

"You are quite mad," Anna says.

"Somehow journalist Sonia Hanson got wind of your deception. Out of fear of losing status and becoming a laughing stock, you killed her and reported your non-existent husband missing. Then you hung up his size seven shoes never to tread the boards as Gerald again. If we ever connected Sonia to you, you had created the perfect scapegoat who conveniently vanished, probably to Australia, leaving you free to assume a new role. What was it going to be: grieving widow or deserted wife? Is that why you reported him missing at all – so you could take on the new part straight away? You didn't have to come to us and draw attention to Gerald. You could have just told everyone he'd gone off on another mission. We might never have connected him to the murder if you hadn't been so desperate to take the lead in a new drama."

Anna shakes her head. "I have to accept that Gerald was living a lie. He deceived me for all our married life. I was duped like everyone else. I couldn't impersonate a man for twenty seconds, never mind twenty years. And how could I have killed anyone?" She pitches the last two sentences an octave higher as if to emphasise her femininity.

"We know about your self-defence courses. After DC Harris saw your certificates on your wall, she had a chat with your tutor. You're a regular unarmed killing machine."

"They are complete fantasists. Do I have to put up with this?" she asks her solicitor.

"Isn't this all a bit far-fetched?" he asks.

"Same height, same teeth, same shoe size, not to mention the biometric evidence; it's all pretty conclusive. And there's something else. Tell them, DC Harris," I say.

She lifts the photocopy from the table. "For the benefit of the tape, I will now read the opening paragraphs of the review of *The Good Woman of Szechwan*, performed at St Maur's Convent School in March 1986.

"The annual performance this year was an ambitious production of the Bertolt Brecht classic. Tour de force Annie Bones, Upper Sixth, was magnificent as not only the female but also the male lead. The role of the girl, Shen Te, was enacted with a subtle blend of passion and naivety. However, Annie's talents were at their best in her scenes as businessman Shui Ta. Annie performed all kinds of vocal gymnastics to imbue the role with deep-set masculinity. Her voice dropped so comfortably into the male register that several parents in the audience gasped in amazement when she was revealed as the actor of both parts. Annie Bones must surely have a great acting future ahead of her."

The eyes of Anna's current audience are upon her. She straightens her back and smooths her hair. Despite knowing she's done for, she seems unable to resist crowing with pride at hearing the review again. With the air of the star performer taking to the awards podium, she delivers a new speech.

"I went to Australia when I was twenty-five. All my school friends married and started producing children but it wasn't for me. I sold my mother's house after she... after her death and went travelling. Quite a thing for a girl alone in the eighties. People said I was ahead of my time." She pauses to brush her hand through her tight curls.

"I was in a village in the middle of nowhere in Western Australia one day when I came across a photography exhibition. It was in memory of a young army photographer who died in a motorbike accident. His widow was selling off everything, not only the prints but also boxes of negatives. It hit me that she was selling off his life. If she'd really loved him, surely she would treasure his work. The photographs needed to go to someone who would appreciate his talent; the man had been an artist. I still had a bit of my inheritance left, so I told the wife, Anna, I would buy everything, a job lot. She couldn't have been more grateful. She said the exhibition had a couple more days to run, but I was welcome to stay with her until she could pack everything up.

"I ended up staying two weeks. She liked having someone around she could talk to about her late husband. He sometimes did undercover work in hostile territory to get reconnaissance photographs. She gave me every photograph she could find, including copies of their wedding photos and pictures from his childhood. I learnt so much about him that I felt he could have been my husband.

"When it was time for me to go, I didn't want to leave him behind. I knew I'd never marry. It didn't really bother me. I was happy with my own company. I didn't need to compromise my life for a partner. But twenty-five years ago our society was geared round couples. Spinster was another word for outcast. I knew it would improve my social standing if I had a husband. It suddenly seemed so obvious. Anna had given me the run of her house, so it was easy to track down Gerald's birth certificate and their marriage certificate. Anna's maiden name was Roper, easy to alter the handwriting to Bones on the certificate.

"I flew to Sydney and stayed there for another month to buy Gerald's clothes and get everything ready. We returned to England and settled in Gloucester. Gerald and I had been married a year by then." She speaks with conviction, as if she believes in the fiction herself.

Harriet takes over. "Over the years you gradually replaced his Australian belongings with British ones. And you made sure he had plenty of cravats. One of the nightclub guests pointed out that Gerald always wore a cravat, a clue we missed at the time. A cravat would have disguised the fact that he had no Adam's apple."

Light flashes on my toffee apple dream of two nights ago. I must have made the link subconsciously. If only I'd latched on when I woke up, Sally Parker might still be alive.

Harriet continues, "It must have seemed expensive, replenishing the wardrobe of a make-believe man. No wonder you fell behind. That was another thing that let you down, but the inspector spotted that straight away."

"The St Michael logo hasn't appeared on new Marks and Spencer products for years," I say. "Gerald's underpants were practically museum pieces."

Anna's face freezes. I can imagine her bellowing at the props assistant but, of course, there isn't one. The error is entirely her own. And it wasn't her only costume malfunction. Tossing a straw hat into the river to suggest Gerald's suicide was a nice idea, except we found the remnants of his original hat among Sonia's burnt possessions. Too many hats spoil the fake-up.

"Everything was fine for over twenty-five years," I say. "You had a husband whose work took him overseas for several weeks so you could have a long rest between performances. You acquired a degree, a career and the respect you'd always craved. So tell us what happened with Sonia Hanson."

The solicitor has put down his bag and folded his arms. With his gaze fixed on me, it's clear he's no advice left for Anna.

She seems to decide for herself that there's no point in holding back. "When Sonia Hanson came for counselling with her husband, she was more interested in interviewing me. Her husband apologised, said she was like that with everyone, always on the lookout for people for her Gloucester Reunited column. It was irritating because I'm a very private person. I don't like to blow my own trumpet." She straightens again, still believing in her own modesty.

She continues, "Then a few days later she turned up at my house still wanting to write the nostalgia piece about me. God knows how she tracked down my address. All counsellors are ex-directory for obvious reasons, but I couldn't see any harm in a story about meeting up with my old school chums. It would be good for them to see what I've achieved. Gerald could be away on government business so there'd be no complications. I told her a bit about my successes at school and since. Stupidly I let her see the photographs on the wall of the plays I'd done at school. She didn't seem very interested. Said she'd let me know if she decided to pursue my story. I didn't hear from her again."

"Until?" Harriet says.

"Gerald bumped into them at the Cross Care Centre three weeks later. He made the mistake of acknowledging them a little too well for people he hadn't ever met. In twenty-five years, he'd never made a slip like that. He chose to do it in front of a journalist of all people. He moved on quickly, pretending that he'd been greeting the receptionist, but the damage was done.

"A week or so later, Sonia was on my doorstep again. This time she dispensed with the charm and came straight out and accused me of being Gerald. I told her to stop talking complete rubbish and I'd prove it. Gerald and I would come to visit her together. It would have to be very early on a particular morning because Gerald had a quick turnaround between assignments in the Solomon Islands. He would be jetting back during the night before catching an early train. It would be best for us if we could meet near the railway station. The cathedral was quite handy. For all her journalistic guile, she bought it."

"So why kill Sally Parker?" Harriet asks.

Her neat curls shake again. "That was Gerald's second mistake. Of all the women he met in nightclubs, the silliest one – with a perfectly reasonable boyfriend – was Sally Parker. He decided she deserved to be strung along, so he accepted her offers to cook supper. As soon as she started on about her school days at a convent school in the midlands, he realised she had overlapped with me by a year at St. Maur's, so he dropped her. That should have been the end of it, but by sheer bad luck she turned up for counselling only a few hours after the Sonia Hanson business was settled. Sally Parker was too much of a loose end to leave undone."

She looks me in the eye. "Gerald went to the cathedral last Monday and to a cottage in Klox yesterday. But Gerald has gone away now."

She seems to think if she says it with enough fervour, it will become true.

CHAPTER FIFTY-SIX

To Tracey's surprise, there's a black holdall slung over his shoulder. She'd half expected him to arrive with only a laptop, but it seems he does intend to stay the night. Hamish leaves his bed to sniff the alien trainers. After deciding nothing is amiss, he retreats to the kitchen. Tracey follows to fetch the man's room key from the rack.

When she comes back, the man is leaning over the visitors' book on the hall table with his mobile phone aimed at a page.

"Can you stop that?" she says uncertainly. "Data protection and all."

He smiles at her pleasantly, taking the key. His gaze lingers on her wound. "Is that infected?"

"A scratch," she says, putting her hand in her apron pocket. Without the bandage, there is more pus than she would like.

"You might need to get it checked by a doctor." He turns back to the book, flicking through. "Don't worry. It's my job to know the laws on confidentiality. Guests don't put full addresses." He holds up the page he's turned to. "Take this one from May, for instance. S. Farrell, Liverpool. I'm sure that person won't mind. Not that you have enough info to track them down and ask."

"Actually, he's passed away." She regrets her indiscretion as soon as she's spoken, even though her words don't seem to shock him.

Another smile slips across his face before he grows serious. "That wouldn't be Sean Farrell? The name's familiar." He pauses, apparently scouring his memory. "Wasn't he the one who was murdered?"

"Aye, but not here," she says quickly. "No one has died at Loch Lomond Guesthouse."

"Of course not. You run an orderly house, Mrs Chiles, I can see that." He scans the hallway, lingering on the dog hairs she hasn't yet swept. "I had no idea of your connection to that case. The business at the cathedral must have been bad enough, but that as well. Did the police talk to you?"

"I've had my fill of police enquiries these last few months."

"Oh?" His glare is penetrating, makes her want to talk. "They pestered you?"

"The hazards of early morning dog walking. I've seen things. My bad luck."

"Poor you. Half the West Gloucestershire Police Force must have been here."

"It is the same officer mostly, a detective inspector."

"Really?" He puts his holdall on the floor and says slowly, "Tell me what she's like."

CHAPTER FIFTY-SEVEN

"I can see how desperate Anna would have been: her fake life about to be exposed in a double-page spread. Do you think she killed her mother for money?" Harriet asks as she hooks her bag over her office chair.

"More than likely. You saw the reaction when we mentioned her. The electric iron that killed her will be long gone, but we can assume Annie Bones tampered with it. At least we've got her for Sonia Hanson and Sally Parker," I say.

"If only she hadn't greeted Sonia when she'd been dressed as Gerald, both Sonia and Sally would still be alive. You'd think after all her years of playing Gerald she wouldn't have put a foot wrong."

"Even Oscar winners slip up sometimes. You're only ever as good as your last show." I sit down opposite her.

"Twenty-five years, though. Never being seen together. How could people not notice?"

"Ever met the boss's wife?" I ask.

"Mrs Richards? Yeah, at the summer barbecue last month."

"With Kevin?"

"No, he got called out to a case," she says. "We all kept her company. Nice lady."

"And at the Christmas party?"

She grins. "The boss was great at karaoke. I don't think I got a chance to speak to his wife that night. Why?"

"They couldn't get a babysitter so she wasn't there. It's an occupational hazard of parenting and – believe me – a good excuse for not attending events you don't fancy. So in your three years working here, when have you actually seen Kevin Richards and his missus at the same time?"

Harriet screws up her face. "You're not saying...? No way...?"

I shake my head. "I have seen them together loads of times over the years, and with their kids. But do you see how feasible it would have been for Anna – or Gerald – to make excuses for flying solo and people not to realise they never saw them out and about as a couple? Anna was adept at creating smoke and mirrors."

"I suppose it shows her acting skills. How many plays have I watched where an actor talks to a silent offstage character? The audience pictures what they're supposed to see: two characters in dialogue. Anna pulled off the illusion because people saw what they expected to see: two halves of a married couple. What put you onto her?"

"The clues were there," I say, squeezing the bridge of my nose. The interview has given me a headache. As I presented my case to Anna Gittens-Gold, I realised how much I had failed. If I'd twigged sooner, we could have made the arrest before Sally died. I should have pieced together the evidence from the comments of those who knew Gerald. Julia, the Cross Care receptionist, said he danced rather too well for the average middle-aged man, and the mother and daughter artists at the nightclub noticed his lack of military bearing. Even Tracey Chiles's dog wasn't fooled. He sniffed him in the intimate way he normally reserved for women.

Kevin sticks his head round the door. "Remanded in custody pending a bail hearing, which will definitely be denied. Good work, you two."

"Thanks, boss," Harriet says, blushing. "But I didn't do much."

"Thanks, Kev," I say.

"You'd better look sharp, Steph. Naomi Thomas is waiting for you upstairs. There's a press conference in ten minutes, and she'd like you aboard."

My jaw hits the desk. From a bollocking to a starring role in five days? Am I back on the Super's good little officers' list? Over the years, I've read out media statements, but never on such a high profile case. My hand reaches up to check my hair, but I snatch it away, ashamed of my vanity. Two, possibly three people, are dead. This isn't about me. But still...

"Quick as you like," Kevin says.

"On my way, boss." I put on my leather jacket. Not ideal in this heat, but it should look okay on camera. Just hope wearing it won't intensify my headache.

En route to the senior staircase, I pass Police Community Support Officer Jess Bolton. "I've heard about the arrest," she says. "I've dealt with wives reporting husbands missing but never one they've made up." She grins as she walks on. "What is it with you and role-playing murderers? Remember the Georgian Gardens?"

How could I forget? The first time I worked with Jess was when she was guarding a crime scene that marked the start of a serial killer's rampage. Like Anna Gittens-Gold, that killer had been playing a make-believe part. Am I surrounded by thespians or outrageous eccentrics?

Talking of which... "Hi – er – Steph." Neil Wright catches me up. "I've been looking all over for you." He rubs his neck.

"Did you try my desk?" I ask, wondering how I'll shake him off without hearing a lengthy geography anecdote.

His face is turning crimson again and I feel bad. Without his input I'd never have made the case.

"Thanks for all you did," I say and add in a rush, "I owe you a pint."

He looks up the corridor, waiting until Jess is the other side of the double doors. "Actually, it's my birthday soon and I'm organising something."

Oh crap. He's having a party and inviting half the station. Another evening with Tony Smith, but at least I'll be able to talk to Nikki. "Sounds great. I've got to dash now." I hold up my watch. "Press conference."

"You'll come?" He's having trouble speaking and his colour stays so high that I scour my memory for my police first aid training. Then his words come out in a rush. "I'll be thirty-six, nothing special, but I wondered if you'd like to... it's not for a few weeks yet... come to dinner with me."

The penny doesn't so much drop as plummet through the carpet tiles. How have I missed the signs? I can spot a make-believe husband but not this. What wrong signals have I given? I never give those out. Not for the last eighteen years. A lesson learnt.

"Well, I..." I'll feign another commitment. Let him down gently. A white lie to save embarrassment and keep him onside. I can't afford to piss off Digital Forensics. "When is it?"

"The fourth of September."

"What a shame, I'm going..." I stop. That's my bloody birthday too. Not in the same decade, but on the same date. If horoscopes are to be believed, does that make us alike? Is my personality the same as someone whose idea of dressing up is a clean Iron Maiden t-shirt? My head throbs as I search it desperately for excuses.

"Are you often this pale? Could be an iron deficiency. Haemoglobin is the molecule in red blood cells that transport oxygen. If iron levels are low, not enough haemoglobin is produced. Are you vegan?"

"It's a headache," I snap and see my escape route. "I suffer from migraines. They're worse in the evenings, so I can't go out much. Sorry."

"Right, of course." His tone shifts from lecturing to over-sympathetic. "I heard about your tumour scare, but didn't realise it was ongoing."

"It's just migraine." So the whole station knows what happened in May. Are they all still thinking about it? Steph the invalid? Steph the weak link?

"Well, I hope it doesn't affect your press conference. Good luck." He turns and hurries away, no doubt embarrassed by my brush-off even though my excuse allowed him to save face. His worn trainers thud along the corridor.

I race up the stairs, head pounding. Despite the worst pain I've had in weeks, I'm determined to put on a professional performance in front of Thomas and the waiting media. Any rumour about my health Neil Wright is about to spread will be squashed before it grows legs.

CHAPTER FIFTY-EIGHT

David Oakley files his copy. *Arrested: Cathedral Killer that Never Was.*

Despite attracting national TV and tabloid media as well local radio and newspapers from across the county, the press conference turned out to be uneventful.

With his hands behind his head, he leans back in his wheelie chair, knowing it was his own reticence that allowed the briefing to progress the way the police wanted. Superintendent Thomas kept looking his way, no doubt expecting his usual volley of smartarse questions, but David was listening. And watching.

Detective Inspector Steph Lewis – the monkey to Thomas's organ grinder. Not given much airtime – hardly a surprise when she was sitting alongside an ego the size of Thomas's – but she provided the press corps with detail whenever Thomas prompted. There was no denying the junior of the two was on top of her brief.

At times during Thomas's slick spin, Lewis's elbows went to the table so her head could rest in her hands. Bore-

346

dom, frustration? Or something wrong? The old dear at the Loch Lomond Guesthouse thinks something's not right. David took a wild punt booking in for a night, but the conversations with Tracey Chiles were more illuminating than he expected, than Tracey realised.

But is the inspector a good copper?

No such thing. Since his arrest years ago while doing his job – why shouldn't he photograph an overpaid footballer out with an actress half his age and not his girlfriend? – David's loathing of the marshals of state censorship has grown. He's ready to scrutinise every high profile police officer and, if necessary, bring them down, one by one.

Starting with Steph Lewis.

AUTHOR'S NOTE

Gloucestershire provided inspiration for my setting. Some landmarks are recognisable, some are altered and shuffled around, and many are completely made up. My version of the grounds of Gloucester's magnificent cathedral is fictional. Although there are some fascinating information boards outside, they are not as described in the novel, nor is there a playground close by.

The lifeboat station at Sharpness does exist, but I've taken liberties with my description of the approach roads and the layout of the operations control building. It is one of the lifeboat and rescue stations operated by the Severn Area Rescue Association. All SARA crews are volunteers and typically conduct well over a hundred operations every year comprising: lifeboat cover for the Severn Estuary and tidal River Severn below Gloucester; land searches for vulnerable missing people; and inland water and flood rescues. SARA holds an annual fundraising open day at Sharpness, a wonderful day out for all ages. I attended two years in a row to research a chapter.

ACKNOWLEDGMENTS

Thank you for reading *Her Charming Man*. I hope you liked the story.

I am grateful to my publishers Rebecca Collins and Adrian Hobart for believing in my Gloucestershire Crime Series and taking on book two. It continues to be a pleasure to work with them. I am also grateful to cover designer Jayne Mapp and copy editor Sue Davison for their hard work on *Her Charming Man*.

I would also like to thank fellow writers Fergus Smith, Peter Garrett and Jessie Payne for their feedback on early drafts. And thank you to Team Hobeck author, Brian Price, for being an extra pair of eagle eyes over the manuscript.

Thank you to everyone who has taken the time and trouble to read, review and/or generally spread the word about my books this year. These include my fellow Hobeck authors, the Hobeck Advance Readers Team, and lots of other bloggers, readers and authors. I really appreciate this support.

I am grateful to Deryck Pritchard of the Severn Area Rescue Association, who gave informative tours of Sharpness lifeboat station at the SARA open days in 2022 and 2023, and to all SARA volunteers for putting on the open days. All errors and omissions for creative purposes are entirely my own.

A big thank you to my family: to my children for keeping my writing in touch with the current decade; and to my husband for being the loudest cheerleader for my books.

ABOUT THE AUTHOR

Rachel Sargeant is a full-time writer of thrillers and crime fiction. Her novels have been translated and sold worldwide. Her short stories have appeared in women's magazines and anthologies, and she is a winner of *Writing Magazine*'s Crime Short Story competition. After many years in Germany, Rachel now lives in Gloucestershire with her family. She likes visiting stately homes, country parks and coffee shops, and she has a PhD from the University of Birmingham. She loves reading in a range of genres and chats about books on her monthly blog.

Visit her website at: www.rachelsargeant.co.uk

Twitter/X: @RachelSargeant3
Facebook: @rachelsargeantauthor
BookBub: @rachelsargeant3

HOBECK BOOKS – THE HOME OF
GREAT STORIES

We hope you've enjoyed reading this novel by Rachel Sargeant. To keep up to date on Rachel's fiction writing please do follow her on Facebook, Twitter/X or BookBub.

Hobeck Books offers a number of short stories and novellas, free for subscribers in the compilation *Crime Bites*.

- *Echo Rock* by Robert Daws
- *Old Dogs, Old Tricks* by AB Morgan
- *The Silence of the Rabbit* by Wendy Turbin
- *Never Mind the Baubles: An Anthology of Twisted Winter Tales* by the Hobeck Team (including many of the Hobeck authors and Hobeck's two publishers)
- *The Clarice Cliff Vase* by Linda Huber
- *Here She Lies* by Kerena Swan
- *The Macnab Principle* by R.D. Nixon
- *Fatal Beginnings* by Brian Price
- *A Defining Moment* by Lin Le Versha
- *Saviour* by Jennie Ensor

- *You Can't Trust Anyone These Days* by Maureen Myant

Also please visit the Hobeck Books website for details of our other superb authors and their books, and if you would like to get in touch, we would love to hear from you.

Hobeck Books also presents a weekly podcast, the Hobcast, where founders Adrian Hobart and Rebecca Collins discuss all things book related, key issues from each week, including the ups and downs of running a creative business. Each episode includes an interview with one of the people who make Hobeck possible: the editors, the authors, the cover designers. These are the people who help Hobeck bring great stories to life. Without them, Hobeck wouldn't exist. The Hobcast can be listened to from all the usual platforms but it can also be found on the Hobeck website: **www. hobeck.net/hobcast**.

ALSO BY RACHEL SARGEANT

As well as writing the Gloucestershire Crime Series, Rachel also writes psychological thrillers.

The Roommates
When a university student disappears during freshers' week, her new flatmates search for her, not realising the danger ahead. Four roommates, four secrets, one devastating crime.

The Good Teacher
A popular school teacher lies dead in a ditch. On her first ever case, DC Pippa 'Agatha' Adams visits his school and meets families who've learned a shattering lesson. Maybe even the good have to die.

The Perfect Neighbours
Helen joins a British expat community abroad and is welcomed by the charming family across the way. When tragedy strikes, she realises her perfect neighbours are capable of almost anything.